Before she started writing books, Helen J. Rolfe worked in I.T. until she came to her senses and studied journalism and writing. She wrote articles for Women's Health & Fitness magazines as well as newsletter content and media releases for a not-for-profit organisation. In 2011 the fiction bug bit and Helen has been writing fiction ever since.

Helen J. Rolfe writes uplifting, contemporary fiction with characters to relate to and fall in love with. In a Manhattan Minute is her fifth novel.

Find out more at www.helenjrolfe.com, and follow her on Twitter @HJRolfe.

Also by Helen J Rolfe

The Friendship Tree

Handle Me with Care

What Rosie Found Next

The Chocolatier's Secret

In a Manhattan Minute

Helen J. Rolfe

Published by Fabrian Books

This book has been edited in British English (BrE) and therefore uses British spellings.

For my husband & my girls who always encourage me to follow my dreams...

I love you all xxx

Chapter One
Jack

Thanksgiving in New York City was one of the biggest holidays of the year. It was a day of national feasting, of gratitude. A day marked by the iconic Macy's Thanksgiving Day Parade, where air-filled balloons would bob along the parade route in the shape of Snoopy, Shrek or the Energizer Bunny, carrying along with them the feelings of hope, promise and new beginnings.

But tonight, Jack Churchill would remember this Thanksgiving for all the wrong reasons.

As the November wind crept through the gap in the back doors that opened out on to the patio of his father's home on the Upper West Side of Manhattan, Jack grabbed his chance for some fresh air before the annual party began. He slipped out the door and rubbed his hands together briskly against the cold. He'd thought he'd be alone, but as his eyes adjusted to the dark he saw Nicole, his father's housekeeper, crouched on the ground in the far corner behind the ash tree.

He moved closer and shivered when the icy wind met his chest, which was only covered in the white dress shirt of his tuxedo. 'Nicole? Is everything all right?'

When Nicole turned around Jack realised she'd been concealing a young woman, huddled beneath a blanket, sitting on the paving stones. In the shadows with the moonlight finding it difficult to battle through the cluster of bare tree branches above, in this tiny slice of

Manhattan, she looked terrified. And when she looked up she locked gazes with Jack, her eyes hollow and lost.

Jack noticed the foil tray on the ground, with a fork protruding and ready to go. 'Nicole, what's going on?'

'I'm just helping her out.' Nicole wasn't only the housekeeper who had worked with his father for thirteen years. She was also a friend, almost a part of their family, which needed all the help it could get. And he'd never seen her look as sheepish as she did right now. She'd always had a confidence about her that had somehow worked with Jack the teenager, Kent the widower. In fact, when Nicole had turned up in their lives, three months shy of Jack's fifteenth birthday and four years following the death of his mother, Cynthia, she'd been a symbol of hope like the first snowdrop of spring. With Nicole the world suddenly became colourful again, and somehow, although he'd never asked her outright, he believed they'd filled an unspoken void in her life too.

The young woman refused to meet his gaze, but Jack winked at Nicole. 'You'd better not let Dad catch you out here.'

Visibly relieved, Nicole said, 'Thank you, Jackson.'

He held up a hand to acknowledge her thanks and left her to continue her good deed as he turned to go back inside. But before he made it to the back door that must've swung right open in the wind, he came face to face with his father.

'Jack, what the devil are you doing out here? It's freezing.' Kent was accompanied by Braydon, an employee of their family jewellery business. 'There was such a draught I came to investigate what was going on.'

Jack had thought he may be able to usher them all inside, but behind his father appeared Marian, Kent's latest woman. He swore his father had had more girlfriends since his wife had died than Jack had had in his whole life, and there was something rather disturbing about that. None of them ever lasted though, and for that Jack was thankful. But this one, Marian, at least seemed to have a bit of common sense, because after checking out their faces as Kent looked past Jack and zoned in on Nicole and the stranger, Marian excused herself to go back to the party.

Jack knew his father and he knew his tolerance levels. He could see his jaw tensing up, his eyes narrowing. No, this wouldn't do. It wouldn't do at all. The Churchills associated with certain people and they did not include a down and out woman who was still sitting on the patio, hands still but eyes focused on the food in the foil container. She was probably wondering whether she'd even get to eat it now.

'What's going on here?' Kent took a step closer, his handsome exterior menacing, negating his usual approachability in company.

'I can explain,' Nicole began. 'I was just help—'

'I can see very well what's going on. Jack?'

Jack held up his hands in defence. 'I'm as surprised as you are.' He almost wished he knew something, that he could start an argument with his father. Perhaps it would shake him into seeing his son as his own person, rather than a clone to carry on the family name and the business.

'Get her off my property,' Kent spat. 'Now!'

Jack's eyes widened almost as much as Nicole's. No matter what the situation was, they never spoke to Nicole with anything other than respect and familiarity. Tonight it was almost as though she was a stranger to Kent Churchill.

Kent took a step towards the young woman. 'You need to leave before I call the police.' His voice low and laced with promise, Nicole stepped in front to shield the terrified stranger. But Kent hadn't finished his tirade. 'Is that mine?' He pointed at the red woollen blanket she was huddled beneath.

Nicole seemed suddenly terrified of this man she didn't recognise. 'You told me to get rid of it.'

'So why didn't you?'

'I didn't want to throw it away when it could be put to better use.' Jack had never heard her voice so small, and when Kent spotted the foil container filled with food, Nicole told him, 'It's just leftovers, scraps. I would've thrown them out anyway.'

Jack watched his father. Surely he wasn't going to use physical force to get his way? He'd never acted like this. Kent was an elitist—Jack got a kick out of it sometimes—but tonight he was acting as though he didn't have an ounce of compassion running through his veins. Yes, the woman was trespassing, and yes, Nicole had given away things from their home, but did he really need to deal with the situation like this? Like it was something else he could control. Sometimes Jack longed to hatch out of the cocoon he'd become wrapped up in as a Churchill, as Kent's son, expected to act, exist and be exactly like his father. Because to Jack, it seemed a bleak existence that lacked real joy or the happiness the man had never regained since losing his wife.

Quietly observing until now, Braydon stepped forward and took a turn. 'You heard the man,' he told the girl. 'You need to go.' The way he sneered at her, his voice full of malevolence, made Jack dislike the man all the more.

Nicole stayed in front of the young woman, hands moving to her hips in defiance, and Jack had to hand it to her for not losing it before now. 'Leave her alone,' she said. 'Go back inside, and I'll see to it that she leaves.'

Kent's hostility carried on the icy wind. 'Don't you dare come back, do you hear? Or I'll call the police.'

The woman stood up, pulling the blanket tighter around herself, and all the while Nicole shielded her from any of them reaching her if they so much as tried.

Jack faced his father and Braydon. He stretched out his arms, ready to block either of them, stand up for the woman who'd been like a mother to him. 'Go back inside, back to our guests before they start wondering where you are and come out to investigate.'

That seemed to get through to him. Every year the guests revelled in the Churchills' Thanksgiving Party; it was even featured in the society pages, and Kent wouldn't want to risk that changing, risk being written up in an entirely different sort of news article for all the wrong reasons.

By the time Jack had ushered Kent and Braydon inside and shut the doors behind them, the woman was already halfway down the steps to run away from the house and Nicole was calling after her.

When she was out of sight, Jack stood behind Nicole looking at the empty space, the darkened path where she'd fled that led out to the New York streets. He put a hand on Nicole's shoulder as little plumes of her warm breath met the air. 'Are you okay?'

She shrugged him off. 'Never better. After all, I know my place now, don't I?'

'Nicole—' His words were futile. She pushed past him and returned inside, slamming the door behind her.

Jack stood outside, his breath fogging into the darkness. His hands were numb and his chest felt the cold snap that wrapped around him. Sometimes he wished he could escape as easily as the woman in the red blanket, get far away from the life he led. But knowing that wasn't the case, he finally retreated inside.

'Anything I can do to help?' He watched Nicole arranging doilies onto a couple of platters, ready to laden them with the finest cooked canapés imaginable. She was a fantastic cook. They'd spent many a night in his teenage years bonding over late night feasts when his father had been working late or he'd been up at night cramming for his exams.

'I've got it, Jackson.' She was the only person who called him by his full name since his mother died. Occasionally she'd forget, slip up and call him Jack, and it always sounded so odd.

'My father isn't a complete asshole, you know.'

When she turned to him, her eyes were filled with tears. 'Language, Jackson.'

He smiled at their familiar banter and took a bottle of beer from the fridge. Soon he'd be offered nothing less than the finest wine or champagne varieties—the Louis Roederer and Dom Pérignon often made an appearance at these gatherings—and a bottle of beer would seem blasphemous. But right now he needed it to kick-start his ability to socialise with people he had nothing much in common with.

'What are you up to?' Nicole eyed the beer. 'Are you trying to make him even angrier?'

Jack hooked an eyebrow. Last year he had purposefully walked into their summer party with a bottle of beer in hand. His father had hated it! Kent had been parading bottles with labels to impress, but Jack had garnered more attention with his cheap brand of beer, even got several requests for one, much to his father's dismay.

'You know how your father feels about you taking part in these gatherings with his business associates and friends. He's already angry enough with me, so don't push it, Jackson.' When he knocked back a swig of beer, she sighed. 'I guess that's why you're doing it.'

He leaned against the kitchen counter as Nicole checked on the Thanksgiving turkey, ran through a prep list and then put the finishing touches to the smoked salmon canapés, topping each one off with a miniature sprig of dill.

'What leftovers did you give the girl?' he asked.

Nicole cast him a suspicious look before she realised he was trying to quell her anger and recover a sense of normality. 'A portion of last night's leftover chicken casserole. It was a modest amount, nothing to make a fuss about.'

'Are you going to tell me who she was?'

Nicole pulled another tray from the oven, this one with creamy sausage and stuffed mushrooms. 'She's someone who needs help.'

Jack stepped forward and loaded the canapés onto one of the silver oval platters as Nicole took the opportunity to head into the cloakroom at the back of the kitchen. She'd always been the same. She was the housekeeper, her role defined, but she always presented herself well at these events and that meant a dash of lipstick, pinning her corkscrew curls up on top of her head, perhaps a spritz of a delicate floral fragrance Jack had always associated with her.

'You go mingle with the guests.' She ushered him with her hands to push him out of the kitchen.

‘I’m finishing my beer. And we’re talking, aren’t we?’

She took the bottle and pushed it onto the countertop. ‘Right now it’s time to go and be business Jack, not my Jackson. And we’ve finished talking.’

He groaned, but lifted his jacket from the back of the chair where he’d left it shortly before the showdown outside. He shrugged it on, adjusted his cummerbund, ensured his bow tie was on straight. ‘Off I go to pretend what happened earlier didn’t happen at all.’

Nicole smiled kindly at him. Jack knew his father was right to get rid of someone trespassing on his land, taking advantage of Nicole’s kind heart and generosity, but he also knew it could’ve been handled a lot more sensitively than it had been. He wondered whether Nicole would speak of it again after the party ended. He was close to her. She’d gotten him through some dark days when there’d been nobody else in the house to soften the edges of Kent’s serious approach, the disappearance of a childhood that had gone in a puff of smoke like a magic trick when his mother died.

Jack took a deep breath and joined his father and their guests in the dining room of the six-storey townhouse. The champagne was flowing readily in this room and Jack took a glass from the silver tray on the sideboard. The table was set, ready for the occasion. Nicole had pressed the white linen tablecloth and napkins that morning, mini pumpkins with tea lights illuminated the centre of the table, hexagonal white plates with gold piping around the edges sat in position, framed by gold embossed cutlery. It was like a scene from a beautiful magazine, a scene from their life, but a life that Jack found increasingly difficult to feel a part of, let alone enjoy.

‘Jack, won’t you join us.’ Braydon, the in-house designer for The Diamond Touch, was a man who had apparently shown his talents first when he joined the company more than two decades ago and later his brashness and lack of social skills. He was a similar age to Kent but much less of a man and Jack neither wanted to socialise with him, nor work with him. Unfortunately, both of those things were unavoidable.

‘Great to see you, Braydon.’ Jack forced brightness into his voice and knocked back the champagne that would undoubtedly get him through the evening. He wasn’t happy Braydon had seen the debacle outside tonight. The man focused on one-upmanship, and Jack had a nasty feeling this was an anecdote he’d no doubt use against them in the future.

‘Let me introduce you to Fern.’ Braydon pulled the woman facing away from him into their space.

‘Delighted to meet you.’ Jack extended a hand in greeting.

Fern draped herself on Braydon’s shoulder, no doubt her attentiveness one of the main attractions for Braydon, who loved to be the centre of attention. ‘Nice to meet you, Jack. I’ve heard a lot about you.’

‘Is that right?’ Jack wondered whether Fern had met his father yet, and assumed the only reason she wasn’t fluttering her eyelashes at him instead was because Kent Churchill had a woman in tow tonight.

Jack was only in his late twenties, but his father was usually the better prospect. A handsome man at fifty-nine, Kent Churchill was distinguished with dark hair, peppered with just enough grey to make it the look women seemed to go for, and he had a natural charisma that seemed to effortlessly win people over. Kent had a slight dimple in his chin that Jack had inherited, and with that, an air of money about him. Chairman of The Diamond Touch jewellery chain, the title made women fall over themselves to get to him first. He was a cobra with his business, squeezing until he got his way.

Jack excused himself from Braydon and Fern and went to greet the Petersons, a couple who were semi-normal and unpretentious. With Clara and Scott Peterson, he talked about the latest winter jewellery collection at The Diamond Touch, the latest jewellery hitting the shelves of their competitors. His mother had been the driving force for the family business that Kent Churchill started in response to his wife's creative flair and talent. Her pieces had quickly garnered attention and become in demand all over the country and internationally, and gradually the business had grown into the empire it was today. Kent and Jack had continued her legacy and Jack felt his pride stir in her memory, something he rarely felt with the daily grind of helping to run a business he had no real passion for.

When Kent came over to join them, Clara was quick to offer a compliment. 'It's lovely to be here again. You throw such wonderful parties!' She clasped her hands together in excitement. Jack wondered whether she got out much.

When Scott Peterson excused himself and his wife so they could find a couple more glasses of champagne, Kent took Jack to one side. 'Braydon has done a wonderful job this season.' He lowered his voice. 'I hope you're keeping things civil between you.'

'Of course I am.' Jack spoke more quietly. 'I've secured contracts with major retailers so you don't need to tell me he's valuable to the business.'

Kent pulled a face. 'I'm not all that keen on him myself, you know.'

‘First I’ve heard.’ Jack was surprised at his father’s candid response.

‘In business, son, you learn to keep your friends close but your enemies closer.’ He tapped the side of his nose.

It all sounded so cloak and dagger to Jack, he wondered what Braydon could’ve done to irritate his father. But the conversation ended when Kent turned to kiss Marian when she ambled up behind him. Jack hoped he hadn’t really seen Marian’s hand caress his father’s ass. It was enough to bring up those canapés again. And they were really quite good.

‘We’ve an early meeting first thing in the morning,’ Kent told Jack. He swilled the whiskey in the bottom of his glass.

‘I’m out tomorrow.’ Jack gave Marian a clipped smile.

‘It’s an important time in the lead-up to Christmas.’ Kent fixed him with a glare. ‘I shouldn’t need to tell you that.’

‘I’ll be back the day after.’ He offered no further explanation and turned when Nicole approached with the remaining two canapés on a tray.

‘How’s it going?’ she whispered when Marian and Kent blended in with the crowd.

‘It’s bearable.’

Nicole nodded and discreetly slipped away. She knew his feelings. He didn’t revel in the high life like his father did; he didn’t feel the buzz that seemed to drive his father forward all the time. Each day, when the jewellery store closed, when meetings were over and negotiations had taken place, Jack was happy to have space and time to himself. He’d run through Central Park, sip a coffee as he wandered aimlessly through the city or take a drive way out of Manhattan to see friends.

But the business was his mother's legacy and he couldn't betray her memory. He was in this for keeps, whether he liked it or not.

During the evening, canapés and champagne were plentiful, diamond rings and necklaces sparkled, business was discussed, family lives were appraised and gossip was devoured—which businessman had left his wife for someone young enough to be his daughter; whose business was in serious trouble; whose kids were running up debts bigger than their trust funds. Appetisers were served, plates were cleared and the main event of the turkey was devoured, with much praise to the Churchills for throwing another annual Thanksgiving Party that would no doubt grace the society pages soon enough.

When Fern's leg brushed against Jack's beneath the table one too many times, his phone ringing in his pocket rescued him.

'Business,' he explained, knowing full well it wasn't. It was Reese, his latest love interest, a tall, leggy blonde who partied hard and was a lot of fun.

'Hey you.' He took the phone up to the second floor and into the bathroom where he could lock the door and have down time away from all those people.

'I'm wondering what time you can come over, that's all.'

He envisaged her lying on the bed, scantily clad, in her studio apartment a few blocks away.

'I won't be able to get away yet, but soon, promise.'

'I'll hold you to that.'

He bit his lip, already feeling better than he had all evening. 'What are you wearing?'

'My heart.'

He knew exactly what she meant: the rose-gold heart pendant encrusted with tiny diamonds in its centre, the gift he'd given her for her birthday in June. He hadn't bought many women birthday presents, he'd never been that serious about anyone, but this one was high maintenance and a gift hadn't been a choice, he suspected, if he wanted to keep seeing her.

'Just the heart?' His arousal was already obvious as he thought of her long, lean body lying on the bed, blonde hair splayed across her shoulders. All legs and a smoking hot body, Reese always eased away his troubles.

'Yes.'

'I'll be over when I can,' he groaned.

He hung up, splashed cold water across his face to calm himself down, and when he emerged from the bathroom he bypassed the festivities and went to the kitchen instead. He didn't need to be sandwiched between Fern, who was getting more touchy-feely by the minute, and Derek, a pleasant man but the firm's accountant and arguably one of the dullest men he'd ever met, for any longer than necessary. Jack sometimes wondered whether he should bring a date to these events to prevent him from being bored senseless. But that would invite questions about his life, assumptions that he was in a relationship when he felt much happier cruising along under his own steam.

Nicole smiled when he appeared in the kitchen. She knew his tolerance for these occasions. He plucked a leftover potato from the roasting pan and popped it into his mouth.

'Didn't you eat enough tonight?'

He shrugged. 'I could never eat enough of your food.'

'Jackson, flattery will get you nowhere.'

'You'll make me fat if you're not careful.'

'Nonsense, you never sit still for five minutes.'

Already he was looking forward to the walk tonight from his father's townhouse over to Reese's apartment. His cummerbund was feeling tighter by the second and they still had dessert to go yet. The high life definitely made the waistline pay if you weren't careful.

'How long has she been coming here?' he asked, spotting the foil container perched at the side of the countertop as Nicole cut the Ginger Snap Pumpkin Pie into slices.

She ignored his question but didn't miss the direction of his gaze. 'It's leftovers, Jackson.'

'I know. For you?'

She hooked a chestnut curl that had escaped her updo behind her ear. 'Does it really matter?'

'Not to me, but it will to my father. Has the woman really gone?'

'Oh yes.' He heard the anger in her voice. 'I don't think she'll ever come near here again. Your father made his feelings quite clear tonight.'

He stepped closer as she moved onto slicing the Cranberry and apple cake. 'Can you understand why?'

'Not really.' She shrugged.

She was holding something back. 'Come on, out with it. You have more to say, I can tell.'

She stopped slicing. 'Do you know how many people there are, homeless on the streets of New York?' He rolled his eyes. 'Oh forget it! I thought you'd have a little common decency, Jackson, that's all.'

'What?'

She harrumphed, shook her head again. 'You've led a charmed life.'

'And what's that supposed to mean?'

'You've never wanted for anything.'

'I think we both know that's not true.' His mom not dying was top of his list.

Her face softened, her voice evened out as she realised what she'd said. 'What I meant to say is that you've never wanted for anything financially.' She finished slicing the desserts and wiped the cake knife before setting it beside the pre-sliced pieces.

'How long has the woman been coming to you for help?'

He got his answer this time. 'I've seen her at the shelter regularly for a while now, at least a few weeks,' she admitted.

'Please say it's only the blanket and the food you've been giving her tonight.'

'Of course. What do you take me for? I'd never do anything to wrong this family, you know that.'

'Tell me about her.'

She wiped her hands on a nearby cloth. 'There's not much to tell. She came to the shelter a few times, and then I'd see her huddled in the doorway of a derelict townhouse not far from here. She's been sleeping on the streets for a while and I don't know her story, I just want to help.'

Jack rubbed his face. 'Nicole, you can't take in every waif and stray.'

'I'm not an idiot. But this woman is different. Something in me wouldn't let me leave her there, I couldn't. I told her this address and told her if she wouldn't come home with me or go to one of the shelters, then she should come here at nine o'clock after family dinner time and I'd give her a hot meal.' She hesitated. 'I've been doing that for three weeks now. And when your father told me to get rid of your mother's red blanket, it was in my arms ready to do just that, but instead of putting it into the bin as he'd asked, I thought right away of Becky.'

'So that's her name.'

'I doubt it. It's unlikely she'd give me her real name. She's no doubt in some kind of trouble. Goodness knows where she bunks down every night. I know the townhouse is no longer an option with the owners renovating, but at least I can think of her as fed and warm now. Or I could until your father chased her away.' She smiled kindly at him as though confirming she knew he wouldn't have behaved in the same way as his father. 'You'd better get back to the party.'

Jack reluctantly returned to the dining room where he was seated next to Fern, and even though she was draped all over Braydon, she still instantly rested her thigh against Jack's beneath the table. The woman was incorrigible, and what had happened tonight with Nicole had made Jack less tolerant of everyone in this room. He looked around at each of their guests in turn, most of them pleasant enough. On the surface it looked like it was a gathering of a close-knit circle. But Jack knew the truth and tonight, the reality had hit. Nicole, the housekeeper, meant more to him than anyone else sitting at this table, and his father's behaviour had been out of character and inexcusable.

The rest of the evening passed slowly. All Jack wanted to do was escape to Reese's apartment, feel her legs wrapped around him and forget about everything else. When the guests had finally gone and Jack took the remaining glasses out to the kitchen ready to be washed, the storm that had been brewing since the altercation on the patio was about to unleash.

‘I trust we won’t be seeing the young woman again.’ Kent stood at the side of the kitchen, cummerbund slightly crooked, bow tie undone no doubt as soon as he’d shut the front door to the last guest.

‘She’s gone,’ Nicole confirmed, rinsing the last of the cutlery that was too delicate to put in the dishwasher. ‘I’m sorry if you feel I’d acted inappropriately, but—’

‘There’s no question!’ Kent bellowed and even Jack took a step away from his father. ‘These people have no morals. They’ll lie, beg, steal—’ His voice broke. ‘They’re not to be trusted. Any of them.’

Nicole reached for a tea towel and began drying the cutlery. Jack wanted to get the hell out of there to Reese’s place but he couldn’t leave them like this. The atmosphere was usually jovial after a party, when all the hard work had finished and it was time to relax. Quite often Nicole and Kent would share a whiskey nightcap in the kitchen before she made her way home, but Jack doubted the top would come off the decanter tonight, let alone make it into the crystal glasses.

‘I believe in giving people a chance, Kent.’ Nicole didn’t look at either of them as she busied herself with her tasks. ‘She wasn’t doing anyone any harm. I don’t know her story, but I think she’s one of the good ones.’

Jack was wrong. The top came off the whiskey decanter in the corner of the kitchen, but only one crystal glass came down from the cupboard. Kent knocked back the double measure almost as quickly as it had been poured.

‘I will not have her type around my house, you hear me?’ Kent looked into the now empty glass. ‘I want your word you won’t give her any more handouts, you will tell her to leave if she ever comes here again.’

Nicole was no pushover and usually it was a quality Jack admired, but tonight when she spoke he cringed because he knew this wouldn't be a happy ending.

'I won't give her anything that belongs to you, Kent, and I doubt she'll even want to come back here after the way you were tonight. But I will give her my help, outside of the time I spend at this house, when and if she ever asks for it again.'

'Then you leave me no choice.' Kent decanted a second double whiskey as Jack and Nicole exchanged glances. 'I want you to leave, Nicole. I won't have someone in this house helping someone like her. I won't have it. I'll send you a cheque with the last of your wages, paid till the end of the week. And I'll speak to the agency about any other payments owed to you.' He left the kitchen with his whiskey and without looking back at either of them.

Jack looked at Nicole, the Sicilian American who had worked with the family for so long she felt a part of it and his heart all but snapped in two, not only for him but for his father.

'He'll come around,' he told her when Nicole snatched her coat from the hook by the back door and put it on.

She calmly fastened the buttons, and tied her scarf, and only then did she look Jack in the eye. 'I've always thought he was a good man.' Her eyes and wobbly voice showed she wasn't as calm on the inside as she was trying to make out. 'But tonight, he's gone one step too far.'

'Let me talk to him. I know he can be a dreadful snob, and maybe he was embarrassed that this was a party and someone could've seen the young woman, but the way he acted tonight was out of character. I've never seen him like that.' In his father's eyes tonight he'd seen anger, hate, misery and even fear. And he had no idea why.

'No, Jackson.' She put a hand against his cheek. 'This is the end, it really is. I've loved being a part of your life. You were my family, all of you, and I'll miss you. But whatever Kent has going on, whatever issues drove him to behave the way he did tonight, without the basic act of human kindness, those issues are beyond what I can understand.'

Her mind was made up, and with only one glance behind her and a raise of her hand to bid him farewell, Nicole left the house, crossed the patio and disappeared into the night.

Jack stood at the back door, watching her go. He dared the icy air to bite at him, sting his lips, nip at his fingers. He was already so numb he wouldn't feel it anyway. When he'd pulled on his tux this evening, ready for another Churchill gathering, he'd had no idea the evening would unfold like this. The father he'd once known hadn't been present since the day his mother died. From that day, Kent Churchill had been withdrawn, too busy to do anything apart from run the business, and Jack had no idea, without Nicole, the glue that had held them together, where they'd go from here. Now they were simply two men, linked by biology. And Nicole was gone from their lives for good.

Chapter Two

Three Years Later

Evie

Evie Jefferson took off her sky-blue bobble hat and shook out her long, curly blonde hair. 'Good morning, Bonnie.' She bustled through the narrow entrance to her boss's apartment. A pre-war, three-bedroomed place in Greenwich Village, with large windows and plenty of natural light, the apartment doubled as the space for The Perfect Match Couture, Bonnie's bridal business.

'Good morning, Evie.' Bonnie spoke without moving her jaw, a pin between her teeth.

'Use a pincushion, would you?' Evie scolded. 'I've got visions of you swallowing a pin one of these days.' Bonnie's eye-roll didn't surprise Evie in the slightest.

'Nonsense,' Bonnie said through gritted teeth. 'There's a fresh pot of coffee in the kitchen. Help yourself.'

'Thanks.'

Evie hung her coat on the wrought-iron stand in the hallway. She shivered, an aftershock of the November winds this morning. Even after twenty years of living in New York, she still couldn't get over the level of cold compared to the south coast of England where her family had emigrated from. And it wasn't even winter yet. The heating in her tiny basement apartment wasn't up to much either. Three small radiators did their best to omit heat, but no matter what the temperature was, it was home now. It was all hers and sometimes she wanted to pinch herself at how her life had taken a complete U-turn, just when she needed it to.

Going through to the kitchen, she rubbed her hands together as they gradually thawed, and then poured a steaming mug of black coffee that she took back with her along the hallway. She leant against the doorjamb of the once dining room, now workroom, sipping the black coffee, abiding by the rules of the workplace: no food or drink would be consumed in the workroom, which saw no plates, no grand meals, no drinks. Instead, the enormous Hogwarts-style dining table was covered in huge swathes of fabric and a myriad of accessories as Bonnie worked away.

'Is that the Carrington bridesmaid dress?' Evie nodded to the dress on the mannequin beside the table. Bonnie was kneeling in front of it, taking pins from her mouth and putting them in the appropriate places.

'It certainly is. What do you think?' Bonnie stood back to admire the shimmering silver bridesmaid dress that would join the other three for the Carrington wedding come December.

'It's gorgeous. And you were right about the buttons down the back, they really add to it.'

Bonnie twirled the mannequin around for the full effect as Evie finished her coffee, her power tool for a full day as a wedding gown designer's assistant.

Evie went back to the kitchen and stacked her cup in the dishwasher in the expansive, eat-in space that could most likely fit her entire apartment, and then she joined Bonnie and set to work. Bonnie was at one end at the enormous table, and at the other, Evie began preparations for another consultation that morning with a new bride-to-be. She gathered the folders of swatches—fabrics for the dress, colour samples—she took out a portfolio of photographs of the dresses Bonnie had designed and made over the years and took everything into the living room at the front where they welcomed clients. She fanned out bridal magazines on top of the walnut coffee table stretching in front of the couch and switched on the two table lamps to give the room a soft glow ready for some lucky woman to dream up her perfect wedding day.

'Thanks for taking charge of the new bride-to-be, Evie.' Bonnie checked her watch. 'The Carringtons will be here any second for the final fitting, but once I've finished that, I'll come and join you.'

'Sounds good to me,' Evie assured her. 'Don't forget the bag and the ring-bearing cushion I made out of the leftover material. They're in the top drawer of the chest.'

'You're the best.' Bonnie smiled. 'What would I do without you?'

'I like using the offcuts to make something, shame to waste them.' She'd made a small cushion out of the leftover satin and embroidered the wedding date in ivory, all ready for the youngest member of the Carrington clan to carry down the aisle. Evie loved her job and she didn't think it was possible to love anything quite so much. She'd been lucky to find it and she'd never let it go.

'Actually, you've reminded me of something,' said Bonnie, retrieving the bag and the ring cushion from the chest.

'What's that?'

Bonnie swiped the screen on her iPhone, tapped in her passcode. 'Okay, if you could sit at the table, perhaps with the bag and the ring-bearer cushion in front of you, clasping one, with a needle and cotton in your other hand.'

'Whatever for?'

'Publicity, dear girl. Publicity.'

Evie wasn't sure she liked where this was heading.

'Come on, Evie. I need to get some action shots and you've resisted me long enough.' Bonnie ushered her over to the table and practically pushed her onto the chair. 'People want to see the faces behind the dresses and the accessories. It makes it so much more personal, I think.'

'But you're much more photogenic than me,' Evie insisted, but to no avail. Bonnie was right, she'd avoided it until now, but with good reason. If her photograph appeared on Twitter, Facebook, their website, it could be only a matter of time before her past caught up with her.

Reluctantly Evie posed at the table, pretending to sew, and then pinning ivory silk around the mannequin and posing there as though in the middle of making a dress. In turn, Evie took photos of Bonnie sitting at the desk with a design in front of her sketched by her own hand. Bonnie looked completely at home pretending to work, much more so than Evie who was beginning to have palpitations at the thought of her picture being seen by people far and wide.

The Carringtons' arrival saw the end to the impromptu photo shoot and Evie was greeted with compliments for her accessories, the extra mile she'd gone for the customer. As the bride had her final fitting with Bonnie, Evie greeted another bride-to-be for her first appointment and the risk of the photos was all forgotten as she immersed herself in one of her favourite parts of the job. Brides rarely came alone for the initial visit and there was always much excitement, much buzz on the initial meeting and this client, Megan, had brought her sister, Annalise, along with her. It always made Evie wonder who she would ask if she ever had the opportunity to get married and choose the way her perfect day would unfold. She loved hearing stories about proposals, engagements, especially those somewhat out of the ordinary. Last month, she'd met a newly engaged woman who'd been proposed to underwater on a scuba diving trip off the Greek island of Rhodes; the week before it'd been a proposal in a log cabin in the Swiss Alps she'd heard about.

Evie ran through some preliminary details. When was the big day? Where would the wedding take place? How big was the wedding party? What sort of gown did she envisage? Some women came in knowing the style, the material, and other times it was a blank canvas and they left it in A Perfect Match Couture's hands. However it happened though, this was how the dream began and forging a client relationship with these women was the most important thing. It'd taken Evie a while to get used to it, but she'd taken Bonnie's lead and now she was comfortable doing this; she felt she'd found her place in the world after two years in a dream job. One day she hoped to move to the design side, but for now she was learning from the ground up and loving every minute. She was learning everything from how to establish good client relationships, advertising for the business, sourcing and maintaining good relationships with suppliers. She knew the difference between tulle, silk, Venice lace and Chantilly lace. She'd worked with silk Duchesse satin, organza, chiffon and beaded silk, and Bonnie had trusted her to get involved with the sewing quite early on, recognising a flair for it when she toyed with offcuts and made added extras.

Evie's skills had stemmed from making her own clothes when she was growing up. Her parents had wanted to dress her in Burberry, Dolce & Gabbana and Moncler play clothes, designer jeans, impractical fussy tops. After one summer hanging around with the new kid in town, Serena, whose parents lived a more modest life, she'd learned all about making her own clothes. Serena's mother had taught Evie and Serena the backstitch, basting stitch, a chain stitch, and they'd practised for hours with offcuts until finally Evie knew enough to start making some of her own garments. She started with a summer top, sleeveless, with essentially two pieces of material and one button on the back of the neck. Then she moved to making an A-line skirt with a small zipper and a waistband. She bought a sewing machine with her allowance and slowly she got better and better. Evie had been making her own clothes since she was fourteen, and she wondered what either of her parents would say if they could see her now.

Evie ignored the twinge of sadness that crept in, and she left the two women flicking through bridal magazines to go the kitchen to pour a couple of glasses of champagne. With a strawberry pushed onto each glass for good measure, she returned to the laughter and chatter and the excited women tossing around ideas of empire waistlines, ball gown dresses and flowing veils made from the finest lace.

Evie took them through various fabrics for the dress first, and then they moved on to the swatches for the veil.

'This one is exquisite.' Megan let the lace fall into the palm of her hand, brushing it lightly with her fingertips.

'It's beautiful, isn't it? Chantilly lace is handmade in France and very delicate,' Evie explained, 'but it's a perfect choice.'

'Is it terribly expensive?' Megan winced.

'Stop stressing.' Annalise was firm. 'This is your wedding day and you've saved long and hard for this.' She put a hand on her sister's arm. 'You deserve the very best.' A look passed between them and Evie wondered what their story was. Was it as gut-wrenching as her own? Would she ever reach the point where she felt she 'deserved' the best?

Annalise moved closer to Evie, and under her breath whispered, '*Is* it really expensive?'

Evie could tell Megan was locked in on that lace. She hadn't taken her hand away from it yet. 'It's priced higher per yard, but it'll depend on the type of Chantilly lace. That one you're looking at now is at the lower end of the price range. From memory it's around one hundred and fifty dollars a yard.'

'And this?' Megan flipped to the next, almost too scared to rest her fingers on the delicate lace for fear of the cost.

Evie leant forward to check the design name. 'Around eight hundred dollars a yard.'

Megan whistled. 'Good thing I like the first one then.'

'Some lace can cost up to twelve hundred dollars,' Evie elaborated, 'especially the beaded varieties. But the one you have there is beautiful. Once you've met with Bonnie and discussed your basic ideas for wedding gowns, we'll have you try on as many as you'd like to find the right shape. And I'll make sure I find out a veil or two for you to try. It may not be the same lace, but you can get an idea of the length and style you'd prefer.'

The girls drank their champagne and Evie had a preliminary chat with Megan about the expectations for the dress. Bonnie eventually joined them and went into more detail before showing Megan and Annalise through to the second bedroom, which had become a dedicated dressing room—Bonnie's husband worked on Wall Street and was thankful he wasn't around the mayhem most of the time—where Megan tried on a few dresses to get more of an idea. She and her sister giggled their way through a slim-fit dress, an empire waistline, an A-line style, a ball gown and a mermaid.

The second Megan and Annalise left, Bonnie got to work. Evie had seen the passion oozing from her during the consultation, her hand almost twitching to get out her design pad and start sketching. Evie had an image in her mind's eye of the dress that would work, and one day she hoped to be able to sketch it out just as Bonnie was doing now.

At the end of her workday, Evie walked to meet Nicole, her closest friend for the last three years. They always met in the same place, at least twice a week, at Thorello's, a favourite café set a few blocks back from the Empire State Building, but tucked away enough that tourists often stumbled upon it rather than flocked there. It was owned and run by Thorello himself; an Italian immigrant he claimed, although Evie had her doubts with his accent that sounded as though he'd done a crash course at a language school, rather than a native Italian who'd gradually picked up American dialect and intonations. The café was also reasonably priced, generous in its portion size and friendly, and Evie thought they served the best coffees and food for miles around.

When Evie pushed open the door to the café, Nicole waved over to her from her table by the window. Dim lights encased in brass shades hung on long wires from the ceiling, and dark wooden furniture was arranged uniformly in the long room. A few paintings adorned the walls—two of the Amalfi coast, another of the Duomo in

Florence, another of the Ponte Vecchio. The whole placed oozed Italian influences, down to the wine bottle candles on each table, lit now the winter sun had completed its descent.

Nicole hugged Evie. 'So, how was your day?'

Evie chatted about new clients, dresses they were working on, plans for the next week. Nicole always asked the same question each time they saw each other, almost a check-in to make sure Evie was still doing well. It had taken a while to get used to, but Evie didn't mind now and chatted away rather than accusing Nicole of worrying too much, as though she was an injured bird that had been rescued from the street and needed watching until her broken wings were mended enough to fly solo. It was important to Evie to be independent, have a place of her own and a job she worked hard at, but she'd never forget the role Nicole had playing in making any of that possible. She'd done everything she could for Evie, and Evie would go out of her way to make it up to her.

They placed their orders: spicy beans and sausages for Evie, spinach and ricotta gnocchi for Nicole, and they chatted with Thorello until extra clientele demanded his attention.

'A winter wedding sounds lovely.' Nicole clapped her hands together when Evie had finished telling her all about today's consultation. She never used names, they were omitted to protect the confidentiality of their clients, but Evie knew Nicole wanted to know about her day in more detail than 'it was a good day', or 'it was fine'.

'What colour will the gown be? Nicole pressed.

'Ivory, we think. And we've suggested a shrug, perhaps fawn, faux-fur, to go round her shoulders. She seems keen on having some of the photographs taken in the snow.'

'And what colour will the bridesmaids be wearing?'

Evie laughed. Nicole knew Bonnie well; it was how Evie had got the job in the first place, and she'd loved the few days she'd spent in there keeping an eye on her protégé when Evie had first started her job. Nicole had been worried something would go wrong. Whether she thought Evie would steal or lie, Evie didn't know, but second chances like this didn't come along for everyone and if they both thought she needed watching at the start, then so be it. After a few days, Bonnie insisted she could 'take it from here' and Nicole wasn't to worry, and Evie launched herself into her new position with gusto.

'The sister says she'll wear anything other than peach or lemon yellow.'

Nicole pulled a face and shook her head. 'Neither of those colours would work with a winter theme.'

'I'm not sure they'd work with any theme!' Evie giggled. 'But I think she'll go for bold colours to contrast with the white of the snow. She's one of the easier clients for sure, and I think she'll make the right choice.'

'Did the really awkward couple return?'

They thanked Thorello when he brought over their food and waited for him to sprinkle both dishes with black pepper and parmesan.

'They picked up the dresses and the wedding is this Saturday,' Evie explained. 'Fingers crossed I won't ever have to see them again. They were demanding, to say the least.' The Fitz family were born and bred on money and didn't mind who knew it, or saw it. From the moment they'd had that first consultation, the bride-to-be, Zara, had been difficult. Evie wondered how many tantrums she'd had as an adult if her behaviour when it came to choosing the dress was anything to go by. She'd huffed and puffed her way in and out of the ball gown style that did nothing for her, she'd become angry when Evie brought out a bigger size in the A-line dress after seeing Zara struggling to get the other dress on, and then all hell had broken lose when she'd received a phone call during a fitting to inform her that her maid-of-honour was already four months pregnant. The poor girl hadn't realised and it meant major alterations to her dress. Evie had done her best to diffuse the delicate situation, and she and Bonnie had been smiles and understanding looks and comments all round until the day the Fitz's had picked up the dresses and they'd shut the door to the apartment block with enormous sighs of relief.

'Let's hope you don't get too many of those.' Nicole popped another piece of gnocchi in her mouth.

'Amen to that. So tell me, how was your day?'

'I worked at the shelter this afternoon after I'd finished with Mrs Mack.' No longer a housekeeper, Nicole shared her time between being a home help for Mrs Mack, an elderly lady who lived in the apartment on the ground floor, and helping at the homeless shelter a few blocks from where she lived on the Upper East Side.

'And how is she?'

'Not getting any younger, so she tells me every day.' Nicole smiled. 'She's a lovely little thing though. Gave me another coffee cake which won't do much for my waistline.' She patted her midriff, but at fifty-seven Nicole looked much younger than her years. Her Sicilian descent had graced her with olive skin and curves in all the right places, her bouncing corkscrew curls made her look younger still, and she had an air of vitality with her joie de vivre and her inability to sit around doing nothing.

'Nonsense, enjoy it.'

'It is good,' she admitted. 'We'll have some tomorrow for brunch if you'd like to come over.'

Evie smiled. Nicole liked to keep her close but she needn't worry. Manhattan was her home now, and the only reason she'd ever run again would be if her past caught up with her. And she had no intention of letting that happen.

'I'd love to. It's supposed to be sunny tomorrow too, so we could have our coffee cake and then walk through Central Park to the shelter. I'm doing the afternoon shift.'

Nicole pushed her cutlery together on her plate. 'Actually, I hope you don't mind, but I've got Doris to fill in for you tomorrow so you can help me collect up any bags donated for the coat drive.'

'Of course, sounds good to me. And anyway, it'll burn off more coffee cake. We could even have two slices.' Evie pushed the last morsel of sausage onto her fork.

'Now you're talking.' Nicole grinned mischievously.

'People have been incredibly generous this year with the coats. We've quite a collection already.' Not everyone was as lucky as she was, and Evie hoped she'd never again have to know what it was like to spend a night on the streets, to be huddled in doorways shivering with cold worrying about where her next meal was coming from. And with winter almost upon them, there was plenty of use for old coats that would be thrown out for the latest label, or because the colour wasn't right or the owner had grown out of them. She and Nicole had leaflet-dropped a week ago, and with each leaflet was a garbage bag with instructions to leave unwanted coats in the bags on appointed days, ready for collection.

They linked arms when they left the café, bracing themselves against the wind chill that lowered the temperature by at least ten degrees. But despite the frosty temperatures, Evie was happier than she'd been in years. She hoped her past would stay buried so that her life wouldn't have to fall apart again, just when she'd just finished putting it back together.

One mistake she'd made. Surely she'd finished paying for it by now.

Nicole

Nicole greeted the doorman at her apartment block in the city. Reggie had been working there ever since she bought the place eleven years ago and he was one of the friendliest New Yorkers she'd ever met. He always smiled, always had something nice to say to everyone and his manners meant he was well respected.

She opened the door to Apartment Twenty-One, dropped her keys on the side table in the hall and breathed deeply into the silence. Three years ago when she'd brought home a stray, as her late mother would've said, the apartment had been instantly filled with warmth and love. She'd stopped feeling lost in a past impossible to change. But since Evie moved out a year ago, the apartment had gone back to being unnaturally quiet and it had marked the first time Nicole had really been alone in fifteen years. She'd been with the Churchills for thirteen of those, and then Evie had brought light into her life for another two.

She hung her coat on the coat stand and looped her scarf on another hook. She went into the kitchen first, then the living room, and turned on lights and lamps. She switched on the television and went back to the kitchen to make a mug of hot chocolate. She liked noise, it kept her company. Of course Evie came over a lot, but she was an independent young thing and Nicole knew she needed to stop babying her as though she were her own, let her make her own way in life. At first she'd worried Evie would take off into the night and she'd never see her again. Experience told her how painful that would be. But gradually she was beginning to trust this wouldn't happen.

With her hot chocolate topped with a few naughty sprinkles from a block of seventy per cent dark chocolate, Nicole took her hot drink into the living room where she set it on a coaster, a habit she'd gotten used to after her time with the Churchills. Kent Churchill was a stickler for having everything just so and had never allowed a drink to be set down without something to protect the expensive furniture.

She bent down to switch on the electric fireplace that did a good job of mimicking the real thing, and then she sat back in the armchair while the pebbles became illuminated with imitation flames behind them. The Portland-stone effect blended in well in the living room filled with soft furnishings of taupe and cream with the occasional mocha-coloured scatter cushion. She watched the flickering orange and her body began to relax. Already she was looking forward to seeing Evie tomorrow for brunch and trudging around the city collecting donated coats. The coat drive had been something she and a few others who helped out at the homeless shelter had come up with. When she'd first met Evie and seen her shivering in a doorway, her thin coat at least a season too early, she'd given her the blanket Kent Churchill had told her to throw away, and it had started her thinking about all the things the affluent discarded without a single thought. She knew she'd been guilty of it on plenty of occasions … shoes barely worn when fashions changed, trousers that were perfectly tailored but weren't a colour she felt suited her any more. Old blankets and coats weren't much to people who had money, but to someone living on the streets, it could mean the difference between life and death. It could mean everything.

Evie had only been staying with Nicole for a week when she'd told her about the coat drive idea and Evie was quick to leap at the chance to help. Evie hadn't divulged much about why she'd been living on the streets, but Nicole hadn't needed to know. All she knew was that Evie had a heart of gold and wouldn't accept any help if she couldn't do something in return. Together, they'd designed flyers and taken them to be printed, put them through doors, covering as wide a spread of Manhattan as they could, pinned them up where they were allowed. More people than she'd thought had been generous and put their old coats into the garbage bags they'd supplied. Nicole had taken charge of their haul and filled the third bedroom in the apartment with them, and slowly they'd washed every single coat and Evie had fixed them up: coats with broken zippers—she'd replaced them all; coats with buttons missing—they'd bought a new set; anything with a tear and Evie had sewn them so you'd never even know. Nicole had ended up buying a sewing machine without telling Evie and pretended she'd had it all the time. The girl was a whiz with the machine, and hand sewing, and eventually her skills had led to securing a job with Nicole's friend, Bonnie.

Nicole stared into the flames. Having Evie nearby eased her pain. It didn't get rid of it all together, but it eased her loneliness, her sense of loss. She thought about the Churchills, something she didn't do so much of these days since Evie had come in to her life, but the coat drive had started her wondering about the family whose blanket she still had, washed and pressed and put away in the linen cupboard. Now and again, on really cold nights, even though the apartment was warm and the fire added cosiness, Evie would visit and they'd sit beneath the red blanket and watch movies: *Miracle on 34th Street* (Evie's favourite), *It's a Wonderful Life* (Nicole's). And each time she stroked the soft, woollen material, she thought of Kent and of Jackson and wondered whether they'd ever regretted anything, like she did. She regretted not making more of a stand, finding out why Kent had reacted the way he did and fired her from the job she'd held for thirteen years. She regretted never telling the truth about herself, her life's journey and all the pain she had endured. But most of all she regretted that she had never been enough for anyone—for Evie to stay, for the Churchills to keep her close, and most of all for the son who'd walked away and never come home.

Chapter Three

Jack

Central Park was closed to traffic at this time and runners were out in force. Jack pounded the road beneath his feet as he ran, hoping this exercise would be a tonic to cope with the rest of the day that lay ahead. Tonight was the annual Thanksgiving Party and for his father's benefit. He'd be there, as he was every year, honouring his mother's memory by working his ass off and schmoozing with people he didn't really like, all in the name of running a successful family business.

Somewhere along the way since his mother's death, Jack, his sister Cameron, and Kent had lost sight of family. It was as though Cynthia was the thread that wound deeply through each of them and when she was no longer there, they unravelled with no idea how to put themselves back together again. With every Thanksgiving, Christmas, New Year's and birthday, Jack had gone through the motions but it hadn't been until Nicole started working as their housekeeper that he'd begun to enjoy those occasions again. She'd come to work for his father a few days after his fifteenth birthday, and rather than resenting a woman stepping into their domain after losing his mother when he was eleven, Jack had welcomed the change and celebrations had returned with a sense of happiness, reflection, laughter. There'd been a sense of fun, a feeling of future despite their fragility.

Jack rounded a corner, dodged another runner, and continued on his way. The sun hovered in the sky like a golden coin, but the wind chill was the constant reminder of an impending New York winter. The bare branches of trees with a lingering frost on their bark crept upwards towards a sky bluer than it had been earlier that morning, when bruised clouds had clustered above the city and the road beneath his feet twinkled with ground frost as it reflected the sun.

As Jack ran, he thought more about his mother. She would've been fifty-seven on her next birthday. She was loving, kind, and had an air of sophistication that didn't come from smart clothes or expensive handbags and jewellery. She'd worn a subtle fragrance with floral notes that lingered subtly in the air long after she left a room, and she'd doted on her children who loved her unequivocally in return. When she died it had left their world with a gap so wide and so deep none of them had ever been able to quite climb out. And the key moments in Jack's life made him miss her all the more—the day he graduated from business school, the successful business that had turned into a fully-fledged, multi-million dollar company, each birthday another he hadn't been able to share with her.

Ever since Jack could remember, Cynthia had been creative, sketching pictures in the park, photographing, entertaining him at home as they made origami frogs, a boat, a car. And when Jack was still in diapers, she'd signed up to a jewellery-making course, more out of boredom as a stay-at-home mom than anything else, and her enthusiasm soared. She made beautiful pieces Jack could still remember now—a brass ring she'd made in one of her earliest classes, the silver horseshoe pendant with cubic zirconia edges, gold and silver leaf drop earrings. Somewhere in the house was a box full of her jewellery, but like the family photographs, his father seemed to have buried it away and Jack wondered whether the pieces would ever see the light of day again. Unlike his father, Jack had a few photos in his condo. His favourite was a picture of his mom, with Jack on one knee and Cameron on the other, laughing away as the camera snapped the shot, their faces rosy and high on family life. They were sitting on a bench in Central Park, just like the benches Jack ran past now, except the trees weren't bare; they had brassy gold fall leaves, which produced the warm backdrop.

Jack turned a corner and upped the pace, pounding his way through the park and all the way back to his condo in the East Village where he paced outside the main entrance to cool down. Despite doing the full loop of 6.1 miles and the excellent scenery in Central Park—every runner's dream—the fog still hadn't lifted from his mind.

Once inside the condo, he stretched, took a long shower, had a power nap and then psyched himself up for the night ahead. When he woke, he ironed his evening shirt, shined his shoes, and pulled on his tux, finishing it off with a semi-butterfly bow tie before heading outside to flag down a yellow cab after it disgorged a businessman and before it had time to pull away from the kerb.

'Come in, son.' Kent appeared behind the housekeeper, Maggie, when the door to the townhouse opened. 'You're prompt.'

'I hate being late,' he said, stepping into the hallway.

'Hard to believe it's Thanksgiving already.' Kent fastened his second cufflink. He was wearing the rose gold set Jack's mother had made, another popular product in the shop. Jack liked to think his father was wearing them for sentimental reasons rather than because he wanted to push sales, but with Kent Churchill you could never be sure. He watched his father look into the mirror in the hallway and adjust his bow tie.

'Yeah, the years go quick.' Conversation was stilted, as though they barely knew one another. Since the worst Thanksgiving in history, the night he'd last seen Nicole, their relationship had grown more tense and Jack wondered how many more times he could don the clothes and adopt the pretence that he enjoyed networking with the people who'd be here tonight.

'How many have we got coming tonight?' Jack mustered up some enthusiasm.

'Twenty at last count, as long as the Dexters don't cancel again.'

The Dexters were notorious late cancellers, but they had five young kids and Jack assumed a lack of willing babysitters, given they were both from overseas. 'Not a bad number. Anything I can do?'

'No, everything's all set. Maggie has the food and beverages ready, so there's nothing for us to worry about except to enjoy the evening.'

Or at least get through the evening, Jack decided. Maggie was a stern housekeeper who seldom smiled on duty, but he knew not one guest would go hungry and they would be lubricated to within an inch of their sanity with an ongoing supply of champagne, wine and spirits.

'Is Braydon bringing Fern along tonight?' Jack winced, praying the answer might be 'no' for once. He'd had enough of her constant habit of brushing past him too many times, or giving him the eye.

'Of course.' Kent shrugged on his dinner jacket. 'She likes you.'

'Exactly.'

'Be flattered, enjoy it. When you get to my age—'

'What a load of bull. You get your fair share of attention. How's Linda?' Jack relaxed a bit. He and his father may not do in-depth chats, but they could manage small talk just fine.

Kent raised an eyebrow and grinned. 'I suppose I do. And Linda's fine. She can't make tonight unfortunately.'

Jack had always wondered why his father had never settled down with anyone since his mom died. He'd been thirty-nine when he lost his wife. He was good looking, rich, not a bad conversationalist when he wanted to be. But it had never happened. He'd had a succession of women, more discreetly at first and then out in the open once Jack and his sister were older, but none of them had stuck around for more than a few months, never been more than casual flings. At first Jack had thought it was because his father was being responsible, putting the kids first, but he'd started to doubt that reasoning. There had to be something else holding him back.

Kent crouched down in front of the mahogany cabinet that ran along the dining room wall and was probably worth more than most people's entire furniture collection. 'Now where did I put the cigars?'

'Bit early, isn't it? Aren't you supposed to have them after a meal?'

He found them in the bottom drawer and then, with one in his hand, sat down at one end of the deep burgundy Chesterfield couch. 'Oh, come on, relax a little. You'd enjoy these things if you did.' Kent snipped the end and inhaled the aroma. 'You can't beat a good cigar.'

'Mom never thought so.' It was a cheap shot to mention his mother, but when his father went all high and mighty and really sounded like a jumped-up dick, he hated it.

'Your mother didn't tolerate smoking, no.' Kent burnt the end of the cigar ready for lighting. 'Things change.' Finally, he stuck the thing in his mouth.

Jack's mother had hated smoke of any kind and it was forbidden inside the house. Even her own father and his pipe had never been allowed within ten feet of her when they were outside. Many a time Kent and Grandpa had gone out post-dinner under the pretence of taking a long walk, when all along they were going for a smoke.

'Care to join me?' Kent puffed a cloud of smoke into the air.

Jack perched on the arm of the Chesterfield at the opposite end. 'After dinner, perhaps.' He'd join the ritual to appease his father. This business was what defined this family now. It was their past and their future and whether that was a good thing or not, it was the way it was.

'Good. A nice way to finish a meal and I can assure you we won't be alone. And Fern will keep her distance.' Kent wiggled his fingertips in the air and pouted, just like Fern did.

Jack couldn't help but laugh. 'She certainly will. Maybe I'll smoke the entire box.'

'Not if I get there first.' Kent took another puff on the cigar. 'Did you talk to Braydon about the diamond marketing campaign?'

'Not yet.' He noticed his father's gaze and sighed. 'Yes, I know. He's good for business. I'll talk to him early next week. We have a meeting, and I'm sure we can get the campaign off to a flying start.'

'Your mother's designs are in the new collection.'

'Good, it's nice we're still doing them. They were always a crowd pleaser.' His mother had been just as popular with customers as her designs were and Jack was glad they still sold well.

'Did you send the figures to the accountant?' Kent poured himself a whiskey and proffered the bottle to Jack.

Jack shook his head at the offer. 'Not yet.'

'Jack, you've got to stay on top of things. What's wrong with you lately? Every time I ask whether you've done something to do with the business it's always "not yet", "haven't gotten around to it" or "I'll do it later".'

'I'm busy, that's all, Dad.'

'We're all busy, but I want to buy the new premises within the next twelve months if I can. It will catapult our business to the next level, having another store for customers to walk into.'

Another store would catapult them somewhere, although Jack wasn't sure where exactly. He wished he had the passion and the drive his father assumed the gene pool had passed on, but he couldn't seem to pull himself out of the lacklustre mood he'd settled into the last couple of years.

'Have you found anywhere suitable yet?' he asked.

Kent shook his head. 'There's a shortage of decent retail spaces. But I've got my eye on a few things, don't you worry.'

Their conversation was cut short and Jack was given a reprieve when the first guests drifted in. This year's guests included a client who'd bought a large consignment of jewellery to sell at retail outlets internationally, as well as neighbours who either owned successful businesses or worked at the top of their game in industries including finance and fashion.

The scene was set—the grand table laid, the fire roaring in the grate and Maggie toing and froing from the kitchen to keep everyone lubricated and satisfied with canapés. The dinner itself was bearable. Jack got lucky this time and sat between Malcolm, a bigwig in the banking world and his wife, Cara, lover of fine jewellery judging by how much was weighing her down tonight—an enormous diamond pendant swinging from a platinum chain, a ring with a rock the size of the Statue of Liberty. Cara was outwardly confident and friendly, and unlike some of the women, she could hold a conversation without one bat of an eyelid or one stroke of his leg beneath the table.

The cigars were passed around at the end and Jack obliged, removed the cellophane wrapper and lit it the second Fern came anywhere near him. At least he could laugh about it. He had to do something to amuse himself at these stuffy events. His father had put on a big party for Fourth of July and Jack had managed to amuse himself by drinking copious amounts of wine, both red and white, and having a competition with Paul Hook, a customer who'd swung an invite after he'd bought his fiancée an engagement ring at The Diamond Touch, a brooch for his mom's fiftieth and personalised cufflinks for his brother's graduation, all in one day. Kent hadn't realised quite how much of a party animal Paul was, and he and Jack had ended up playing drinking games that only ended when Paul introduced a game of dizzy astronauts to the mix and cut his head open by bashing into the sideboard.

Jack couldn't help the laugh escape as he remembered.

'You're a happy boy tonight.' Fern had crept up behind him without him realising.

He took a drag from his cigar and blew it in her general direction. If she didn't leave soon, he'd have no choice but to blow it in her face.

'Just enjoying the party and the company,' he told her.

Fern lowered her voice. 'It's a nice night to be out on the patio.'

She was nothing if not forward. 'Bit cold, isn't it?' He saw Braydon weaving his way over to them and this time he was glad of the man's company.

'Great cigars, Jack.' Braydon looped an arm across Fern's shoulders and immediately she began nuzzling his neck in a sickly fashion that made Jack want to get the hell out of there. And he would if he wasn't so damned polite to his father's guests. Instead, he stood and listened to Braydon harping on about brands of cigars, lots of crap Jack didn't give a shit about.

'Gurkha His Majesty's Reserve has to be the world's most expensive cigar.' Unattractively, Braydon showed his prowess and puffed gloomy smoke rings into the air. 'It's the Rolls-Royce of the cigar world.'

'Is that right?' Jack's voice dripped with disdain, but Braydon didn't pick up on it.

'They start with a rare Dominican wrapper,' he went on as though Jack was remotely interested, 'which covers a secret blend of filler tobaccos from all over the world.'

'Yeah, well if you can afford them then we're paying you too much.' Jack slapped him on the back a little harder than was necessary and left him droning on to his audience of one about a unique infusion process, something to do with an entire bottle of cognac. The guy was a total idiot.

Jack found their accountant, Nigel, also smoking a cigar but much more pleasant to talk to.

'How's the house you bought, Jack? In New Haven, isn't it?

'That's right. I haven't done much with it yet. It's in bad shape, which is why I could buy it so cheap.'

'Don't tell me you're going to move into it yourself. It's hardly commuter distance.'

'Some people do the commute, I'm sure.'

'Yeah, those who do it in exchange for space, a family home. But there's only one of you.'

Jack grew irritated at the reference to his bachelor status. He liked to keep a firm line between the business and his personal life. 'I was going to fix it up and rent it out for a while, or I could keep it as a weekend home.'

'So why buy in New Haven and not here in Manhattan? If you're going down the rental route, you could've made a lot of money.'

For some it was always about the mighty dollar, but not for Jack. 'I'm sure I could, Nigel, but I have my condo in the city. I saw this house by coincidence when I was passing through on my way to Hazelbrook, and well, I was impressed.'

The truth was, he'd fallen for the place, but he wasn't going to elaborate. He could imagine the blank faces if he talked about how the day he'd closed on the house the fall colours of New England had made him catch his breath, how the russet red and gold leaves skittering across the road in a kaleidoscope of colours and the crinkling sounds passing through his open car window as he looked at the house, had ignited a passion in him that he hadn't felt for years. The sunlight bathed across the roof of the dilapidated house had dared him to imagine another life, a life separate from the one he was standing in now. With a large front porch, an attic at the very top with a latticed window and an overgrown garden that he longed to trim back, it was like a fresh start being dangled in front of him.

‘Well, when you’re ready to start work on the place, let me know,’ Nigel insisted. ‘I’ve got a list of contractors as long as my arm and it’s always best to go by recommendation.’

‘I’m sure it is. And thank you.’ In the first burst of excitement after buying the property, Jack had dreamed of doing all the work himself, but never having tackled anything more manual than lifting boxes of jewellery before, he suspected renovating a property would be as new to him as talking was to a baby.

Jack’s head hurt by the time the party ended and he left the house, but it felt good to be out in the cold air now. It’d been a full few days leading up to Thanksgiving, with back-to-back meetings yesterday with buyers from some of the major department stores in Lower Manhattan.

He turned the street corner, and pulling his coat tightly around him, he looked up at the moon hovering above as the air around him threatened more snow. Even now he loved to look at it. His mother had had a fascination with astrology and loved to talk about how the sun, moon, stars and planets could influence human actions. She’d talk about it for hours, Jack and Cameron would giggle, and their father would roll his eyes even though you knew he secretly loved the passion in his wife’s voice. Every night, all four of them would wait for the sun to go down and the moon to come out from its hiding place, and they’d stand out on the front steps of the townhouse and look up to the skies blanketing Manhattan. They’d talk about how far the moon was, whether there was any life there, which was a topic of endless fascination for Jack when he was younger, the shape of it—crescent, full, a sliver—and they'd desperately try to see beyond the buildings and skyscrapers that hid the stars too well, the lights of the city that made it almost impossible to distinguish between mother nature and what western civilisation had added.

Jack treasured his memories, and when the moon was as full as it was tonight, shining as if to say 'look at me, Jack, I'm still here, what happened to you?' he'd remember those times. Tonight, his memories were with him as he reached his condo ready to sleep off the dinner and the cigars, and tomorrow he'd make his escape out to Hollyhock Farm, the only place his life seemed to make sense.

Chapter Four

Jack

Jack left Manhattan earlier than planned so he could stop off at the property he now owned but had done nothing with, and with every mile he travelled away from the city toward the simplicity of Connecticut the tension fell away from him. Who knew, perhaps getting started with renovation plans could help him to see clearly, give him some direction in his life, a clue as to what to do next.

The house sat at the end of a long road on the outskirts of New Haven. It had enough land to afford privacy, yet the facade of the vintage home still sat prominently enough to belong to the rest of the neighbourhood. By the time he pulled up in the driveway, in front of the garage with crooked, rotten doors and a huge gap looming between them, the rain had started. He ran from the car up to the porch and beneath the shelter, threw off the hood of his charcoal-grey Harvard hoodie and pulled the bunch of keys from his pocket, cursing that he hadn't figured out which one fit the front door and put a sticker on it the last time he was here. Metal keys jingled together as he worked his way through them—there were keys for internal doors, one for the rear door of the garage, another for the dilapidated shed at the foot of the garden. At last he found the right key and let himself in.

It was cold inside, but out of the wind a strange sense of calm fell over Jack. It felt warming to know this place was his. Cobwebs hung from the ceiling—the beneficiary of the deceased estate had just wanted to get rid of it so hadn't bothered to clean it up at all before presenting it for sale. He walked up the stairs from the hallway, thankful they were sturdy. He'd noticed the smashed window as he'd pulled up outside and it was noticeably colder up here. He wasn't worried about the temperature, but he didn't want wildlife making its way in, if it dared to come out in the Connecticut winter, so he looked around for something to board up the window. He found cardboard in one of the bedrooms and put it up against the window, somehow wedging it between the wall and the frame. He'd have to come back on his way home from Hollyhock Farm with some duct tape and fix it properly.

Jack took out his phone and snapped away, taking pictures of all the rooms. His passion had been quietly simmering when he'd talked about this place with Nigel, and this morning on the drive up it had begun to boil gently, but now it was bubbling away nicely. He wanted to make plans, get started on a path that would lead him away to something else entirely. Walking around the rooms, he took pictures of as much as he could: cracked walls, the old fireplace, the hideous bathroom with the brown stains where water had run down the once-white sides of the enamel bath. He photographed views from the windows over the back yard that stretched out before him, bordered by trees of all shapes and sizes. Already he could feel the buzz of spring, a garden he could work on until it was filled with a riot of colour.

Jack checked his watch. He needed to get going out to Hollyhock Farm as he'd originally planned. He stood at the front door for a moment, looking back into the hallway. It was light enough even in winter, and already he could see what it would be like come summer with reclaimed wooden floorboards, a curled oak bannister leading upstairs.

With a spring in his step, he locked the door behind him. The rain had lessened but he still pulled his hood up, and he was about to go down the steps of the porch when he stopped. Something was moving beneath a grey blanket at the very end and if it had been there when he'd arrived, he hadn't noticed. He looked around and picked up a fence panel discarded at the opposite end. He armed himself with it and walked over to the blanket.

Was it a cat? Maybe a racoon? As he advanced he decided it couldn't be either. It was too big. He prodded the blanket with the fence panel, and prodded a little harder when whatever was beneath it didn't budge.

He jumped when the blanket curled back to reveal a kid who couldn't have been much older than sixteen. The kid cowered, covering his filthy face with hands encased in gloves that were either fingerless or had fallen apart.

'What the fuck do you think you're doing?' Jack demanded.

The boy held up his hands, staggered to his feet, not daring to get closer to Jack. 'I didn't mean any harm.'

'This is my property!' Jack lowered the fence panel. This boy was half his age at least, and he wasn't going to use violence, at least not yet.

'I'm sorry, mister.' The boy gathered up his blanket, along with a black garbage bag.

'What have you got there?' Jack snatched it from him, wondering what he'd pilfered from the property.

'It's nothing, just my stuff. I didn't steal anything.'

Jack peered inside and saw nothing except a half-empty bottle of water, a sweater and a box of cereal. He gave the garbage bag back, convinced. 'Well, you are trespassing. I've a good mind to call the police.'

The boy braved moving forwards past Jack, sensing a truce. 'You don't need to do that. I'm leaving now. I won't come back.'

Jack glared at him until he was out of sight, swallowed up by the neighbourhood. He leaned against the porch railing until he realised the rotting wood probably wouldn't hold his weight much longer. But at least he knew one thing for certain now. He didn't want some squatter staying here, so the sooner he started renovations, the better. He'd have this place alarmed, well-lit and regularly maintained so he wouldn't get any more trouble.

*

'You're looking more relaxed since you arrived.' Julia handed him a mug of steaming hot coffee.

Jack sat opposite Julia, his best friend Nate's fiancée, in the kitchen of their house at Hollyhock Farm in Hazelbrook, a simple town out past New Haven, Connecticut, and before you reached Hartford. Hollyhock Farm had been Jack's sanctuary for years. At first he'd only come out here to visit Nate, but he'd soon become accustomed to the wide, open spaces as he cruised away from Manhattan in his Lexus sedan, away from thc skyscrapers, the brownstones, the concentration of so many people in one space. Out here was an America he rarely got to see, an America many New Yorkers may not even be aware of when they were buried deep in their everyday lives in the metropolis.

'You know me, Julia. I'm always relaxed when I come here.'

'Even after finding an intruder at the house?'

'He wasn't an intruder as such. He was outside.'

'But it's your property, he was trespassing.'

Jack nodded. He agreed, of course, but since he'd driven away from New Haven all he'd been able to think about was the moment his father had thrown a homeless woman off their property three years ago. He'd shuddered at the realisation that he may be more like his father than he cared to admit.

'Nate won't be much longer,' Julia told him. 'He's in the far field, bundling trees ready for shipping today.'

Many people confused the ownership and running of a Christmas tree farm with a business that only demanded attention around that special time of the year, but Jack knew what a full time job his friends had on their hands. It was year-round activity, fertilising the soil, monitoring plants for animal pests or diseases, replanting and planning for the years ahead. Nate and Julia had inherited the family business, a far cry from the jewellery business that was handed to Jack on a silver platter, and life in Manhattan couldn't be more different than here at the farm. The city was fast and exciting, and for a time Jack had wanted nothing more; but since Nate had settled down with Julia and Jack had been coming out to visit them, he felt a weight lift every time he made the two-hour drive from New York City. Hazelbrook was a picture-perfect small town. A white, curved sign welcomed you and stood beside an iron clock on top of a post. The clock had the town's name on it, and beyond the clock, lining either side of the small street, were shops and amenities including a post office, a bakery, a bank, a small convenience store and a pub. It was a town with a big country feel, and once you'd passed through, the road continued on until ten minutes later Hollyhock Farm came into view.

'People don't wait long after Thanksgiving to get on with the next celebration, do they?' Jack laughed. 'How's business anyway?' He blew across the top of his coffee before he took a sip.

'So-so.' Julia's blonde hair hung around her face until she hooked it behind both ears.

'Sounds dubious.'

'We're hoping for a good season for Christmas trees, put it that way.'

'Didn't the fruit do too well this year?' Hollyhock Farm operated a Pick Your Own service for peaches, strawberries and raspberries, and Jack could vouch for how good the produce was. He swore food grown on your own land, or seeing exactly where it came from, made it taste so much better. He'd even begun to think he might plant a vegetable patch or some fruit trees on his new property one day. He'd better be careful; he was sounding almost domesticated!

'The fruit did fine, but Mom and Dad should've handed the reins over long ago. I'd offered to help, but they'd encouraged me to go away to college, forge my own path, to only come back to Hollyhock Farm if this was what I really wanted.'

'And is it?'

Julia smiled. 'It really is. Hazelbrook is my home and always will be. Nate and I tried the big city; we lived in San Francisco for a while with his job, and we went over to Europe. All the while I was waiting for a switch to trip in my brain and tell me that I actually wanted more than Hollyhock Farm.'

'But it didn't happen, did it?' Jack sipped his coffee.

'Nope. But I'm glad my parents put me on the path, made me try a different life. Otherwise I may never have known how much I wanted what I already had. I just wish they'd not let it get in such a state over the years. The Christmas tree section is fine, and I'm hoping the rest will follow suit as we clear more land, replant. And thank you for all your work clearing the maze.'

'Not a problem. I'm enjoying it.'

'Well, Nate told me how hard you've worked. It's something that's been on the list for a while but had been pushed to the bottom with everything else going on.'

Jack gulped down the rest of his coffee. 'I think I'll head down there now, see how my pride and joy is coming along.'

Julia smiled. 'You never were fit for an office, Jack.'

'Ain't that the truth.' He pulled on the rain boots he'd brought with him, the extra thick coat, picked up the gardening gloves to protect him from the elements as much as anything else and left Julia organising supplies for making Christmas wreaths. He tried to focus on how lucky he was to be inheriting a well-oiled family business that would provide for years to come. Nate and Julia had worked far harder than he ever had, or at least it seemed that way when physical labour was involved, but perhaps it was different when it was also a labour of love.

He walked over to the field closest to the lane that ran around the perimeter of the property. Many years ago Julia's father had planted conifer saplings, and in the first of two framed photos in the hallway of the farmhouse, the maze her father had lovingly made from scratch and cared for as long as he could was on display. In the other photo, her father was shown crouched down, pushing the first sapling, some eight inches tall, into the ground. Those saplings had grown and the maze had taken, looked promising, but when illness ran through the family, the maze had been neglected. It hadn't been pruned for years, light and rain hadn't reached the parts it needed to and the paths running between the almost twelve-foot-high conifers had ended up overgrown and impassable.

Last spring Jack had walked around the property with Nate. It had been an unusually warm start to the season and in the lull between Christmas and the start of fruit picking season, which began in June with strawberries, elderberries and this year, blackberries, the men had found themselves at the entrance to the maze with a beer each in hand.

'What the hell is that mess?' Jack sat on the grass area in front and swigged his beer as they looked at an overgrown area of land that looked as crazy as a plate of tangled spaghetti, except it needed more than a garden fork taken to it.

Nate, cowboy hat on his head, sat down on the grass next to him.

'You could clear up the area and plant more fruit, pumpkins maybe, they're always popular.'

Nate grinned. 'Julia won't do that.'

'What, she's attached to this mess?' Jack lay back, propped up on his elbows.

'Once upon a time, it was a maze.'

'No kidding.'

'You've seen the pictures hanging in the hallway of the farmhouse.'

Jack whistled through his teeth. 'It's unrecognisable.'

'Julia's dad planted it years ago, but when he was sick they let it go. They couldn't manage everything.'

'Was it open to the public?'

Nate shook his head. 'Trust you, with your business head on. No, it was only ever fun for him. He did it for his kids.'

'Could've been a nice money earner, people love that sort of thing. Mom went to England once and I remember seeing the photos of her and dad in Hampton Court Maze. Fun for adults and kids.' He grinned.

'Be my guest.'

'What do you mean?' Jack sat up now, pushed his sunglasses on top of his head.

'If you want to clear it, go for it. I'd like to see you get your hands dirty for once.' He grinned. 'And I've got plenty to do this year with the fruit field and keeping those Christmas trees shipshape until December, replanting more.'

'Yeah, looks like you're flat out, sitting around on your ass with a beer!' Jack nodded to the bottle.

'Very funny. It's a quick break then back to it.'

Jack looked at the mess in front of them, and as he stared into the tangled branches, the ground barely visible beneath, he began to get excited about restoring the maze to its former glory. It would certainly distract him from his own family business, and perhaps here, he'd found his calling.

'You're on,' he announced.

'What?'

'I'll clear it for you,' said Jack. 'I'll come up on weekends and I'll get it looking like it does in the photo in your hallway.'

'You're serious?'

'Of course.'

And that was how his maze project had started. It'd been a turning point for Jack, the moment he'd begun to fully appreciate the wider world that stretched beyond Manhattan, when he'd realised the emotional stretch outside of the city.

Now, jeans, a roll-necked jumper and a puffy jacket replaced last night's party tux, clumpy bottle-green rain boots took the place of gleaming, well-fitted shoes, and Jack's tidy dark-brown hair was covered in a grey waffle-knit hat. He made his way down the lane adjacent to the fruit fields and on to the maze that looked so much better already. Over the last six months, he'd hacked away the overgrown branches and leaves, taken the electric hedge trimmers to the conifers. Julia had been there to supervise—he'd told her it was unnecessary, but she said it wouldn't be good for business to end up with a disfigured body stumbling out of the maze. It had been exhausting work with so much debris put into wheelbarrows and wheeled out following the maze's unique pathways each time, but soon enough the paths of the maze were clear. He'd planted some more saplings, closely monitored them for diseases, and he'd kept them shaped. He'd rearranged some of the conifers and brought in a couple of more established trees at the start of the maze to cover the most obvious gaps and present the attraction in the best way he could. It was a labour of love and he'd fallen for it well and truly, revelling in the juxtaposition to his office job, the fresh air, the simplicity of outdoor life.

The farm had a good irrigation system in the other fields, and some kind of watering system in the maze, but it needed improvement. It was on the list for Nate and Julia when they had the funds and Jack knew if he paid for it they'd feel indebted to him forever, and that wasn't what he wanted at all. So here he was, hooking up the garden hose to the outside supply near the lane. Once the maze was fully established, it would be easy to maintain if they kept on top of it.

Jack took out the wheelbarrow from the lock-up tin shed adjacent to the maze. The muscles in his arms strained as he manoeuvred it up to the entrance, and when his phone rang he tutted, pulled it out of his back pocket and saw it was his father calling before he switched it off. Whatever it was, it could wait. There was nothing in the business that couldn't allow him a little leeway and some time out. With the wheelbarrow, Jack followed each part of the path in turn, hedges wider now he'd trimmed them back and shaped them. The widening was also necessary if Nate and Julia wanted to open the maze to the public—there'd be strollers or wheelchairs, both of which required the extra space.

Jack pulled out weeds, lifted up debris, dropping it into the wheelbarrow each time. He finished off by picking up the hose he'd connected earlier and watering beneath the trees, the area not always reached when it rained, satisfied for now that the conifers were looking good. The ground itself was more hardened than usual, but it was inevitable with temperatures plummeting with the season. He'd done a bit of research and discussed with Nate how important it was to deal with the soil compaction before it became troublesome and prevented proper draining, which would negate all his hard work.

As Jack wound up the hose and removed the heavy-duty gloves, Nate wandered over from another field.

'Jack.' His friend shook his hand and patted his opposite shoulder. 'Good to see you. How's your maze looking?'

It had become 'his maze' the second he'd offered to do something with it, and Jack didn't mind in the slightest. As they walked back to the house, he explained what he'd done, how it was looking.

‘I’d like a few more of those conifers to take and become more robust and we’ll be good to go,’ said Jack as they took their boots off at the door.

‘Where’s Julia?’ Jack asked, already welcoming the warmth of the farmhouse compared to outside.

‘On the phone with her sister. It could be a while.’ Nate made coffee and handed one to Jack, before settling down in the armchair to the left of the fire. Jack sat opposite and let the mug warm his hands. Despite the gloves, the winter chill had still nipped at his fingers.

‘And how’s life in the big smoke?’ Nate asked.

‘Same as usual.’

‘That good?’

Jack smiled. ‘You know what it’s like. Making money, keeping Mom’s dream alive.’

‘Julia was in The Diamond Touch last week.’

‘Yeah?’

‘She picked up the wedding rings.’

‘That’s great.’ Here was his friend getting married to the love of his life and Jack didn’t even have a date. ‘How are the plans going?’

‘I’m leaving it all up to her, to be honest … too many cooks and all that.’

Conversation moved to ice hockey, a sport they’d both enjoyed over the years. Nate had played for a time but preferred to watch it now and shout at the television when things didn’t go the right way for his team, the New York Rangers. Jack liked to rile him up, particularly because he followed the New Jersey Devils … whenever their two teams were up against one another, Julia couldn’t stand to be in the same room as the men. Too much testosterone for her liking, she claimed.

Julia emerged from the bedroom and settled the phone back into its cradle. She perched on the arm of Nate's chair and he rested his hand on her thigh. 'The maze is looking great, Jack. And people in town have already been asking about it.'

'That's a good sign.'

'You've worked hard, man, we owe you,' said Nate.

Jack dismissed the compliments. 'You're the ones who've done me a favour. Working outside, getting rid of my pent-up city frustration has been a godsend.'

'How's Kent?'

'His usual self.' He knew he wouldn't get away with the flippancy. 'He's hungry to find new premises and open up another retail outlet which apparently will take us to the next level. And he's still smoking those jerk-off cigars.'

'They're not so bad.' Nate laughed until Julia shot him a look. 'Don't get your panties in a twist. I didn't say I smoke them. Couldn't afford them even if I wanted to.'

'He's always liked the finer things in life,' Jack went on. 'But since Mom died it's as though he can't stop himself. If he has expensive wine and champagne he needs to know it's the best, he buys new suits when he has a dozen of them already, he buys pieces of furniture he doesn't need because they're "the thing to have". He even has his fair share of women.'

'You know it's better than him moping around.' Julia sat on the raised hearth by the fire and stretched out her hands to warm them. 'Imagine if he sat around depressed every day. You'd hate it.'

'I know. God, I'm awful.'

'That wasn't what I meant exactly. It's just that perhaps he's coping in his way and you cope in yours, and for some reason neither of you are meeting in the middle.'

Jack grinned and pointed to Julia as he looked at Nate. 'She's way too clever for you.'

'Don't I know it?' Nate blew Julia a kiss. Domestic bliss was beginning to feel like a fairy tale to Jack, something in which he'd never play a starring role.

They talked some more about Jack's mother. Julia's antennae had shot up at Jack's negativity about his father, as he'd known it would.

'Does your father talk about your mother much?' she asked.

Jack shook his head. 'Only occasionally, but then it's the briefest of comments before he'll change the subject.' Whenever Cynthia's name was mentioned, Jack would notice his father's demeanour change and he'd wonder how much he still hurt inside, how much he'd buried so deep that the surface showed no ripples of grief any more. He longed to talk to his father about his mother, smile about her, even laugh, but his father was closed to conversation about the woman who still meant so much to both of them.

'Well, you and your father need to somehow get on the same page, Jack, and to do that you need to talk to him, tell him how you feel.' Julia hesitated. 'Tell him why you come up here, Jack. That'd be a start. I wouldn't mind putting money on the fact that you tell him you're coming to see Nate and he thinks you're in it for the men's camaraderie, the bonding, the talk of women and sport. I bet he has no idea you're really coming for the farm, the setting, the escape.'

'I can't, Julia.'

'Why not?' This from Nate who shared his fiancée's opinion, Jack knew.

‘Because it was my mother’s dream. The Diamond Touch was the empire her love and talent started. Without the business, she’s really gone.’

Julia came over to Jack’s chair and crouched down at his feet, looking up at him. ‘And what about your dreams, Jack? What’s happening to them?’ She patted his hand, and as she made her way over to the kitchen area and opened the fridge, said, ‘Just promise me you’ll think about it.’

He agreed and Julia brought dips, breadsticks and torn up pitta breads back to the living room.

‘We’re thinking of starting up the carriage rides and sleigh rides.’ Nate scooped up a globule of red pepper hummus with the end of a breadstick.

Jack sat up. ‘First I’ve heard.’

‘Julia’s sister still keeps the horses in the field closest to town and she’s a whiz at training them. They’ve been at halter, even in the harness, and they’re almost ready.’

‘We’ll need a decent carriage and a sleigh,’ Julia added, a piece of pitta in hand, ‘but it might have to wait until next year. Maybe the maze will raise the profits a bit and we’ll have a good summer with the fruits.’

Jack beamed. ‘Well, if anyone can get there, it’s you two.’

Nate changed tack completely. ‘I forgot to ask. How was last night’s party?’

‘It was pleasant enough.’

‘And how’s the lovely Fern?’ Julia smirked. ‘Still all over you like a bad rash?’

‘Yup. Braydon either doesn’t notice or likes feeling jealous. I’m beginning to wonder whether it’s some kinky game between the two of them … she hits on me, he gets jealous, then punishes her later, if you know what I mean.’

Nate laughed. 'I've never met the man, but he sounds like an idiot. Then again, Fern doesn't sound much better. Did you get rid of her when the cigars came out?'

How well they knew him. 'Works like a charm, every time.'

'You know,' said Julia, 'sometimes women just want a bit of honesty.'

Jack and Nate looked at each other, and when they both fell back laughing, Julia knew she wasn't going to win this one and ended up giggling as they talked more about the party, the life that was so different to the one on Hollyhock Farm, the stilted atmosphere at social gatherings compared to this one with three friends totally relaxed in one another's company.

By the time Jack left Hollyhock Farm in the early evening, armed with duct tape so he could stop off in New Haven and board up the window at his property properly, a light flurry of snow had decorated the farm. He made his way towards Hazelbrook, and as he came into town the clock stood guard like a sentry over the shops. By this time people had gone home, to wives, husbands, family, at the end of another day. Benches at either side of the road were covered in a thin layer of white from the snow which was coming down harder, creating the blank canvas that come morning would let some lucky soul be the first to make their mark in it.

Jack pulled up before he reached the end of the street. He didn't want the day to come to an end, so he climbed out, shrugged on his jacket which, filled with duck down, was enough to tackle the worst American winter, a wool hat and a pair of gloves. A snowflake spiralling down from above kissed his nose as it fell. The rest of the snowfall shone against the honey glow of the streetlamps. A giant Christmas tree bedecked with hundreds of coloured fairy lights marked the end of the street, and other trees that come spring would have leaves and lush foliage lined the shopping strip and dazzled with the white twinkly lights wound around their trunks.

He looked up to the top of the enormous Christmas tree and beyond, let the snow settle on his cheeks. He closed his eyes, parted his lips slightly to feel the cold sensation on his tongue, and when he opened his eyes and looked up, saw the moon and stars twinkling all around him in a sky so very different to the one he was used to in Manhattan.

His mother had always said, 'Trust in the stars, Jack,' as though they would always show him the way, as though they had the power to change everything. But was that even possible? Would he ever find what he was looking for, without betraying his father or the memory of his mother?

Chapter Five

Evie

The Manhattan streets throbbed with Christmas shoppers as Evie left work to meet Nicole. People walked every which way, somehow managing not to collide, and skyscrapers made their presence known, decorated with lights that shimmered across the city. Window displays competed for attention, red canopies over doorways were framed with sparkly lights, a gold Christmas tree made up of tiny lights went from the ground to the top of a building on one corner, and on another, a gigantic red bow made up of glowing lights illuminated passers-by. Window boxes had said goodbye to the flowers of spring and summer and instead green foliage interspersed with silver lights lit up the smiles of Christmas shoppers.

Evie and Nicole linked arms as they wove their way through the throng, people jostling for cab rides across the city, to get into shops, to make it home to loved ones. Even after three years of relative normality, which involved a comfortable apartment of her own, a job she loved, food on the table and even the odd luxury every now and then, Evie still found it hard to completely let go of where she'd once been, to stop the heartache from eclipsing the joy of the season as her memories crept in. But slowly she was beginning to believe that even she deserved to be happy, and it was a good feeling.

They made a beeline across West 34th Street towards Macy's. Up above the entrance were Christmas trees, a sparkly invitation for shoppers to come in out of the icy wind, to defrost in the heated shop the second you stepped through the doors. The window displays on the Broadway side attracted thousands of people every year and today was no exception. On Thursday last week, they'd watched the Thanksgiving Day Parade with the thousands of other people as Santa came to town and put delight on the faces of kids all over New York. Giant balloons had bobbed up and down the street, different characters from last year and the year before that. Evie had timed it well yesterday and managed to see several window displays at major department stores and designer outlets when the crowds were at their smallest, early in the morning before she started work. She'd seen giant versions of Christmas ornaments, the holiday adventures of Charlie Brown, wintry depictions of the world's greatest natural and man-made wonders, and she'd seen a song sheet illuminating the window of a store with the notes and lyrics to 'White Christmas'.

'What do you think of this, for Mrs Mack?' Nicole had already located her first gift after only entering America's largest department store minutes ago. She held up the camel cashmere scarf in Macy's for Evie's approval.

'It's beautiful.' Evie couldn't resist stroking the material. 'I think she'll love it.'

'I'll take it,' Nicole told the sales assistant. 'Do you have the gloves to match?'

Evie grinned. Nicole was a shopper—she could've done it as an Olympic sport if such a thing existed. They'd already bought earrings for Madison, an old school friend of Nicole's, a posh pen that had cost an extortionate amount for Patrick, a man in his sixties who lived in Nicole's building and was quite the writer—last week they'd been into Barnes & Noble on 5th Avenue and seen his titles in there—plus a beautiful hand-crafted abacus for two-year-old Freya who lived with her parents in Nicole's apartment block and whom Evie suspected Nicole wished was her grandchild most of the time. The child had one of those angelic faces and loved Nicole to bits. Evie had seen them together and it'd always made her wonder why Nicole had never married, never had a family of her own. She was the type: motherly, caring, kind, and most importantly, not a pushover.

They shared the shopping bags between them as they joined the escalator going up. Evie had finished all her shopping, not that it was much. She only bought for a friend at the shelter—they did Secret Santa and maximum spend was five dollars so she'd bought Selina, an art student, a furry notepad with a feathery pen—for Nicole, and for her boss, Bonnie, she'd made up hampers full of their favourite things: candles, bubble bath and hand lotion for Nicole, chocolates and a trendy, new pincushion cuff for Bonnie in a bid to stop her holding those pins between her teeth.

They bustled through the crowds surrounding the perfume counter. 'There are still four weeks to go till Christmas and we're nearly done,' Nicole whispered excitedly. 'I do so like to get it all ready, wrapped and out of the way early. Then I can concentrate on everything else.'

'The food you mean,' Evie teased. The woman's passion for feeding other people was nothing short of amazing. She always cooked too much—two freezers solved that problem, as well as donations to Evie.

'What's on the menu this year?' Evie asked. 'If it's anything like Thanksgiving …' She puffed out her cheeks to show she'd burst eating the same amount all over again. They'd had Thanksgiving dinner with a couple of volunteers from the shelter and then worked the evening shift, where patrons had pestered them into joining the festivities, eating the turkey, the yams, pigs in blankets. Evie had relented when a regular at the shelter had offered the pumpkin pie because he looked as though his heart would break if she didn't accept the bowl.

'The usual,' mused Nicole as she perused the bottles of designer fragrance and cologne on display. 'Turkey with all the trimmings.'

Evie adjusted the bags looped over her arms. For a small amount of shopping they were surprisingly awkward to carry, but it didn't help that the temperature was tropical in here compared to outside. She was already carrying her coat, and her jumper would be next to come off. 'Christmas pudding and brandy sauce to finish?'

'And mince pies,' Nicole grinned mischievously.

'Just remember how much there was leftover last year,' Evie warned.

'Ah, don't you worry about that. It didn't go to waste.' She'd frozen plenty and taken mince pies, boxed up, to the neighbours the next day, as well as handing them out at the shelter.

Evie picked up a bottle of Chanel Mademoiselle and inhaled the heavenly fragrance. It smelled expensive even before you'd checked the price tag.

'I still need to get you a little something.' Nicole lifted the bottle as soon as Evie put it back.

'Not at that price you don't.'

'It's Christmas, let me spoil you.'

Evie shook her head. 'You've already done so much for me, and all I want is your company, that's all.'

'But I need to get you something.'

'Fine,' Evie relented, 'but nothing that expensive.' She ushered Nicole along as the sales assistant, sensing a customer whose fingers itched to grab at their purse and open it, poised herself, ready to swoop in. 'Let's go upstairs and have a look what they've got there.'

They took another escalator up and wandered about the floor until they came to the cold weather accessories. 'What about this?' Evie picked up a ruby infinity loop scarf, checked on the price tag that it wasn't horribly expensive, and hooked it over her head, winding it around again.

'It's gorgeous!' Nicole felt the wool, soft as a baby blanket. 'And it's just your colour. It matches the rosy glow you've got going on.' She reached up and pinched Evie's cheek lightly.

'That's the freezing cold weather and being plunged into the tropics in here.' Evie admired her reflection in the nearby mirror. She was about to take the infinity loop off and give it to Nicole, grateful it cost a fraction of the bottle of perfume downstairs, when a tall, well-dressed man stopped in front of them. He glanced at her but was transfixed with Nicole who was rummaging through racks, no doubt to find some accessory to match the infinity loop, determined to buy more for Evie than she already had. Generosity had to be the woman's biggest fault.

'Nicole?' The man wore a suit, a cashmere coat, and a swanky deep red scarf hanging loose around the collar. His outfit looked like it cost more than all the items in Evie's wardrobe put together.

'Jackson?' Nicole froze for a moment. 'Oh my God! Jackson!' And then she threw her arms around the man who towered almost a foot above her. 'I don't believe it.

How are you? I haven't seen you … since … well, you know.'

Jackson took her hands in his and stood back looking at her. 'You disappeared. You wouldn't take any of my calls.'

She looked to the floor, shaking her head. 'I couldn't, I was so embarrassed after what happened.'

'You had no need to be. It's us who should've been embarrassed. You know, Dad never talks about what happened.' He still held both of Nicole's hands in his. 'Why didn't you keep in touch, with me at least?'

Tears sprang into her eyes. 'I didn't want to make it worse for you. I know you and your father have a difficult relationship. I didn't want to meddle with that.'

He sighed exasperatedly, and they seemed to have forgotten Evie was there until she moved to remove the infinity loop from around her neck.

'Oh, where are my manners?' Nicole let go of Jackson's hands, wiped her fingers beneath her eyes. 'This is Evie, my good friend.' She hugged Evie to her. 'Evie, this is Jackson.'

Evie stared at the man. He was gorgeous, no doubt about that, but she'd seen him before, she knew it. She just couldn't place him. And if she wasn't mistaken, he was looking at her in much the same way. He had soft toffee eyes, hair the colour of roasted chestnuts and a smile that showed well cared for teeth, much like hers were now. She'd not allowed Nicole to spend much on her over the years, but Nicole had put her foot down with some things, including dentistry. When Nicole had rescued her, Evie had been doing her best to keep a dental hygiene routine going, but it was hard when you had no home to call your own. One of the first things they'd done was get her medical insurance and see a doctor and a dentist. Her health was fine, but the dentist had given her a filling, an all-round clean and six months later they'd given her braces! She'd avoided them in her teen years and then orthodontics became a luxury item when her mother got sick and the family business failed. But Nicole's gift had given her a smile that still took her by surprise on occasion, when she caught sight of herself in a store window.

Evie shook hands with Jackson, eyes locking at the same time as their skin touched.

'I'm sorry, have we met?' he asked, still holding her hand, obviously trying to place her, as she was him. He only dropped her hand when a bubbly Amazonian beauty appeared out of nowhere. She'd clearly been to the fragrance department given the waft that came with her.

'Aurelia,' said Jackson, 'this is Nicole, an old friend of mine.' His eyes were on his girlfriend but didn't take long to flit over to Evie's direction again. 'And this is Evie, a friend of hers.'

Evie smiled back at Aurelia, let Nicole introduce herself and make small talk about Christmas, the business of shopping. Evie bit the side of her mouth nervously, unable to figure out where she recognised him from.

'Well, we'd better go,' said Jackson as Aurelia linked his arm proprietorially. 'I need to choose a present for Dad.' Aurelia's other arm hugged her shopping equally as possessively: a Burberry bag and a Louis Vuitton, no doubt filled with all the luxuries she'd ever want but probably didn't really need.

'It was lovely to see you again, Jackson.' Nicole kissed him on the cheek, touched her hand to the stubble around his jaw. 'Please do give my best to your father, won't you?'

Whatever was between Jackson, his family and Nicole, the strong emotional ties were written over both their faces. Over the years, Evie had become adept at reading people without talking to them; she'd had to in the darkest of days when her parents were no longer around, and then when she had no home to go to or anybody to care for her. She'd soon learned whom she could trust. And now, she didn't miss Jackson gulp as he said goodbye to Nicole.

'I'll tell him I've seen you,' he assured Nicole. 'Take care of yourself.' He didn't seem to want to leave, but the shopping bunny on his arm was raring to go.

'I feel like I've seen him before,' she told Nicole when Jackson went on his way and they took the infinity loop over to the checkout.

'You have seen him before.' Nicole sucked in her breath. 'That was Jackson Churchill.'

'Churchill?' The name was familiar, but it took a moment to fall into place. 'As in the Churchill family who fired you?'

'The very same.' Nicole took out her purse as they lined up to pay.

'And that was the son, the one who found me before his father appeared?'

Nicole nodded. 'I'm sorry, I didn't want to say who you were.' She clasped one of Evie's hands as much as the bags on her arms would allow her to. 'Not because I'm ashamed of you, but for your sake. I didn't want him judging you because of your past. I wanted him to see you as my friend.'

'Thank you.' Evie tilted her head to the checkout when it was their turn. This encounter had clearly affected Nicole more than she cared to let on, and it was obvious she and Jackson had an incredibly strong bond that neither of them wanted to sever.

'Maybe we could sneak upstairs and have one of those frozen yogurts you like so much,' said Evie as the sales assistant wrapped the infinity loop and put it into a bag.

The sparkle was back in Nicole's cheeks. 'Pomegranate for me.'

'I'll have the peach passion.' Evie smiled and hugged her friend to her, the only mother figure in her life now. 'Can I ask you something, Nicole?'

'Of course.'

'Do you regret not going back to see them? You seemed quite emotional when you saw Jackson.'

Nicole popped her receipt into one of the shopping bags as they walked away from the checkout. 'I was close to him. His mother died before I started working for them, and I don't think that family ever got over it. There was a lot of deep-set anger, a lot of words unspoken, and Jackson doesn't get along with his father.'

'He was a scary man.'

Nicole smiled. 'Not when you really get to know him. Underneath that bellowing voice and behind the expensive suits, I really believe he's one of the good ones.'

Evie let it drop for now, but once they'd gone up to another floor and bought their frozen yogurts and she was enjoying the peach passion, she asked, 'Do you think he recognised me? Jackson, I mean.'

'I don't know.' Nicole grinned.

'What?'

'He couldn't take his eyes off you!'

'Stop it!' She knew it was true, although unlike Nicole was insinuating, Evie suspected it had more to do with trying to place her than finding her attractive. Aurelia hooked on his arm told her his taste in women was a stratosphere she was unlikely to ever enter.

Wrapped up in their coats, scarves and gloves once more, they left Macy's, and as Evie walked home to her apartment, she wondered what Jackson Churchill would think when he realised who she was.

The second she got home, she flicked on the fairy lights around the front door inside, the line strung beneath the overhead cupboards in the kitchenette, the trees lights and the lights strung across the top of the small window that looked out to nothing but brick. She filled the kettle and clicked it onto its stand before flicking the switch, dropped a fruit tea bag into a sky-blue mug from the set of four she'd bought herself when she moved in, and let the teabag steep for a couple of minutes. She rubbed her hands briskly in front of the radiator, begging all heat to come her way. The single bedroom apartment was tiny—a bedroom just big enough for a double bed, at basement level with minimal natural light and a bathroom that had seen better days—but it was all she could afford on the Upper East Side, and she'd wanted this specific location so she'd be near Nicole, the friend who wanted to keep an eye on her. It felt like a lifetime ago that anyone had even cared.

When her tea was ready, she sat next to the fake Christmas tree in the corner, clutching her cup between her hands. She smiled at the twinkly lights surrounding her now, the tree dressed in the only set that would be packed away at the end of the season. She'd bought the tree in the sales at the end of last year at a bargain price for something most people couldn't stand the sight of for another eleven months. The day after Thanksgiving she'd teased its branches into shape again after it had been rudely squished into a box, and she'd adorned it with gold baubles that glowed against tiny white Christmas lights, silver beads that began at the top and wound all the way down like a shiny helter skelter. She'd picked up a few decorations in the sale too when she'd bought the tree, and she had snow-sprinkled pine cones and a round, china Santa bauble from Nicole. The bauble had a china bell inside that tinkled every time you accidentally knocked the tree, walking past in the compact apartment. Lizzy, who lived in the apartment upstairs, had given her a set of three silver reindeer. In return, Evie had made a batch of oatmeal and raisin cookies, which Lizzy had devoured. As a doctor, Lizzy worked ridiculous hours and, Evie suspected, rarely cooked a thing in her life, surviving on takeaways given the number of times the delivery guy had knocked on her door at the basement by mistake rather than taking the few steps up to the entrance of the main building.

Evie touched her fingers to the end of one of the branches. With her job going so well, maybe in a couple of years she'd spend a bit extra and treat herself to a real tree. Not every year—it was so extravagant—but at least once so the scent of pine could fill the room, sneak into the bedroom off the living room and wake her each morning with its heady scent.

When there was a gentle knock at the door, Evie hauled herself up, checked through the peephole first and then opened the door to Lizzy's smiling face.

'Come in!' she ordered. 'It's freezing out there, where's your coat?'

Lizzy did as she was told. She brushed flakes of snow out of her red hair that hung loose around her shoulders. 'I was only coming down from upstairs.'

'Can I get you a cup of tea?'

'I can't stay, I'm afraid.'

'That's a shame. Work? Or hot date?'

Lizzy grinned. 'The latter, I'm happy to say.'

'Who with?'

'Carl.'

'Wow, what's that … the fifth date?'

Lizzy smiled sheepishly.

'I'm happy for you,' said Evie. 'He seems lovely.' Since Evie had moved into the building and made friends with Lizzy, who'd rescued her on moving day when the first thing she'd done was stumble down the steps to the basement and cut her knee, Evie had seen a few men come and go, but this one was sticking.

'I came down to tell you that a guy was here looking for you.' Lizzy's eyebrows lifted up and down as she teased Evie.

'Who?'

'You tell me!'

While Lizzy had had her fair share of boyfriends, Evie's love life had stalled five years ago when she was twenty-three, right before everything began to go so horribly wrong. Lizzy had suggested setting her up with a guy she worked with, but Evie had told her not to. Meeting someone was something she hoped would happen in time, but she was in a good place right now where she knew what was what. She didn't want to upset the equilibrium.

'I really don't know. Didn't he leave a name?' Evie asked.

‘No, nothing. He just said he’d be back again another time and there was no need to pass a message on. He was a little old for you though.’ She pulled a face.

Evie gulped as reality began to dawn. ‘How old was he?’

Lizzy thought about it. ‘Fifty-ish. Maybe a bit older. But I’m useless with ages.’

‘Did he ask for me by name?’

‘Yup. First and last name. He knew who he was looking for.’

Evie’s mouth felt like sandpaper. ‘What else do you remember about him?’ She’d told Lizzy nothing of her past.

‘Fairly tall, thinning dark hair, kind of one of those office faces like he should be sitting behind a big banking desk.’

It was possible it was someone from the shelter. She’d befriended so many lovely people, men and women included, and maybe somehow they knew where she lived. But deep down, Evie knew this was wishful thinking.

‘Well, I’d better go.’ Lizzy rubbed her arms, bracing herself for the cold again. ‘Time for my hot date!’

‘Watch out for the icy steps,’ Evie called, watching her friend trot up the steps from the basement, turn around the railing and take the other set of steps to her own front door.

‘See you, Evie! Dinner next week, okay?’ Lizzy yelled when she was already out of sight.

Evie shut the door behind her, locked it and drew the chain across. She did the same thing every night, but this evening she didn’t want to wait. She leant against the door, listened to the sounds of New York City still wide awake around her, sounds of people calling out into the night air, cars whipping past, a group of women giggling as they passed by the top of the steps at street level.

Evie huddled up on the comfy poppy-red couch, pulled her knees in tight and looked deep into the branches of the Christmas tree, but even the fairy lights with their magical sparkle could do little to lift her spirits.

If this man was who she thought he was … she could be about to lose everything.

Chapter Six

Jack

Jack swigged the last dregs of coffee from the disposable cup, aimed the empty vessel at the trash can and succeeded in getting it in first time. He yawned as he looked out of the office window from the space that sat above The Diamond Touch flagship store, across at a bakery, a fashion store. If you stood close to the floor-to-ceiling window on your left, you'd see the magnificent Washington Square Arch, but Jack had been up here so many times he rarely registered its presence anymore, let alone its beauty or history.

He yawned again. Even the caffeine hit couldn't wake him up this morning. These days, much of their business came from online, but a physical presence still carried a lot of clout and this week he'd been to Cincinnati, Chicago and Seattle. He'd spent four days discussing retail strategy, meeting with staff and clients, meeting buyers, only to return to New York to race all over the city and check out new properties with his father. And now, this morning, he should have been tackling the accounts, losing himself in figures and collating spreadsheets, but all he could think about was bumping into Nicole Capra in Macy's the other week.

Jack hadn't seen Nicole since his father had fired her three years ago. She hadn't been back once, and at the time he'd been hurt, upset. They were close, and when she'd left, a gaping hole in the household had opened up even though Jack had moved into his own apartment many years before. He'd tried phoning her, sending her emails, writing her old-fashioned snail mail in the hope it'd get through to her, but nothing had worked. The letters had been returned to him, the emails ignored, the phone calls unanswered; eventually he'd been forced to accept that what his father had done, and what he'd been party to that night, had alienated Nicole forever.

Jack loaded up the spreadsheet from the Seattle store. The sooner he got this done, the sooner he could get onto the website redesign, something that at least interested him slightly. It was preferable to staring at figures and writing reports at any rate. But his mind still hovered on Nicole, and more predominantly, the young woman she was with. She was familiar, no doubt about it, but Nicole had no family to speak of, at least not here in America, so who was she? He turned the name, Evie, over and over in his head but came up with nothing.

When Braydon knocked on his office door, he stopped thinking about Evie and turned his attention to the range of bracelets his colleague had brought in. Jack had seen the initial designs on the computer, but now they'd been crafted at the company warehouse, they were even more spectacular. Blades, pliers, soldering equipment and brushes had pulled together some fantastic items, and Jack took turns with Braydon to use the loupe and inspect the diamonds set in the bracelet that dominated the collection in its beauty as well as its expense. He wouldn't mind betting Fern would have her eye on that for her own jewellery box.

Before Braydon left, his father came in to see them both and discuss the company website, and all Jack's thoughts of escaping to see his latest girlfriend, Aurelia, were crushed. Aurelia was the assistant to a bank manager as old as their combined ages, and Jack suspected she'd rather be his assistant any day, at least in the bedroom.

'The diamond flower earrings on the Home Page are a part of the store's history,' Jack insisted when his father tossed up the idea of a new approach. 'I think they *should* be the feature. Simple, sleek, elegant, the image we're trying to convey.'

'Exactly,' said Braydon.

'What do you mean?' Braydon couldn't possibly agree with him for once, could he?

'The design is part of the store's *history.*' Braydon looked over to Kent. 'But is it a part of the store's future?' Perhaps sensing he was touching shaky ground, he added, 'All I'm saying is that we need to be forward thinking, keep up with the competitors. Otherwise, we'll constantly be a step behind and we'll drown.'

Braydon took the floor and pulled up some images on the Smart Board. 'Here are the home pages of our competitors.' He swiped the screen periodically, scrolling through. 'They're clean, simple, classy, no fuss, allowing customers to delve for specific items using the search criteria.'

Jack couldn't read his father. If he disagreed, he was keeping it well hidden. But they needed to come to some sort of agreement and move forward.

Eventually Kent nodded. 'Let's put our proposals out to the web designer, give him *all* our thoughts and let him work up what he sees as the best ideas. We've worked with him long enough now, we can trust he understands what we're trying to achieve.' Kent ignored Braydon's lift of the eyebrows, pissed he hadn't got his way and it was still to be decided.

‘How did we do with the marketing campaign for wedding designers?’ Jack moved on, a sure way to placate Braydon.

‘Good,’ Braydon confirmed, his face still pinched.

‘How many stores have agreed to take part?’

‘A hundred stores,’ he announced proudly, mellowing. ‘Every store I approached was happy to feature the poster in their window, hand out flyers to customers for ring designs, wedding day jewellery.’ Braydon flourished an image of the poster on his iPad for maximum impact as he talked, his heady enthusiasm for the marketing campaign a tonic for not getting his way, the conversation a reassertion he could still do the job as well as any Churchill. He and Jack had devised the marketing campaign together, with Braydon happy to approach stores as Jack went around the country doing business.

‘It’s an inexpensive campaign,’ Braydon continued, ‘but it’ll have maximum impact. Already, from the customer feedback box on the existing website, we see it brought in two online orders this morning before eight am. And they weren’t even for wedding-specific jewellery. One order was for a watch, the other for a christening bracelet.’

They talked more about the marketing campaign, but Jack’s niggling temptation to meet up with Aurelia for a more physical lunch than one sitting at a table with business associates was thwarted when Kent reminded him of the working lunch at a top seafood restaurant that afternoon with Braydon and a buyer from Bloomingdales.

Half an hour later, Jack and Braydon walked the three blocks to the restaurant as Braydon prattled on about his golf technique. Jack had gone along to golf several times with his father, to the driving range with the fairway jutting out over the Hudson River. It was the cigars all over again, all the little things that added up to showing Kent Churchill that his son could keep up with his father in whatever he was asked to do. If Jack was asked to chair a meeting, he did it with ease; if he was asked to play golf, he hit the ball like a pro, if he was expected to live the high life in Manhattan, he did it without question or rancour, at least on the surface.

'Hang on.' Braydon stopped at the street vendor on the corner of the next block and lifted up a Bridal Magazine.

'You and Fern getting serious?' Jack laughed. He blew into his palms and rubbed his hands together, the outside temperature unforgiving.

'Shut up and give me a minute.' Braydon flicked through the magazine, and when he found what he was looking for, he held it open for Jack. 'It's our new Christmas advertising feature, I thought you'd want to see it.'

Jack took the magazine. 'Impressive.' He'd seen the feature before it went to press, but kudos to Braydon, a man who was more than just the jewellery designer at The Diamond Touch, an almost unconventional business where all employees wore different hats at some time or another. In fact, Jack felt sure Braydon could run the entire business himself given half the chance. But it didn't make the man any more likeable. Short in stature, bald on top but clinging on to the remaining hair he had at the sides, Braydon was outwardly loyal but inwardly shifty.

'You buying it or what?' the street vendor called out to them. If he was worried about two men running off with a magazine filled with white dresses and lace veils, he was sadly mistaken.

As he moved to return the magazine, Jack's fingers slid between another two pages and revealed another article altogether. He looked at the front cover, dug in his pocket, and without taking his eyes off the feature, paid the street vendor. 'Keep the change.'

They stood at the corner and waited for the sign to change to Walk from Don't Walk, all the while Jack mesmerised by the article in front of him.

'What do you want that for?' Braydon asked, nodding to the magazine.

'I'll show Dad.'

'I expect he's already seen it,' Braydon said, bemused. As they crossed the road, he wouldn't let it go. 'Come on, truth time. You're perving on someone in there! Be honest.' His laugh made Jack want to punch him, but as he entertained the thought Braydon snatched the magazine from his hands.

'Give it back.' Jack's tone was deadly serious and it wasn't long before Braydon did exactly as he was told. Braydon knew better than to mess with him, at least so directly.

Jack read on. The feature was about a local business, The Perfect Match Couture, and there looking back at him was a picture of the young woman he'd seen in Macy's with Nicole. He read some more. She was the assistant to her boss, Bonnie, and he skimmed through the article trying to find more information, uncover where he knew her from, but all he drew were blanks.

'Put that away, would you?' They'd reached the restaurant and it was time to turn his mind from the mystery woman to lines of jewellery this client could stock, how they could retail The Diamond Touch products to reach more customers.

*

'That went well,' said Braydon when once again they were out on the Manhattan streets.

The snow that had begun to fall when they were in the restaurant had stopped, and in the gutter the telltale black slush splashed against car wheels. Frost still lingered on the tips of roofs and the cold went straight through Jack as he pulled his coat to him.

'Let me see the advert again.' Braydon held out a leather-gloved hand for the magazine tucked safely under Jack's arm.

Jack handed it over, but Braydon didn't turn to the advert for the company, he went straight for the page with the dog-eared corner. 'I don't get it,' he claimed. 'What's so fascinating about this article?' He read an excerpt out loud. 'Bonnie Chesterfield successfully launched the business nine years ago … blah blah blah … assistant Evie … blah blah.' He looked at Jack as they stopped at an intersection and waited behind the crowd of people crossing the road, pushed back when a yellow taxi mounted the curb and yelled out his window as though they were all in the wrong.

'I was thinking we could pass on the poster and the flyers to them,' Jack attempted.

'It says here that she works out of home. What, you want her to plaster a poster in her front window?' Even his laugh was annoying.

Almost back at The Diamond Touch, ready to take the side door leading straight up to the office, Braydon stopped. 'Hang on a minute. This young woman, Evie, or whatever her name is.' He looked up to the sky and smirked at his light bulb moment. 'I knew I'd seen her before!' He poked a chubby index finger at the page. 'I'm right. It's her!'

Jack stopped at the foot of the stairs that led up to the office. 'It's who?'

'The woman from the streets. Three years ago I think it was, and your maid, hot-looking woman with curly hair—'

'Housekeeper, not maid,' Jack bristled. 'And her name's Nicole.'

'Whatever. She was passing out food and who knows what else to this person.' He stabbed his finger at the page again, at the woman in question. 'Your father threw her off the property. Told her to get out and then fired Nicole's sorry ass.'

It all clicked into place. The young woman had been using a different name back then, but Jack should've guessed who Evie was as soon as her eyes had locked with his in Macy's. The night he'd first seen her had lingered in his memory for months afterwards as he tried in vain to contact Nicole. He'd even had dreams about what had happened and she'd featured, her eyes an intense blue as she'd looked up at him from beneath the blanket, terrified as she cowered on the patio outside his father's townhouse. Her hair was blonder now than he remembered, and her face a picture of health, no longer diminished beneath the turmoil of being on the streets, but finally he had a name and an explanation for where he knew her from.

'Well, well, well,' said Braydon when they reached the top of the stairs. 'It seems someone has come up a bit in the world. We need to show this to Kent.'

When Braydon shrugged off his coat, Jack took the opportunity to snatch the magazine back. 'No, we don't. And you don't need to mention it either. What went down that night was a woman getting fired. It's hardly something to be proud of.'

Braydon pulled a face as if to say what's your problem? And then he stalked off, chuckling to himself, muttering under his breath about the girl, how she'd come out of the gutter. He was like a dog tugging at a trouser leg, unwilling to let go until he'd ripped it to shreds.

Jack went into his office, but it was only when he'd clicked the door shut behind him that his feeling of sympathy for this young woman turned to one of suspicion, anger even. He finally began to unravel the last three years in his mind and realised that this Evie was the reason Nicole had walked out of his life without so much as turning back. And it dawned on him that Evie had latched onto Nicole's kindness, taken advantage of her kind nature and generosity to get her own life back on track. And now, who knew what liberties she was taking with the woman who'd been the closest he'd come to a mother figure in his life for a very long time.

When there was a knock at the office door, he turned to see his father.

'Everything go well at lunch?' Kent asked.

Jack gestured for him to sit as he breathed deeply trying to let his anger subside. He told his father all about the buyers, their approach, what they'd agreed. He didn't mention Evie or the newspaper article. He hadn't even said anything about bumping into Nicole last week, even though he'd told Nicole he would pass on her best to Kent. In truth, he wasn't sure of what his father's reaction would be. He and Nicole had been good friends for a long time, and the way Kent had acted towards

Nicole three years ago had shocked Jack; it was so out of character.

'A good outcome then,' Kent concluded. 'They'll bring a lot of business our way. Great job.'

'Let's hope so. We have a good relationship with them.'

'And the marketing campaign was genius.'

Jack's gaze shot up. He'd been unable to truly look his father in the eye until now. Had Braydon shown him the magazine? 'You saw it?'

'I approved the mock-ups.' He laughed. 'Anyway, I'll leave you to it.' He stood to go, rubbed his shoulder and left his hand against his chest.

'Something wrong?' Jack watched his father's face change, his usually relaxed features pulled tight.

'A bit of indigestion, that's all. I've got some antacids in my office.' He turned to walk away, but Jack wasn't convinced.

'Dad?' He shot to his father's side.

Beads of sweat gathered on Kent's forehead. He loosened his tie, undid his top button, grabbed hold of the door handle for balance but missed and stumbled to the floor.

'Dad!' Jack flung open the door, yelling to the first person walking past. 'Call an ambulance, now!'

Chapter Seven

Evie

Evie helped the bride-to-be, Julia, into the ivory strapless ball gown. The dress had been designed over a few meetings and taken close to five months to make and to perfect the delicate beading and crystals embroidered on the bodice. Looking at Julia's reaction as Evie fastened the last of the Duchesse satin buttons at the back, it had been more than worth the wait.

'Are you happy with it?' Evie asked into the mirror as she fixed the silk sash around the middle and tied it in a bow at the waist. It was the finishing touch, the final extra that took the dress from beautiful to jaw-droppingly stunning.

Julia remained silent.

'Julia?' Evie's hand settled on her shoulder and she stood upright. 'Is everything okay?'

Julia took a deep breath in, widened her eyes as tears threatened to escape. She flapped her hands in front of her face. 'I won't cry, I won't cry.'

'What is it?' Her sister, Ella, pulled back the curtain to the changing area Bonnie had fashioned in the corner of the spare room. 'Oh … My … God.'

'I know!'

Evie deduced that these were threatening tears of joy rather than tears of anything else. She'd pretty much seen it all in her time here—tears of joy, tears of fear, tears of regret at making the wrong decision. But these tears were her favourite kind and assured her that all the hard work had paid off.

'I'd hug you if I wasn't scared of ruining my dress,' Julia squealed. She turned to Evie. 'You've done an amazing job, you really have. It's a dream come true.' When Evie reached for the Chantilly lace veil on the table at the side of the room Julia said, 'Oh no, if you put that on me I'll completely lose it.'

Evie took a tissue from the box on the mantelpiece over a fireplace, which hadn't been used in years and now housed an arrangement of Mexican Poinsettias and verdant greens. In the summer it would most probably be replaced with a simple collection of spring roses or a chic display of flowers ranging in colour from pinks and oranges to soft creams and yellows.

She handed Julia the tissue. 'Here, wipe your eyes, because this veil *is* going on. This is the second to last fitting and I want to ensure everything is as it should be.' When Julia had wiped her eyes, Evie carefully lifted the veil into place, securing it in Julia's gorgeous straight blonde hair with the attached comb and two extra hair clips. 'Have you decided what to do with your hair?'

'I'm thinking natural, perhaps pin the top up, but I've got a friend coming to have a play around with styles.' She giggled. 'My fiancé says he won't be around for that one.'

'It sounds very girly, and definitely not something he needs to be involved in. Now, turn around and take a look.'

Julia turned round to look in the mirror and gulped. 'It's perfect. Everything is perfect.'

'And …' Evie held up a finger to say wait, scurried over to the chest next to the table and took out a small bag in the same ivory silk as her wedding gown. 'Now I know you didn't ask for it, and there's no extra charge, it's just I hate seeing offcuts of material go to waste.

You can use it to put lipstick in, a few hair pins just in case, maybe a tissue or two.' She grinned.

'Evie … it's beautiful. I don't know what to say.'

'You don't need to say anything.' She went back to the drawer and took out something else. 'And a little something for you,' she told Ella, this time brandishing a tiny bag in midnight blue sateen. 'It'll match your bridesmaid dress.'

'Oh Evie, it's gorgeous.' Ella smiled at Evie and then looked at Julia. 'Thank you for making my sister's wedding day so perfect. The dress is simply stunning.'

'Oh nonsense, it's not just about the dress. It's the day that'll mark the rest of your lives together,' she told Julia. 'That's the biggest focus.' But when she noticed them both frowning cheekily at her she giggled. 'Okay, so it's ninety-nine point nine per cent about the dress!'

Julia admired the dress some more, and Ella tried on the bridesmaid dress one last time so that Evie could make any final adjustments. Once they were finished, she tucked the gowns and accoutrements safely into special garment bags and hung them on a rack, where they would stay until collection just after New Year's when they would do one final fitting to make sure everything was perfect.

Evie saw the sisters to the door as they giggled about rationing Julia's food this Christmas to avoid any weight gain. But as Evie went through to the kitchen to reheat the fried rice leftovers she'd brought from home, Evie suspected Julia would come to the final fitting no different to the size she'd always been. Over time she'd got to know Julia, as she did with most brides; one reason Evie liked her so much was that she wasn't the type to flash around the cash and make demands. In fact, from conversations held in her presence, she knew this dress was the biggest extravagance for the day, the day to be held out in Connecticut, away from the glitz and glamour of New York City that so many other brides were ready to be a part of. Evie loved the way Julia spoke about her fiancé too, with a fondness and respect that showed how deep her feelings ran. This was more than about just one day to Julia; this was about the rest of her life.

After lunch it was back to work sourcing fabrics from their supplier. Evie had always thought summer the busiest time for weddings until she started working at The Perfect Fit Couture; Christmas weddings seemed to have shot up in popularity these days.

'Did we get the Rouleau button loops for the Morrison dress?' Bonnie poked her head around the doorway, cup of tea in hand.

Evie looked up from the laptop where she was engrossed in the supplier's website, requesting samples of new fabrics from Milan that Bonnie had agreed to try. 'They're in the top drawer.' She nodded to the chest of drawers at the side of the room

'Thanks. Would you be able to fix those on this afternoon?'

'Sure thing. I'd noticed you've got another new client scheduled this afternoon. We're getting lots of new custom lately, it's great.'

'Tell that to my husband,' Bonnie quipped, although Evie wouldn't mind betting he enjoyed having a wife who was independent and had made a success of her own business. 'And I have some more good news for you.'

'Oh?'

Bonnie took a deep breath, barely able to conceal her smile. 'I've secured The Perfect Fit Couture a stand at three major Bridal Expos next year, including the prestigious New York International Bride Week!'

Evie's mouth fell open. 'No way!'

'Way!' Bonnie's eyes lit up. 'This is a major deal and it'll be all hands on deck. This will boost our reputation and,' she crossed her fingers on one hand, 'if sales increase, it could see us expand to new premises.'

'Bonnie, that's fabulous, it really is.' It hadn't taken long in the job for Evie to realise that this was her calling. Her motivation came from the creative licence, the thrill of having a hand in designing and producing exquisite gowns, delighting customers from far and wide. One day she dreamed of opening her own place, perhaps having her own label, and hearing about the expo was a step in the right direction. Surely nothing could step in and spoil this now.

Evie's phone chimed, but she didn't recognise the number. 'Hello?' Holding the phone between her shoulder and her ear, she moved over to the main table, looking at the design for the Morrison's dress that was laid out, ready for her to begin fixing on the button loops. But that was as far as she got before the voice sent her in to a panic.

*

'I told them not to bother you at work.' Nicole shook her head when Evie arrived at the hospital and told her the nurse had telephoned. 'I only got upset because my wrist really hurts and I won't be able to help out at the shelter tonight.'

'Oh, you silly thing.' Evie did her best to hug her friend, despite the injured limb encased in a sling against her chest. 'You should've called me yourself.'

'I would've let you know.'

Evie pulled a face.

‘I would’ve … eventually.’

‘So what happened?’

‘I slipped when I was out for a walk this morning. I was only trying to be healthy, but typically, I found the one patch on the ground that hadn’t thawed, and before I knew it I’d slipped on the ice and I’d fallen.’ She grinned. ‘A handsome man helped me up and made sure I was okay.’

Evie smiled, glad she was in good spirits. ‘Is your wrist broken?’

‘I don’t know. I’ll have to find out what the X-rays say. The coat drive might be a challenge for a one-armed woman though.’

‘Don’t you worry about that, I’ll go round collecting, enlist someone else’s help if I need to. Sometimes, Nicole, you really do need to learn to put yourself first.’ She said it knowing it’d never do any good. Nicole was a helper and helping others came as naturally to her as taking corners at speed came to a racing driver.

‘Another buyer was sniffing around the shelter yesterday,’ Nicole added glumly. Evie knew that wasn’t good news. ‘And locals have been campaigning to get rid of us, even started a petition.’

Evie slumped back in her chair. ‘I thought the community were supportive.’

‘They are, they give us their coats,’ Nicole harrumphed. ‘But that doesn’t mean they want us anywhere near them. It’s the same old story. They’re sympathetic to the plight of the homeless, as long as it isn’t happening on their doorstep. I suppose I can’t blame them.’

Evie lowered her voice. ‘We should point out that the people coming to the shelter could very easily have been one of them, if they’d lost their way.’

'Oh, they won't listen, they don't want to. They'll throw money at it, but like I said, they don't want to see it every day. I think our days are numbered.'

'But it's not like we have neon signs out front,' Evie argued. That'd been one thing they'd never done. The shelter where Nicole and now Evie volunteered wasn't like the bigger ones in New York City. They were a small operation started by a New York family, the O'Briens, who'd since moved away but handed over the reins in every aspect except the finance to volunteers. The building was near a prestigious shopping precinct, nestled between a clothing store and an old-fashioned candy store, the sort that sold Salt Water Taffy by the caseload and where jars lined the walls with multi-coloured candy and a gum-ball machine stood out front. The stone façade of their building was old and the glass needed replacing, but it had been relatively inconspicuous until word of mouth meant they'd been filled to bursting point most days.

'The building will be sold in less than twelve months.' Nicole sighed. 'Both of the O'Briens passed away recently, and when I spoke to the daughter she told me she's not interested in keeping property here in New York. I explained everything to her, but she's returning to Ireland with her children.'

'I do wish she'd reconsider.'

'Oh, Evie, we don't know her story. I couldn't press her on it after she told me her plans.'

'Is there any way we could raise the money?' She knew she was clutching at straws from the look on Nicole's face.

'I'd buy it myself if I could, but it's prime retail space and far too expensive. I was hoping to get government funding before I had to tell anyone about this, but with the locals petitioning, I doubt it's even worth the effort.'

In the waiting room, new patients were called, loved ones murmured between themselves as they waited for news on relatives, a baby grizzled on his mother's lap.

Evie covered Nicole's good hand with her own. 'Try not to worry, we'll sort something out.'

They both knew it wasn't true. They couldn't work miracles.

Nicole gasped. 'And what about Christmas dinner? How will I cook one-armed?'

'You've always got me. I may not cook as well as you, but I have my uses.' Evie looked up at the doctor approaching. 'Looks like we're about to find out what's going on with you.'

It turned out Nicole's wrist was broken and she went off to have it put in a cast. It'd take a while too—it seemed Nicole wasn't the only person today to have slipped and broken or fractured something in the icy streets of New York.

Evie sat and read the newspaper for a while, but when she'd had enough and her bottom had turned numb from waiting around, she went down to the main foyer of the hospital. She followed the selection buttons on the vending machine, and when she reached the black coffee option she clicked, deposited her coins, waited for the cup to drop and the liquid to splash into it. She pulled the cup from its grasp, appreciating the warmth through the plastic, and turned to find a place to sit and read the book stowed in her bag while she waited.

'Watch it!' A man yelled as she sent her coffee flying all down the front of his impeccable suit.

'Oh God, I'm so sorry!' Her eyes shot up to his and she froze.

He didn't say anything, but raised his eyebrows as though to tell her to move her arse out of the way of the vending machine, pronto.

'It's Jackson, isn't it?' She tried to be friendly. Nicole seemed to like him after all.

He glared at her. 'It's Jack.'

How was she supposed to know? She wasn't psychic! 'I apologise, once again. Nicole introduced you as Jackson, that's all.'

Oh dear, the mere mention of what she presumed was his full name didn't please him in the slightest. She'd been tempted to suggest paying to have his expensive suit dry cleaned but the look of disgust on his face told her the help probably wouldn't be appreciated. So she turned to walk away, pulling a tissue from her pocket to dry the drips that were all over the side of the now half empty coffee cup.

'Don't think I don't know what you're up to,' he shouted after her.

She turned on her heel, slopping coffee again, except this time the tissue she was clutching absorbed it straight away. 'What did you say?'

He lifted his own cup from the vending machine. 'I know exactly who you are. It took a while, but I figured it out.'

She exhaled. 'Figured what out?'

'You're the one we threw off our property a few years ago.'

'Well done, Einstein.' Who did he think he was? Just because his family owned a fancy home overlooking Central Park didn't make him any better than anyone else. 'Big deal,' she snapped. 'So you remembered. You can go to the top of the class.'

When she turned to walk away, he followed her, stuck closely behind.

'You're using Nicole and I'm not happy about it,' he accused.

'You what?' She kept her hand in check, tempted to sling the rest of the coffee right in his face.

'You reeled her in well and truly. You got her fired and then you've muscled in on her life. Oh, you might have a job now, but I bet she had something to do with that. You sure as hell landed on your feet, didn't you?'

Tears sprang into her eyes, but she was tough. She didn't go down without a fight. 'I didn't get her fired. Your family did that all on its own, not willing to see another side to the story. She worked for you for years and you repay her loyalty by terminating her employment and throwing her out of your lives like an overused teabag!'

He had the good grace to look shocked at her outburst, and she wasn't finished yet.

'Nicole did help me to get a job, yes. People in my situation need help. We don't live on the streets because we like it! So next time you accuse me, please make sure you do it in front of Nicole. I'm sure she'd be very interested to hear your opinions.' And before she could talk herself out of it, her wrist flicked and sent the rest of the cup of coffee in Jack's direction, soaking the front of his dark grey suit, the white shirt and burgundy-striped tie that sat beneath.

Shit, she shouldn't have done that.

'Evie!' Nicole appeared behind them, coat draped around her shoulders, wrist encased in fresh plaster and nestled comfortably in a sling. 'Jackson? What on earth's going on?' She looked at Jack standing there lost for something to say, Evie refusing to open her mouth.

‘What happened to you?’ Jack returned Nicole’s question with one of his own as he took a tissue she handed him from her pocket and dabbed at the coffee.

‘I slipped and fell. But don’t change the subject. I want to know what this is all about.’ She looked from Evie to Jack and back again.

‘It was an accident,’ he told her. ‘Wasn’t it, Evie?’

Evie’s mouth sat in a hard line. ‘Yes, sorry about that. I don’t know what happened.’ She wasn’t sure why he was covering it up; she’d be happy to tell Nicole everything, but for some reason he didn’t want to. Maybe he knew Nicole wouldn’t listen. Evie had done nothing wrong. She stood on her own two feet, always had done.

Nicole clearly didn’t believe a word of it, but maybe because she was exhausted at having been at the hospital for hours, she let it go. ‘Why are *you* here, Jackson?’

‘My father.’

Nicole clasped a hand to her chest. ‘Is he okay?’

‘He’s fine. He had a heart attack.’

When Nicole stumbled, Jack was at one side and Evie at the other. They led her over to a chair.

‘Take it easy.’ Jack crouched down in front of the chair and held Nicole’s hand. ‘It was a mild heart attack. Sorry, I should’ve opened with that.’

‘You think?’ Evie muttered under her breath.

Jack shot her a look, which Evie saw fit to ignore. ‘Dad will be fine. He gave me one hell of a scare, and he’s going to have to make a few changes to stop it from happening again, but he’s as strong as an ox, remember.’

The colour returned to Nicole’s cheeks.

‘You could go up and see him, if you’d like,’ said Jack.

Nicole looked as though she was considering it, but she shook her head. 'It's been too long. No, Jackson. Too much was said that night, I can't.'

Still crouched down in front of Nicole, he said, 'What's done is done, and I know he reacted harshly towards you that night, but I also believe he's regretted it ever since.'

Nicole reached out with her good arm and put her hand to Jack's cheek. 'You're a good man.' She looked to Evie. 'I need to use the restroom and then let's go home. I'll cook us something nice.'

'You'll do no such thing,' Evie admonished. 'You'll put your feet up in front of the fire and I'll wait on you hand and foot.' She took Nicole's handbag to make it easier for her to negotiate the restrooms.

'Sounds like a good idea to me.' Jack pushed himself to standing.

As Nicole left them alone, Evie wondered whether he thought it a good idea for Nicole to rest or a good idea that she became the servant for the night. She wanted to believe it was the former but doubted it very much.

'Don't worry, I'm not going to rifle through it.' Evie indicated Nicole's bag before Jack had a chance to say anything.

'I didn't say you were.'

'I'll bet the thought was there.'

'Feisty little thing, aren't you?'

'Oh, fu—' Her words stopped when he put his fingers to her mouth to stop her.

'No need for that language.'

She only breathed again when he took his hand away to wave over to the doorway. The sensation left her lips tingling as she watched another man enter the foyer. He was dressed as impeccably as Jack had been before the coffee incident and something about him was oddly familiar. He was nothing like Jack though. Jack was tall, athletic, strong. This man was short, balding and had the paunch that told the story of the high life.

Evie took a seat and opened up her book again as she waited, but she didn't lose herself in the words, only Jack's accusations. She was a friend of Nicole's because Nicole had opened her heart, and contrary to Jack's opinion, their friendship had nothing to do with Nicole opening her purse. She was angry that Jack could think anything else, but more than that, she was angry at her reaction to his touch when he put his fingers against her lips. She'd wanted to hate it, but instead she'd found pleasure in it.

A shadow appeared over the page she was at, and when Evie looked up, the short, balding man was hovering over her, with Jack in the wings.

'Can I help you?' she asked.

'Now there's a question.' He plonked his hands firmly on his hips.

'What's that supposed to mean?' Evie stood, unafraid of confrontation.

'I know your type, you're all the same.'

'Braydon, let it go.' Jack tried to usher him along. 'Go up and see my father.'

'Just a minute, I want to talk to the lovely girl who's fallen on her feet.'

Evie shot a look at Jack. He looked angry, but was he angry with her or this horrid little man?

She felt the man's hot breath when he took a step closer to her, and in that moment she realised exactly why he made her skin crawl. She'd seen him before, beneath the darkened New York City sky, as menacing as he looked now.

‘Like I said,’ he continued, ‘I know your type. How did you get the good job with the fancy wedding designer? How did you get to be wearing such fine clothes?’ When he reached out an arm and ran it down the sleeve of her jumper she cringed, her past flashing through her mind, her previous meeting with him all she could think about. ‘I suppose good looks go a long way in this city.’

Jack grabbed Braydon’s arm and yanked it back. ‘That’s enough.’

Braydon shrugged him off and took a step closer to Evie, backing her against the wall, his stocky build making his presence known, his stomach protruding so it touched against hers. ‘I wouldn’t mind betting somewhere along the line you slept your way to the top.’

He moved closer still, trailed a finger beneath her chin and up to her lips, and for a moment she was paralysed. But then instincts crept in.

She parted her lips, let his finger graze her bottom lip and then … she stuck her chin forwards and bit down as hard as she could.

The scream brought Braydon to the attention of each and every person in the foyer, alerted a security guard, made Nicole stand stock still as she emerged from the restrooms. Braydon drew back a fist, but Jack dived between them, blocking Evie.

Evie’s heart pumped so hard she swore she could hear it. He’d been about to hit her, she was sure of it.

The security guard was on the case. ‘Is everything all right over here?’

‘It’s fine,’ Jack assured him. He stayed where he was, his bulk protecting Evie. She could smell the dry-cleaning scent on his expensive suit, even now that it was covered in coffee, his subtle cologne that made her imagine he was nicer and sexier than he actually was.

'Braydon, go up to see my father. Now,' Jack instructed.

Braydon smirked, shook his finger at her as if to say 'you'll keep'. She noticed she'd drawn blood and she hoped it hurt like hell.

Nicole was by Evie's side seconds after Braydon retreated. 'What on earth's going on?'

She couldn't look Jack in the eye. 'Could we please just leave?' She didn't wait for an answer and walked straight for the door, out into the icy open air, letting the cold blast wipe away the revulsion of another man who was hungry to get exactly what he wanted, what he felt was owed to him. And although Jack had leapt to her defence, she couldn't help thinking he was no better. They both represented a world of pretence, of entitlement, and a world she never wanted to be a part of, not ever.

Chapter Eight

Kent

Since he'd returned home from the hospital five days earlier, Kent was certainly being looked after. Cameron had flown in from Toronto to check he was still in the land of the living, Maggie had been her usual efficient self around the house but paying more attention to him—something he guessed Cameron had put her up to—and Jack had taken the reins with the business alongside Braydon.

He picked up the first newspaper from the stack Maggie had brought in and piled onto the side table next to the couch. He'd not read or seen the news when he was in the hospital. Instead, he'd slept, read an entire novel—he couldn't remember the last time he'd been able to do that—and he'd enjoyed friendly banter with other patients who had nothing to do with jewellery, weren't looking for a promotion, and weren't trying to chat him up. He flicked from the front page of the periodical through to more doom and gloom. The world seemed to be getting worse, not better.

'Can I get you a cup of tea?' His housekeeper was back again.

'You must have a million and one things to do, Maggie. I take it this is Cameron's doing?' The sheepish expression told him he was right. 'Well, I can assure you I don't need to be fussed over. I'm alive and kicking and I'll yell if I need anything, I promise.'

Maggie left with a smile. She was a good worker and her efficiency had wowed him from the start, but he'd never formed the same bond with her as he had with Nicole.

He sipped from a glass of water and reached for a different newspaper, hopeful it'd be more positive than the previous. But it was the same old thing … and he may have only been away five days, but he wondered how he'd ever read these over his breakfast, then again in the evenings, convinced he could have missed something vital.

He sat back against the couch, closed his eyes and let his thoughts drift to Nicole. Had she found work quickly after their altercation? He'd felt wretched after it had happened, and hadn't seen her since she'd gathered up her things that day and left the townhouse for good. But he hadn't fired her only because she'd been giving handouts to a homeless person, he'd had to get rid of her because of who she was. And what had started out as a platonic relationship had soon developed into a friendship, and later the gradual realisation that his feelings ran so much deeper. And when he'd told her to leave that night, part of the reason was because he couldn't carry on the pretence any longer.

His feelings had blossomed a few days before Christmas, during Jack's final year at college. It seemed a lifetime ago, but thinking about it now, it felt like only yesterday. Kent had flown in from Seattle one morning, and with the business not expecting his return until the following day, he'd experienced a rare day out and about in New York City, his birthplace.

He'd gone right to the top of the Empire State Building and out onto the main deck on the 86th floor where he'd soaked up the three hundred and sixty degree views taking in Central Park, The Statue of Liberty, the Brooklyn Bridge, Times Square and the Hudson River.

Along with the mesmerising views and the fresh air, he'd taken in a city that was almost a stranger to him. He went from home to the office, the office to home each day with not much in between, but up there, he'd realised the world was a big place if only he could open his heart to it.

He'd continued his adventure like a big kid, perusing the Christmas windows in Macy's, and just as he was contemplating a show at Radio City Music Hall, something he hadn't done since Cynthia was alive, he bumped into Nicole, dazzled by the blades on the white skates looped over her shoulder by their tied laces.

'You look like a professional,' he'd told her, flummoxed at their unexpected meeting outside the confines of his townhouse. 'You never mentioned you were a skater.'

Over a mulled cider each that Kent had bought from a street vendor, who was so embroiled in the festive spirit he'd filled their polystyrene cups up at least twice as much as they should be, they got to know each other a little more.

'I'm sure I've mentioned ice skating over the years,' she told him.

'You probably have.' He looked around them, appreciating the hustle and bustle, the myriad of characters walking past going about their business. He felt like his head had been buried beneath a heap of sand, unable to see or hear anything much other than his own thoughts and concerns.

'How often do you practice?' he asked her.

'At least a handful of times every year.' The breeze made her corkscrew curls dance beneath a beige bobble hat.

'How could I not know that?' He shook his head.

‘Because *you* never asked.’

He finished his mulled cider, and as Nicole finished hers, he took both empty cups and dropped them in a nearby trash can. ‘Well, I’ll let you get over to the ice. I might even watch for a while before I head back to the house.’

‘You’ll do better than that.’ She grabbed his hand and off they went.

‘Oh no.’ He shook his head when he realised they’d joined the line at a booth to pay for admission, rent him some skates. ‘I don’t think I can.’

‘What a load of nonsense.’ She grinned back at him and kept hold of his hand as though he were a small child about to make a run for it.

By the time they took to the ice, Nicole, with a prowess he never dreamed he’d find, and Kent, with all the grace of a deer who hadn’t yet learned to walk, he knew he was in trouble. They’d twisted and turned—her much more gracefully than him—they’d laughed and become far more than employer and housekeeper, and when Jack had spotted them on the ice together and seemed only happy to behold the rare sight of his father having fun, Kent had allowed himself to follow the spiral of falling for Nicole, this woman he liked, admired, laughed with. He’d pushed away his feelings of how wrong it was, any misgivings at getting involved; he’d told himself of course he couldn’t possibly fall in love with the woman who was so closely linked to his wife’s death.

Now, sitting in the living room of his townhouse, Kent flicked through the newspaper pages and scanned the headlines until the doorbell chimed and Maggie announced he had a visitor.

'Jack, good to see you.' Over the years since his wife had died, he and Jack had gradually drifted further apart, and what had once been a close father and son bond had morphed into more of a formal relationship, garnered mainly during talks about the business. On the surface they looked as though they had a good relationship, but the strain came more from what was left unsaid than what was said out loud.

'How are things with the business?' He couldn't help himself. Old habits died hard and business talk always prevented awkwardness.

Jack loosened his tie. 'Business is just fine. More importantly, how are you?'

'Sick of people asking me how I am.' Kent smiled ruefully, dumped the newspaper on the table and took a sip from the glass of water beside him. 'Sick of drinking nothing but this or herbal teas. I could do with a neat Scotch to take the edge off.' When Jack shook his head, he said, 'You think I'm kidding? I've had your sister pampering me day and night and she only left yesterday.'

Jack laughed. 'A visit from Cameron is enough to drive anyone to the Scotch bottle. I love her dearly but she goes into mom mode, and not just with you.'

'Yes, well, she's a great mother, but she does tend to forget we men don't need mothering. She was forever plumping up my pillows, the cushions.' He gestured to the scattered pieces on the couch. 'She subscribed to just about every newspaper in the country. She's even been instructing Maggie on "heart-friendly recipes".' He put the last bit in air quotes, enjoying the unusually relaxed banter and seeing Jack smile so much.

'She left me with strict instructions too.'

'So that's why you're here?'

‘I would’ve come by anyway. Hey, I wouldn’t be surprised if she’s managed to link up my iPhone and track it so she knows I’m doing the right thing.’

Kent shook his head. ‘She says she’ll bring the children next time.’

‘Good, haven’t seen them in months. And it’ll ease the pressure off us if she has them to chase after. Dad, I—’

Maggie appeared with some dainty sandwiches, much like the type you were served for a fancy brunch at an expensive restaurant. There was a pot of tea beside the vintage silver tray and two cups, and without a word she left them to it.

‘You were saying?’ Kent had suspected there was another reason for Jack’s visit. He didn’t ever just drop by to see how he was, something that could easily be checked with a simple phone call.

Jack poured the tea and put a couple of sandwiches onto a plate for himself, a couple for Kent. ‘I saw Nicole.’

Kent’s hands froze as he took the plate from his son. ‘When?’

Jack popped the miniscule tuna and cucumber sandwich into his mouth before he filled his father in on both occasions he’d seen their former housekeeper and friend.

‘Why was she at the hospital?’ Kent toyed with the tiny cheese sandwich on his plate.

‘She slipped on the ice and broke her wrist, but it’s all set in a cast. It won’t be long before it’s as good as new.’

‘Oh, that’s a relief.’ He hesitated. ‘Is she still very angry with me?’

‘She didn’t really say. But it was a long time ago now.’

'Three years,' he confirmed, remembering it like it was yesterday. 'And is she well, apart from the arm?'

'She seems just fine. She was with a friend, actually.'

A male friend? 'Oh?'

'The young woman, Dad.'

'What young woman?'

'From the night of the party. Her name's Evie.'

Nicole was a good woman. She had a heart of gold, and she was a target for someone to take advantage if ever there was one.

'Apparently they're very close,' Jack continued, 'and it's all above board. Nicole says she knows exactly what she's doing.'

Kent didn't miss the undertone of his son's remark. 'But you don't think so?'

Jack helped himself to another sandwich. 'I hate to think of someone taking advantage of her. But for what it's worth, she seemed genuinely happy.'

'I don't suppose it's any of our business anymore.'

Jack didn't say anything. Kent knew that most of the tension between them had well and truly started the night after he fired Nicole, and he'd never stopped feeling guilty for that. But he'd been left with no choice.

'It was great to see her,' said Jack.

'I'll bet it was.' He let a smile creep across his face, relief that after all this time they knew she was fine. He knew Jack had tried to find her after that dreadful day and she'd ignored all his efforts, but knowing she seemed happy was the main thing. 'Is she working? Did she find another job after …' His voice trailed off.

'I don't know anything else, I'm afraid. But she asked for me to send her best, so I'm doing that.'

Kent ate a bite-sized ham and mustard sandwich. He'd wondered time and time again whether to get in touch with Nicole, but under the circumstances it almost felt like what had happened had been a reprieve. He would no longer have to deal with falling for the wrong woman, admit to her who he was or, worst of all, tell Jack everything.

'Well, thanks for the brunch.' Jack picked up one last bite-sized sandwich. 'I'll stop by the kitchen quickly on my way out, thank Maggie. Apologise for my sister's behaviour.' He grinned.

'Wait, we haven't discussed anything to do with the business yet.' Kent slid his plate on to the table.

'I know.' Jack's smile reached his eyes. 'It's been nice to see you.'

When Jack left, Kent's mind wasn't on the business at all. It was on Nicole. When she'd left the house that night, he hadn't tried to get in touch with her. Part of him knew he should, to apologise, but the other part told him to let it lie. But now Jack had seen her, his curiosity was back with fervour. He wanted to fill in the details of the last three years, know that Nicole was all right, that his actions hadn't ruined her life. And most of all he wanted to know whether this Evie was trying to take advantage and gunning for any money Nicole may have put aside. He wanted to be reassured that his former housekeeper wasn't trying to replace the past with the present by opening her heart and her home to a total stranger.

Nicole

It was the morning of the coat collection for streets to the north of their immediate neighbourhood, and Nicole followed Evie as they went on the final round. Winter coats were surprisingly heavy, but when they'd organised the flyer drop, they'd given different allocated days to different streets so they didn't have to do the collection all at once.

'I'm sorry about this.' Nicole pulled a face and looked at her wrist, still encased in a cast, helplessly sitting beneath her coat.

'It's fine. It'll keep me fit,' Evie assured her. 'And for the last time, stop apologising!'

Nicole smiled. Evie didn't need any help keeping fit. She was careful about what she ate and rarely slouched around with nothing to do. Since they'd met all those years ago, Evie had always been a doer rather than an observer. She liked to help whether at home or in the shelter; she loved to walk whenever she could rather than take the subway as though now she was okay she didn't want to miss a second of living, a moment of how special the world could be when it was on your side. Evie was an attractive young woman too, even more so since she'd had the dental work and the life and confidence to smile broadly every day. The dental work had been one of the few indulgences Nicole had been allowed to spoil her with, and Evie's smile rivalled any in Hollywood. Her long blonde hair sprayed out from beneath her sky-blue bobble hat and cascaded around her shoulders. She was tall and leggy—something Nicole had never been able to pull off—and she had the kiss of youth on her side.

'People have been generous this year.' Evie hauled the last of the bags off the apartment steps and dumped it with the other four at the bottom ready to take home. Both women had a rucksack each, and they shoved single coats into those before Evie grabbed the other bags.

‘They most certainly have.’ Nicole took one bag with her functioning arm. She thought of the petition against the shelter. She supposed she couldn’t blame people for their objections. Residents in this area had worked hard to get where they were and they didn’t want a shelter to be a danger to them or their families. If only they could see the bigger picture, come and meet some of the people who deep down were no different from them. But Nicole doubted any explanation would help to change their minds. The mindset of the people in these houses was most likely as strong as their bank account.

‘So …’ Nicole caught up with Evie as she marched across the road. ‘Are you ever going to tell me what was going on at the hospital?’

‘What do you mean?’ Evie strode on.

‘You know exactly what I’m talking about, young lady. You haven’t said a word since that day, since we saw Jackson.’

‘Oh, that.’

‘Yes … that.’ Nicole hadn’t pushed it before now because she’d seen the anger simmering beneath Evie’s calm exterior as they’d left the hospital and she hadn’t wanted to upset her. Even though she knew Evie was happy, Nicole always had the fear that the girl would run and she wouldn’t see her again. ‘Slow down, my legs can’t keep up. And be on the lookout for ice. You don’t want to break a bone like me.’

‘I’ve got good grips on these boots.’ Evie snickered. ‘And you’re getting unfit. What happened to all the walking in Central Park?’

‘That’s enough sass from you.’ But she laughed all the same. ‘Come on, Evie. What happened with Jackson and that man?’

Evie stopped. They were almost at the apartment, but it seemed the weight of the bags or what was on her mind prevented her from going the last few paces. 'That revolting man was apparently there the night of the party when you were fired and I was told, in no uncertain terms, that I wasn't welcome.'

'Ah, I thought I recognised him.'

'Horrible little man.' Evie made no attempt to hide her disgust. 'He implied that I was sponging off you, that he knew what people like me were after. He implied I'd offered myself around to get ahead, to get a job, nice clothes, etcetera.'

'You mean prostitution?' Nicole was horrified. How low could some people go?

'Uh-huh.'

'I'll give him a piece of my mind if I ever lay eyes on him!'

'I can look after myself.'

'I'm not saying you can't.' She hesitated. 'But why throw the coffee at Jackson?'

'I didn't. I—'

'It's no use arguing with me, I saw you do it. My wrist is broken, not my eyesight.'

Evie exhaled hard, a plume of silver air heading up to the sky. 'We were arguing about you.'

'Me?'

'He didn't accuse me of quite the same thing as his friend, but he doesn't think my intentions are honourable, put it that way. He thinks I'm using you, taking your money, your hospitality. It's them and us.'

'What do you mean?'

'People like Jack, or Jackson, or whatever his name is, they see people like me as "different". There's no middle ground. To them it's clear-cut. They're probably not too dissimilar to the signatories on the petition … do-gooders, as long as it's from a distance.'

'You may be right.' She hesitated. 'I was thinking I might go to see Kent. Perhaps I should've made the effort to stay in touch with the family, at least with Jackson.'

'What? No! You're too nice, Nicole! One fired you and the other stood by and let him do it.' Evie's voice softened as she picked up the bags again. 'If I were you, I'd stay well away from that family. Come on, let's get home and warm up. Never mind slipping on ice, I think I'm about to lose one of my extremities if we're out in the cold much longer.'

As they walked on against the cold, Nicole wondered what Jackson's part had been in all of this. She wanted to believe he wasn't of the same ilk as this other man who'd accused Evie in the worst possible way, but it'd been years since she'd last seen him and there was every possibility he could've changed. Maybe Evie was right. Perhaps she should leave it alone, but when she'd been fired she hadn't only lost a job, she'd lost a family and had been heartbroken. And she'd never stopped missing them. So many times she'd been tempted to go and see them, talk about what had happened, anything to not be shut out of their lives. And didn't everyone deserve a chance to explain themselves, a chance to put things right?

Evie

When they reached Nicole's apartment, Evie dumped the bags of coats in the third bedroom. This was the first port of call after another collection, the sorting room where all coats would be pulled out and the pockets emptied. Then they'd go to the laundry or get in line for a visit to the drycleaners if necessary, after which they'd be ready to mend and made to look like new before taking them to the shelter to hang on portable coat stands.

Evie began taking coats out of bags, emptying rubbish from pockets, when the doorbell to the apartment rang.

'I'll go,' Nicole called on her way past the bedroom door. 'You keep doing what you're doing.'

Evie pulled out old tissues—she'd wash her hands next—coins she put in an old plastic tub in the corner of the room … they'd quite a collection now and would take it to the shelter when it was full, use it to buy more supplies: toilet rolls, kitchen towel, more cutlery. She pulled out subway tickets, a flyer for the Empire State Building, a paperclip, a cigarette lighter.

'Here's another one for you.' Nicole came in and dumped a plain black garbage bag inside the doorway. 'How about a mug of hot chocolate?'

'Now that sounds lovely.' Evie smiled.

Humming away, Nicole went to make the drinks and Evie emptied out the pockets of the last few coats, laughing when she took out a plastic whistle, grimacing when she pulled out a sticky wrapper containing the remains of a Hershey Bar. She opened the unmarked garbage bag that had just arrived. The smell was oddly familiar as she took out a black mid-length man's coat. It was reasonably new with no signs of the usual damage: missing buttons, a torn pocket. It wasn't as musty as most items they received either, items that had been stashed away and forgotten about for months, until the coat drive had done the owner a favour by taking away their unwanted goods. No, this coat had been worn recently. It still had the pungent smell of cheap cologne.

'Here you go.' Nicole came through with two mugs of hot chocolate and the smell overpowered anything else.

'Put it in the living room and I'll wash my hands, take a break. Who delivered this, by the way?' She held the latest bag aloft.

'I don't know. Reggie brought it up before he went home from his shift. He said it was by the main entrance with your name on it.'

Evie had got to know so many people who volunteered at the shelter, chatted with others who had left their marked garbage bags out for collection. It was probably one of them being even more generous and far too modest. She smiled at the spirit of the season.

'I'll turn on the fire,' said Nicole as she walked away, back to the living room, 'so we can sit and gossip while we drink our hot chocolates.'

Evie loved it when they chatted the evenings away, when they forgot the time, forgot the circumstances that had brought them together in the first place. It made her feel as though she'd truly found her place in life, her happiness, her way forward. She pulled out the contents of the last of the pockets in the remaining coat, and that was as far as she got before her heart thumped against her chest and she felt as though she'd almost stopped breathing.

Evie held a single photograph. She stared at it, eyes welling with tears.

She had a nasty feeling her happiness was about to take a serious nosedive.

Chapter Nine

Evie

Evie was up early the next morning. The evening with Nicole had been cut short after finding the photograph because Evie had been unable to get the image out of her head. She'd feigned a headache, feeling guilty with every lie that came out of her mouth, and she'd left for home before nine o'clock. She'd walked back to her apartment paranoid someone was following her, and as soon as she'd arrived, she'd locked the door behind her, drawn the chain across and pulled the curtains. She'd kept the lights off too, even the twinkle lights on the Christmas tree and around the door and cupboards.

Sleep had come eventually, but Evie had tossed and turned and after a fitful few hours she'd got up before sunrise to take a long walk around Central Park. Usually, a walk did the trick and ignited her energy levels, but not this morning. And when someone had tapped her on the shoulder, she'd jumped a mile before realising they were merely passing her the packet of tissues that had fallen from her pocket to the ground. She'd ended up taking off at speed in the direction of her apartment, and hadn't stopped until she'd safely slammed the door behind her and locked herself in all over again.

Evie stayed below the shower jets until the mediocre water tank ran cold. She dressed, tried her best to eat a bowl of muesli and drink a glass of juice in the hope something, anything would put a spring back in her step, but nothing. She wrapped a long scarf around her neck, covering the bottom of her face to keep away the winter chills, and made her way to work, venturing through the New York City streets which didn't seem anywhere near as friendly as they had been twenty-four hours ago.

*

'Is everything okay?' Bonnie hovered in the doorway to the workroom where Evie had plonked herself at the enormous table in the middle the moment she'd arrived. Since then Evie had kept herself busy scrolling through their social media, replying to any comments. Sharni from Long Island wanted to know how much notice she'd need to give them to make her dress; Rhianne from Brooklyn wondered whether they made clothes for groomsmen; and there was a post to approve from the Henderson's wedding last week, shots of the bride's dress alongside a big thank you note.

'Everything's fine,' Evie didn't look up from the screen. 'I just didn't sleep too well last night.'

'Don't you dare come down with anything, Evie. I need you!'

It was true. Work was full on crazy right now. There were final fittings to do, last minute touches to make to dresses and accessories, and the rush for summer wedding attire seemed to have begun early with two new clients booked in that afternoon. And that was before they even thought about working towards the upcoming expos in the New Year.

'I want to run through some ideas for March's Bridal Expo when you've got a moment,' said Bonnie. 'I want your opinion on the designs that'll make the most impact.' She clapped her hands together in an excitement Evie did her best to share and went to answer the door to the client who was stopping by to collect her dress for her wedding at the weekend.

Evie stared at the screen. She looked at the banner across the top: The Perfect Fit Couture written in lavender on the left and a backdrop photo of herself and Bonnie for all to see. She'd agreed to it when she hadn't really wanted to. She'd also agreed to a magazine article, and of course with that had come more photographs. She'd sat here at work as the professional snapped pictures of her, all the while thinking surely after all this time her uncle would've been well rid of her and moved on to something or someone else. But after seeing that photo when she'd pulled it out of the coat pocket last night, the disgusting image she longed to forget, it seemed he hadn't moved on at all. In fact, she suspected he was enjoying every minute of the chase, like a cat pinning a mouse down by its tail and watching it wriggle, deriving a kind of perverse pleasure as it squirmed and tried to get away. She wondered where he was going to turn up next, what he was going to do with the other photographs she knew he had.

Evie shook herself. Right now she needed to focus on her job, the part of her life she loved, the part she could control. In half an hour, she'd need to be ready to greet the next new bride-to-be and make this moment about her. She plastered a smile on her face, pinched her cheeks to give them a bit of the colour she suspected had drained as she obsessed about what might happen, and went out to the formal living room to prepare.

Evie had changed her life once before, and as she arranged the magazines into a perfect fan, lit the lamps to emit a warm glow and polished the glasses ready to offer champagne, she knew she couldn't let anything take away everything she had worked for. She thought about the man with Jack at the hospital, how he'd judged her and looked at her as though she would never be good enough to turn her life around. She'd seen his feelings in those mean, pinny eyes, heard it in the condescending tone of his voice. But she would fight him and everyone like him who got in her way, just as she'd had to fight the first night she'd ever seen him.

Jack

They finished the video call with the Seattle outlet and Jack gathered his papers together.

'That went well,' said Braydon. 'They've got the displays set up, as we discussed, the best lines out there for the customers. Jack, are you even listening?'

'What? Oh, sorry. Yes. Good meeting. Progress.'

Braydon rolled his eyes and Jack walked away before he'd say something he'd regret. Since the day at the hospital, he hadn't been able to look his colleague in the eye. He'd disliked him before that, but never had he seen him so downright nasty. Jack had let the man see his father but he'd excused himself to go to the restrooms where he'd splashed freezing water on his face before walking away, back to the foyer where he hovered until he saw Braydon leave the building. The man was an ogre and his father's insistence that he was good for business did little to show Jack that he belonged with the company. In the interests of his father's health, he'd keep quiet about his concerns for now, but there was only so much he'd put up with.

Jack ran in Central Park after work, pounding the pavements venting his frustration. He finished with a loop of just under two miles in the southern part of the park by the Tavern on the Green where he stopped for a moment, paused for breath. Plumes of white filled the air as he regulated his breathing, paced back and forth, and stood out of the way for a couple heading inside, past the planters surrounding the perimeter, and into the Tavern for dinner. The trees outside sparkled with twinkly lights wrapped around their once-bare trunks, as enchanting as the flowers would be come spring when the bistro-style white iron tables would come out to announce the season of hope and fresh starts.

Back at his apartment, he poured a glass of juice and slouched on the couch of his bachelor pad, feet up on the cushions the way he'd never been allowed to in the house he grew up in: a place for everything and everything in its place. Apart from a few photos of him over the years, the Churchill family residence was more like a show house than a home. His father had packed away all the photographs of Jack's mother, his own wife, as though by not having them around it could ease the pain of their loss. But it didn't. The only reminder now was a photograph of the family all together for Cynthia's last Thanksgiving with them, taken beside the fireplace by a family friend. And that photograph had been relegated to Kent's office, an identical one here in Jack's apartment, reminding him of how happy they'd once been and how precious life was. The problem was, you rarely realised that until it leapt up and smacked you in the face by being so cruel.

The next morning Jack did something he never did. He called in sick. He left a message on the company voicemail to tell Penny, his father's executive assistant, he had a migraine. He may as well have said menstrual cramps given how believable he sounded.

And that was how he found himself driving from Manhattan to Hazelbrook in the early hours of a Thursday morning. A thick frost had set in, but with barely any traffic on the roads, the drive calmed him as he followed the familiar route through Hazelbrook and onto Hollyhock Farm. So early in the morning he snapped off his headlights as he arrived at the farm, anxious not to wake Nate or Julia. It was unusual for him to appear mid-week, but he had plenty to do. Aside from any cutting back and maintaining the maze, he wanted to help Nate construct the new shed, and then there were Christmas trees to haul onto a truck and drive into town as Nate did each day. It was a simple life with a hell of a lot of hard work, but there was a love, a passion behind all that effort. And sometimes, Jack wished to God he could trade places with his friend.

The land at Hollyhock Farm was big enough that Jack could park away from the house so he wasn't heard as he made his way down to the maze. The sun wasn't due up for another hour and the frost presented the conifers gloriously, lining the hedges of the maze, twinkling silver and white beneath the moonlight. Kitted up in scarf, gloves and winter jacket, he pulled an old raincoat from the trunk of his car and followed the familiar route of the pathways that, stretched into a straight line, would amount to over a half a mile. He chuckled when even he, who'd spent many hours in this maze, took a couple of wrong turnings.

Eventually he found his way to the centre and there he spread out the old raincoat, lay down and looked up into the darkness that settled over Hazelbrook like a comfortable blanket. A thousand stars congregated above him, more than he could ever see from the townhouse or his condo in Manhattan, and he thought about his mother, how this sight would've mesmerised her for hours. He wasn't a religious person, nobody in his family was, and he knew it was a silly notion, but since his mother had died, he liked to think of her being among the stars looking down at him. When he was little she'd taken him to the organised events in Central Park where Jack could run free with other kids, waving their glow sticks in a familiar colourful dance in the air as their parents listened to the astronomers sharing views through telescopes of planets or star clusters.

As he lay there in the centre of the maze, Jack's thoughts drifted to Nicole, then to Evie and the pair of them three years ago, the pair of them today. Evie was feisty enough not to take any of his crap when he accused her of sponging off Nicole, but could he really trust her? Nicole had been like a mother to him, and he'd done his best at keeping in contact with her, but her refusal had left him no choice but to move on. Maybe if he'd told her what she meant to him, what she'd become over the years, she would've gotten in touch after that night. Perhaps if, for once, he'd disagreed with his father and not allowed it to happen, confronted him rather than falling in line, none of this would've happened.

Who was he kidding? He hadn't ever stood up to his father and actually told him what *he* wanted to do with his life.

Jack fidgeted at the uneasy thought, at the sense he still hadn't manned up to his father. He gazed up at the sky willing the stars to give him answers, show him how to escape the life he felt increasingly stuck in.

Was he asking for the impossible?

Chapter Ten

Nicole

Nicole stood at the front door she'd not knocked on in over three years. In fact, she hadn't knocked on it much before that, either; she'd had a key for the back entrance leading from the patio into the kitchen.

When the door opened, she came face-to-face with a woman, a housekeeper given the white apron and the air of efficiency about her.

'I'm here to see Kent.' Nicole's voice shook as she got the words out. No matter what her feelings were back then, she could do this.

'Certainly,' said the housekeeper. But before she could do anything else, such as ask for a name or invite her into the hallway, a familiar face appeared behind her.

'It's fine, Maggie.' Kent didn't break the stare between himself and Nicole. 'Please, come in.'

When Maggie had disappeared once more to the rear of the house, Kent stood back and held out a hand, gesturing Nicole to come in to the hallway.

When she stepped inside, it felt as though she'd been here only yesterday. The same mahogany side table was positioned on the left, just far enough from the front door to enable visitors to enter with ease. The same ornate coat stand stood beside the antique gilded mirror fixed to the wall. There weren't any photographs here, only a couple of expensive pieces of artwork Nicole had never much cared for and that didn't express the personalities of anyone in the household. The only difference in this house between then and now appeared to be the time and space that had sat between Kent and Nicole for three years. The house even smelled the same. Home-cooked meals, a hint of cologne Kent had worn then and still did now, the smell of clean surfaces, sandalwood polish and vacuumed carpets, the floral aroma she associated with the Churchill residence.

When she'd first started working for Kent Churchill, Nicole had soon realised that aside from not having many personal items lying around, everything was pristine and very much in its place, even with a teenager in the house. One day she'd been out walking and passed by a flower seller, and hadn't been able to resist buying a small bunch of traditional white daisies and another of deep fuchsia spray roses. She'd intended to put them in water for the rest of the day and take them home to her apartment, but when she'd let herself into the kitchen Kent had complimented her and said it was nice to have flowers in the house again. She'd assumed he meant since his wife had passed away and she hadn't had the heart to tell him they weren't for him. Nicole had found a vase in the very top cupboard above the cooker and arranged the flowers and found a place for them on the table in the hallway. She'd even seen Kent pause to feel the silkiness of their leaves, lean in to smell them, lost in his own thoughts as though another living thing in his home was taking some getting used to. And from that day on she'd bought flowers for the house every four to five days.

Nicole looked down the hallway and saw that even now, three years since she'd left, the tradition she'd begun more than a decade ago was still holding strong. A clear vase hugged an arrangement of white gladiolus with deep green foliage beneath, lighter green stems standing tall and proud.

Kent stood in front of her. 'Can I take your coat?' Nicole shrugged it off, careful to ease it over the cast on her wrist. 'You must be freezing, go through to the living room and I'll have Maggie bring us some tea.'

It was strange, even now, to hear of somebody else making the tea and no doubt taking out a plate to fill it with a morning snack of some description. It'd been her job once upon a time and for so many years.

When Nicole went through to the living room, it too was exactly as she'd remembered it, apart from the new rug in front of the hearth and two ornate silver candlesticks sitting on the mantelpiece. Kent had always had expensive taste and kept his townhouse impeccably furnished. Everything from the ebony wood flooring and Italian crystal lamps in here, to the French silver-leaf spare bed she'd slept in one night when they'd been snowed in, to the top-of-the-range cookware in the kitchen, spoke of wealth, of extravagance, of a man who needed those things because he lacked something else, something Nicole had never managed to work out in her time with him and his son.

Sometimes Nicole had felt sorry for Jack, the teenager unable to hang loose anywhere in this house. But Jack had taken it all in his stride. It was the way Kent was and had been, she assumed, for a very long time. Jack had always sat properly on the furniture, been polite to any guests who appeared, even worn all the designer outfits Kent bought him when casual, inexpensive clothes would've been far better. Nicole sometimes wondered how quickly after his wife's death Kent had fallen headlong into the business, how soon he'd begun to drift away from his own son, like two pieces of a shipwreck ending up with miles and miles of ocean separating them.

'Please, sit.' Kent came back into the room and left the door ajar, presumably for Maggie.

Nicole sat on the edge of the couch nearest the fire, sinking into the leather that had softened over the years.

'It's good to see you.' Kent sat the opposite end of the couch. To someone who didn't know him, or to a business colleague, he looked relaxed. But Nicole could sense his edge of nervousness, ever so slight but there nonetheless.

'It's good to see you too.' She cleared her throat. 'I bumped into Jackson and his young lady at Macy's.' She began the small talk, hoping to disperse the tension. The closeness they'd once shared had been extinguished, but it still felt good to see him again.

Kent smiled. 'I'd forgotten how you always called him Jackson.' He looked at her for a moment, his expression unreadable, before he went on as though the spell between them had been broken. 'Jack said you'd seen him at the hospital, too. How's the wrist?'

She patted the cast with her opposite hand. 'It doesn't hurt anymore. There's the occasional itch, but nothing more sinister. I'll be in the cast for another few weeks and then it'll take some time to get my strength back. I'm not as young as I once was.'

'None of us are.' His blue eyes flickered back at her and for a moment she was back where she'd once been, three years ago, laughing and smiling together, and it made her sad. 'And you've managed okay, since … you know …'

'I've been fine since I left here, yes.' She appreciated his concern and wondered how much he'd thought about her over the years, whether he'd replayed what had happened over and over in his mind like she had. 'And how are you? Your hospital stay sounded a little more serious than this.' She lifted her wrist.

As Kent told her about the minor heart attack, the list of dos and don'ts from the hospital, Nicole wondered whether Jack had mentioned what happened at the hospital with his colleague, with Evie, but she doubted it or Kent would've mentioned it already. He was a strong man, never one to hold back on letting his feelings known. She knew that much from experience.

'I can imagine Cameron fussing around you.' Nicole smiled after he told her all about his daughter's flying visit from Toronto. Cameron had been away at college when Nicole started working for the Churchills but they'd met a few times and Kent's daughter was as headstrong as her father.

'She didn't bring the kids in case it was too much.'

'Maybe she had a point,' Nicole agreed.

He dismissed it with a flick of his hand. 'Nonsense, there's life in me yet.'

After a moment's pause she said, 'Jackson looked really well. He's always looked so handsome and together in a suit.'

'He most certainly does.'

The awkwardness evaporated as they launched into a conversation about Jack as a teenager, how he'd hated dressing up formally, his graduation with a first class business degree, shopping for a new suit for his first day on the team at The Diamond Touch.

'I always wondered whether Jackson would do something entirely different,' said Nicole.

'You mean not work at the family business?' Kent looked surprised. 'Why wouldn't he? He's a natural.'

Indeed, he was, but Nicole had seen moments of doubt in Jackson's eyes even before he started on the team. She'd never seen him look that way throughout his college years, despite the stress of coursework, the impending exams. He'd always been the life and soul of any social gathering with his friends, always chatted so freely, but the moment he'd stepped up to take on the family legacy something inside him had flickered, like a candle about to burn out if the draught got too much.

'The business needs Jack,' Kent concluded. 'He's family and he'll inherit it all eventually. The more we build it up now, the better.'

'I suppose you're right.'

Maggie brought in a pot of tea and two cups with a side plate of coffee cake, and although she was hungry, Nicole couldn't eat a thing. She accepted the cup of tea, and when the heat came through the china and warmed her hands, she said, 'I'm sorry about what happened.' When she looked at Kent she knew he'd cast his mind back to the night in question.

'I think it's me who should be apologising.' He offered her a slice of cake, but she shook her head.

'No, it was wrong of me to have someone on your property without permission, and it was wrong of me to give away food and the blanket without asking first.'

Kent set his tea and cake aside. 'Was she homeless?'

'Yes, and very scared.' She hesitated, and then, 'She never asked for my help. Believe me, it took a lot of convincing to get her to accept anything in the way of handouts. She's been through a lot … I'm not sure what exactly, but I do know she's a good girl. Eventually, with my help, we got her started in a job and she was offered an apprenticeship.'

'And did she live with you?'

'Of course, she needed a start.'

'So you took her in as your own?'

'She lived with me for a while—' Nicole stopped talking when Kent stood and moved over to the fireplace. She watched him rest one hand on the mantelpiece, unable to look at her. In years gone by she'd seen him do this many a time, but she'd never been the cause.

Nicole continued. 'Once she was settled with her job, Evie found her own apartment.'

'She saw you coming, didn't she?' His eyes followed the flickering flames.

Nicole slammed her cup onto the coffee table. 'She's a genuine girl, one of a kind, and I won't hear a word against her. I wouldn't back then, and I certainly won't now.'

Kent's face softened as he turned to look at Nicole. At over six foot, he towered above her and she saw the strong man he was, but couldn't ignore the words that had come from him. She'd always thought of him as mellow when he was at home, away from the fight and hunger of his business, but today he looked different. He reminded her of the man who'd sent her away.

'You were special to me, and to Jack,' he explained. He gestured for Nicole to sit down, and again he sat at the opposite end of the couch. Neither of them touched the drinks or the food. 'When you left there was a void, and just because we weren't in contact doesn't mean we didn't think about you or worry.'

'Jackson did try to contact me.' From Kent's face she knew this was news to him. 'But I turned him away. I didn't answer calls or letters, and eventually he stopped. I didn't want to come between you both.' Her voice faltered. 'It was only when I bumped into Jackson that I realised none of us should've left it this long.'

'You're right.' He looked deep into her eyes. 'But I'm sorry too, for what happened. I didn't need to fire you. My actions that night were completely over the top. I know Jack thinks so.'

She warmed at the thought of Jackson on her side. 'I need you to know that Evie never took advantage of me.'

'But you gave her money.'

'I did. How else can anyone ever get off the streets and start over? She deserved a chance and, yes, I was the person who gave that to her.'

'So she's moved on now?'

'She no longer lives with me, but we're close. And she's a wonderful girl. She's become like a daughter to me.'

She didn't miss the way Kent bristled. Unable to sit still, he went back to the fireplace once again, next to the flames that licked against the throat of the chimney.

'Why do you see things so black and white?' she asked.

He turned around. 'I see things the way they are. I know when something is right and when it isn't.'

'Like firing me? That wasn't right and you went ahead and did it anyway.'

'It's not the same thing.'

'You're prejudging Evie, like some of your guests prejudged me.'

'What?'

'Yes, that's right. Plenty of times I was sneered at by guests at your parties who thought I was the lowly hired help. And you like those people? You call them your friends? I'd rather be in a room of ten Evie's than a single one of those pompous business associates you have.'

When he said nothing, Nicole could see no way forward. It was time to leave.

She stormed out of the room, grabbed her coat, wincing when she accidentally knocked the wrist in the cast against the coat stand in her haste.

'Nicole, please don't walk out,' Kent came after her, his footsteps close behind. 'This solves nothing.'

She spun around. 'I don't know why I came here. For some reason I thought things might have changed, you might have learned to look at situations from more than one angle. But I was wrong.' She flung open the door and left it so wide it blew spatters of rain into the hallway as she left.

And to think, she'd once had feelings for that man.

Kent

He watched Nicole leave, pulling her coat tighter around herself with her good arm, battling against the wind and the rain, her chestnut curls bobbing in the wind as she marched away from him again.

He shut the door, and by the time he returned to the living room, Maggie had already discreetly cleared away the food and tea, wiped up the spill from Nicole's cup. Deflated, he flopped onto the couch. When Nicole had shown up at the door almost an hour ago, his heart had leapt. Jack had already told him about Evie, but he hadn't expected Nicole to be quite so involved in setting her on the straight and narrow. To take someone in off the streets was a big thing, but he shouldn't be surprised; it was in her nature to care more than she should. And her past made her vulnerable to sympathising with someone like Evie. But whether that was right, he had no idea. She couldn't replace the child she'd once lost, but he couldn't tell her so, because he wasn't supposed to know. Nicole Capra had never had any idea how much he knew about her and how little she really knew about him.

Nicole had come into this house and this family, wanting nothing in return, and slowly it had become harder and harder to tell her the truth. He'd kept his secret closely guarded for twenty years, and though he'd started out trying to make sense of his own loss through getting to know the woman who was unwittingly at the centre of it, he'd ended up getting too close. Nicole had gone from a generously paid housekeeper to a friend, a member of the family, and then she'd become the first woman he'd fallen in love with since his wife.

Evie

'Thanks for helping, Evie.' Nicole moved the bags from yet another coat collection with her foot, into the third bedroom at her apartment. 'Are you off anywhere nice tonight?'

'I'm out with Lizzy, from upstairs, introducing her to Thorello's.' She grinned. It was a cheap and cheerful place she doubted Lizzy had ever tried. Lizzy's culinary experiences seemed to be on opposite ends of a see-saw: on one end were the fancy restaurants she frequented with her boyfriend, and on the other, it was takeaway cartons and pizzas in huge cardboard boxes where she found her sustenance. Tonight Evie intended to redress the balance, and besides, when she was out with her friend, Evie wasn't scared of her past catching up with her. Having company gave her confidence, rightly or not.

Something was up with Nicole tonight though, Evie was sure of it. For a start she could see the other woman had been crying. But when she'd asked about it, Nicole denied anything was wrong. And when Evie had gone to put the bags of coats in the spare bedroom, a room that had been Evie's once upon a time, Nicole had insisted she do it. She'd pushed them gently with her foot into the doorway and pulled the door shut, but not before Evie had seen the windowsill with a photo of Nicole and a little boy. A photo she hadn't seen before. The boy looked about fourteen and too old for a cuddle from his mum, but there they were, cheeks pressed together, laughing, Nicole's eyes dancing in a way they hadn't been tonight. Evie wondered whether he'd been from the shelter, perhaps one of the cases Nicole hadn't managed to jump in and save.

Evie hugged Nicole and left the apartment, took the elevator and bid farewell to Reggie in his usual position beside the door, ready to leap forwards and help someone out of a cab, ready to open the door for someone who had their hands full or bid a family goodnight. He was a man of few words, but somehow he was someone you knew you could trust and rely on implicitly. She headed away from the apartment towards Madison Avenue, past designer clothes outlets, coffee shops, a macaron café, and cut down a side street before walking two further blocks that led towards Thorello's. She loved the crisp, night air against her skin and finally she was beginning to relax again. Her uncle seemed to have crawled back in to whatever hole he'd come out of, at least for now.

Lizzy, sitting at the table, removed her purple hat and matching mittens as Evie arrived at the café. 'You've got impeccable timing! I just got here myself. I ran, I didn't want to be late for you.'

Evie unwound her scarf and hung it on the back of her chair with her coat. 'You didn't have to rush, I'd have waited.'

'Nah.' Lizzy waved a hand dismissively in front of her. 'My meeting was boring as hell anyway. It should've been over hours ago.'

The waiter came over and embraced Evie, took their order of two beers.

'Come here often then?' Lizzy giggled after he sauntered off.

'Just a bit. It's a favourite of mine and Nicole's.' Evie opened her menu. 'I can recommend the nachos.'

'Now, they sound good, but not much better than takeout. I thought you were educating me on eating healthily.'

'I am! The nachos come with red onion, peppers, cheese, and a side salad is served with everything.'

Lizzy perused the salad section on the menu, which had everything from a basic green salad to a Cobb salad or Caesar.

'If you're looking for more of a meal, there's the roast chicken, which comes with corn on the cob and Thorello's speciality coleslaw,' Evie suggested.

Lizzy shut her menu. 'I'll go for that.'

'Make that two,' said Evie when Thorello himself appeared with the two beers they'd ordered.

'And a big welcome to your friend.' Thorello nodded to Lizzy, his Italian-American enthusiasm evident. He committed their order to memory and off he went. This place was the best. It was so relaxed. Chairs and tables were old and worn yet still bright, red gingham, wipe-clean tablecloths sat on square tables, there was an old-fashioned jukebox in the corner and chatter buzzed at a medium level as they sat at their table next to the window and watched a dusting of snow fall from the skies.

'So?' Lizzy sipped on her beer.

'So?'

'Any news on the mystery man?'

Evie wished she hadn't brought it up. She didn't want to think about her uncle tonight, let alone talk about him.

'I've no idea who it was,' she lied. 'I expect he was from the shelter.' She fiddled with the label on her beer and looked out of the window. 'The snow's coming down thick and fast now. It hadn't even started when I left Nicole's.'

'We might get a white Christmas.' Lizzy grinned. 'And nice change of subject, by the way. There I was thinking you were going to tell me something exciting, like you had a secret lover on the streets of New York. Mind you, he wasn't exactly who I'd have paired you up with if I'd been the one to choose.'

Evie smirked. Her uncle had never been much of a looker, even in his younger days, although he'd behaved as though he was the next best thing to Richard Gere. She shuddered at the thought, at the memory of his eyes on her the first time she'd changed for the pool.

Their food arrived, and Lizzy was so ravenous the dinner silenced her for a while.

'You should make time to eat proper meals, you know.' Evie smiled, watching her friend devour what was in front of her.

'I know, I know. One of these days I'll do it right. At least I've got you to keep an eye on me.' She dragged a piece of chicken through the thick, salty gravy and after she'd finished her mouthful, said, 'Now, I don't want you to get upset …'

'Why do I sense there's a "but" coming?'

Lizzy cut another slice of roast chicken. 'But,' she began, 'there's a guy at work, new in town, and I'd love to set you up on a date.'

'Oh no, absolutely not. No way on this earth!'

'Come on, Evie. I've never known you to have so much as a one-night stand, let alone a relationship.' She paused then, eyes wide. 'Oh God, I'm such an idiot. I never thought to ask.'

'What do you mean?'

'Well … you're not … you know.'

Evie almost spat out her beer. 'I'm not gay, no. Why, are you worried I fancy you?'

'Don't be crazy. And stop changing the subject.'

So she hadn't forgotten the mention of the mysterious man, the link to her past that Evie wanted to bury.

'I'm not changing the subject, I'm just not interested. I will go out with someone, when I find someone *I* like.'

'But you'd like him. He's gorgeous. Tall, dark and handsome—'

'Is he a movie star?'

'He's a doctor. Oh, you're messing with me—'

Evie laughed. 'Thanks for trying, but I'd prefer to find my own dates, thank you.'

'Have it your way. This chicken is delicious, by the way, really tender, and the gravy is so good, it—'

Lizzy's voice trailed off as Evie looked out the window and saw a man crossing the road, wool coat pulled up against his neck, collar turned up against the snow.

Jack Churchill.

She was about to look away when he looked up and locked her gaze.

'Hello,' said Lizzy, realising what had got her friend's attention now. 'I don't think there's any need for me to meddle and set up a blind date.'

Evie looked away, embarrassed she'd been seen looking. 'Him? Oh God, no. He's not someone I'd date.'

Lizzy shook her head.

'What?'

'You're both into each other, I can totally tell!'

'No we're not.' Evie scooped up the remains of the coleslaw, filling her mouth so she couldn't speak for a bit.

'And you're blushing!'

Reluctantly, she finished chewing. 'I'm not!' Jack had already gone on his way.

'You are so, Evie.'

'If you must know, he's a bit of an ass.'

'Oh? Tell me more.'

'That's all I'm saying. He knows Nicole, and take it from me, I'll be steering well clear.'

Thorello appeared and cleared away the plates quickly and efficiently, and they ordered another couple of drinks. When he left, Evie added, 'He's really not a nice person.'

'No? He looked all right to me.'

'Looks can be deceiving.'

Lizzy shook her head, unable to stop grinning.

'Lizzy.'

'Don't "Lizzy" me. You need to get out there, get some man action! And I don't mind saying, *he* was gorgeous!'

Evie rolled her eyes. 'Anyone would think a girl can't function without a bit of sex.'

'Oh, we can function all right, but we need oiling and maintenance every now and then, if you know what I mean.'

'Yeah, well, not him.'

They relaxed over their second beers and changed the chat to Lizzy's upcoming visit to her parents for Christmas. 'Always a stressful time,' said Lizzy, referring to the messy divorce they were going through. They discussed Evie's plans to spend it with Nicole as usual, and by the time they left the café, Evie was back on an even keel, less worried that what she'd built up could be snatched away from under her, like a tablecloth whipped from a table, taking everything piled neatly on top and smashing it over the floor.

'Dinner same place, same time, next week?' Lizzy was about to take the steps up to her apartment as Evie hovered at the top of the flight to go down to the basement.

'So you liked Thorello's?'

'I'm sold. It was a lovely place, very you: simple, yet elegant in its own way, with a warm atmosphere.'

'I'll let Thorello know you'll be writing their next review then, shall I?'

'I'd love to.' Lizzy smiled. 'Goodnight, Evie.'

'See you.' Evie carefully took the icy steps down to her basement studio and took out her keys. She'd have to throw salt onto the concrete first thing in the morning; the winter weather made it treacherous, and she didn't fancy breaking a limb simply going to work.

About to put the key in the lock and cursing that she hadn't fixed the security light above the door yet—something Nicole regularly nagged her about—a figure stepped out of the shadows and her keys crashed against the concrete below.

How could she ever have doubted his persistence?

She froze, her breath held. She backed up to the door, unable to go any further, and he closed the gap. He breathed against her face as he began to speak, his eyes pinning her to the spot.

'Good to see you again, Evie.' His voice sent shivers right through her.

Deep down she'd always known it'd only be a matter of time before this happened.

Chapter Eleven

Jack

Jack hadn't meant to stare like that when he saw Evie in the window of the café. He was in the middle of Christmas shopping and was hunting in his pocket for loose change to grab a newspaper from the street vendor before he went back to meet Aurelia at Barney's. The look Evie had given him was akin to how he felt about her—the look of distrust, an unfounded dislike.

'What about this perfume for Halle?' Aurelia spritzed the scent in the air beside the fragrance counter and Jack turned away before he sneezed.

'That'll work.'

Aurelia rolled her eyes. 'I want to get my sister a nice present, not something that'll just *work*.'

Jack pretended to be distracted with the men's cologne. Aurelia was better shopping on her own anyway. He wasn't even sure why he was here. They'd only been seeing one another a couple of months, and apart from the sex, Jack knew they had little in common. Aurelia had no interest in the things he enjoyed—she wasn't interested in driving out of the city at weekends, she didn't want to go for a long walk around Central Park, cook together and chat or laugh over a bottle of wine at either of their apartments. But he guessed he suited her image, a party girl who liked the limelight, liked to be seen and liked to be treated to lavish gifts on regular occasions.

He leant against a counter and pretended to read his newspaper until Aurelia had finished. She must've sprayed every fragrance in the store. How were you supposed to tell one from the other? He wondered whether Evie wore perfume. She wouldn't suit the powerful scent Aurelia had asked him to smell first—Poison, if he remembered correctly—which was an overwhelming spicy fragrance. No, Evie would suit something more subtle, light and sexy.

'Are we done?' When Aurelia walked over to him, bags looped over her wrist, he closed his newspaper.

'You're so impatient.'

He pulled her to him. 'Let's go back to your place.'

And with smiles, off they went.

An hour later, sated and rejuvenated after a quick post-coital shower at Aurelia's place, Jack walked home. He had his own Christmas shopping to do, but the offer of a session in bed had been far more tempting; long limbs wrapped around his, taking him to places that made him forget everything else.

It was dark now except for the city lights, and all that remained from the snow earlier was its coating on skyscrapers, in the grooves of windows on brownstones he passed, on cars parked for long enough to let winter cover them up. He passed the same café he'd spotted Evie in, and even though she wasn't there now to quiz about her intentions, he went in. He sat at the same table he'd seen Evie sitting at, ordered a large cappuccino from the waiter with a funny Italian-American accent, and wondered whether he should get in touch with Nicole. It'd been so wonderful to see her again, and the best way to make sure she wasn't being taken advantage of was to be friendly and keep an eye on her without her even realising.

His phone rang and he answered it quickly. He hated it when people had loud conversations in places like this, and although he'd not wanted to answer his father's call—it was bound to be work related—it was too late, he'd tapped the accept button rather than decline in his haste to stop the ringing. Kent asked a few fleeting questions about the business, but Jack suspected that wasn't the only reason he'd called.

'Anything else?' Jack probed when the conversation lulled.

'Nicole came to see me.'

'Oh.' He hadn't expected that. 'And how did that go?'

'Not too well. We got onto the subject of Evie. I'm not sure I like the situation, Jack.'

'Nicole assures me she's perfectly fine to look after herself and that Evie isn't taking advantage.'

'Do you believe that?'

Even Jack had to concede that seeing them together at the hospital, they'd looked more like mother and daughter than a woman with someone following her around to take her money and who knew what else. 'I'm not sure, but I don't think it's any of our business.' Either it was all true and perfectly innocent, or Evie was an incredible actress, able to convince Nicole.

Kent sighed. 'She was like one of the family.'

Jack, taken aback by his father's honesty, eventually said, 'I think you've hit the nail on the head. Nicole *was* like one of the family, but she's gone her own way now. I think we need to accept that.' He didn't admit he had every intention of catching up with Nicole again and making sure she was okay.

When he ended the call, Jack finished his coffee, paid and tipped the waiter and set out onto the city streets again, towards home. When he reached the first intersection, he briefly clocked the homeless man sitting huddled in a doorway, his head beneath a brown hoodie, fingers blackened and unprotected against the cold. That would've been Evie a few years ago, and the realisation sent a bolt of shock cascading through him. Being female she would've been more vulnerable, and he wondered how often men like him had passed her by without a second glance, or worse, whether she'd been hassled.

The thought coursed through his veins as he made his way home to a warm apartment and safe bed for the night. But he didn't sleep as well as usual. His dreams were plagued with Evie, homeless on a street corner, Nicole trying to help her and ending up hurt.

He wanted to trust this young woman, but how could he? He was worried Nicole had taken on far more with Evie than she could really handle.

*

It was business as usual the following day. Jack met with the web designer and Braydon, and they agreed on a final design. He went through tedious accounts and figures as he did every month to see where their sales were dipping, where they were increasing. He booked a meeting with the manager of the Chicago store, their worst performing outlet, to discuss strategy.

It was already dark when he left work, save for the bright Christmas lights that brought the city to life. He smiled. As a kid he'd marvelled at Christmas lights whether on trees, houses or in store window displays, and nothing had changed. It still gave him a warm buzzy feeling. He crossed the street before a yellow taxi whizzed past, and when he crossed the next he saw the same man he'd passed last night, the homeless man, huddled in the store doorway. He wondered whether he'd been there since last night or whether he'd gone off elsewhere and returned to what he'd deemed a safe place. His head was dipped against the cold, against the world. Jack couldn't see his face, but he'd seen it yesterday—unshaven, dirty. He wondered how long the man had been on the streets. What had happened to him that had ended in this? He wondered whether it was a man, or perhaps he was just a boy. What was his story? Everyone had one, yet this was the first time he'd ever thought about it. Usually he passed these people by without a moment's thought.

Jack found his feet coming to a stop. The café across the street, with its window bedecked in fairy lights, was still open; and dodging a taxi coming from his right, and another on his left that honked rudely at him as he ran, he went in and scanned the menu. He ordered a cheeseburger and a large cappuccino to take away, and retracing his route, found himself back opposite the man at the very same intersection.

Jack crouched down. 'Hey, man.'

The man said nothing. He looked panicked.

'Here.' Jack handed him the bag with the burger and set the coffee down beside him. He suspected the man smelled, but the biting cold and the frost on the bricks beside him and the ice on the step where he sat on an old shaggy black blanket, meant it was impossible to smell anything tonight.

Jack estimated the man to be in his early twenties at most, and when he looked up Jack saw green eyes that told tales of happier times, times that hadn't always been this bleak. The gold flecks in them stood out against his grubby face and begged to ignite change somewhere along the line.

'Take it.' Jack pushed the bag at him again. 'There's hot coffee in the cup.' He'd never so much as dropped a dollar in the pot for a homeless person, let alone talked to one of them or bought them something to eat.

'Thanks.' The man picked up the bag, wary as though it were some kind of trick, but eventually took out the burger and immediately started devouring it in huge bites. 'Thanks, man,' he said between mouthfuls.

'Don't forget your coffee.' Jack pushed himself to standing.

The man held out a hand to shake Jack's as a thank you, and reluctantly Jack touched his palm to the cold, rough, filthy skin on this young man's hand.

Jack nodded to him and went on his way without looking back. It felt good to have done a good deed for someone he knew nothing about. He thought back to the night on the patio when his father seemed to fear Evie, a young woman he didn't know, his fear so great he'd fired his own loyal housekeeper in a moment's panic. It was as though the not knowing and the air of mystery brought some deep-veiled threat to his father's life, and Jack had tried to make sense of it then and now, but still couldn't.

Jack walked on, past Christmas shoppers with bags dangled over their arms, others bracing against the cold or ducking into nearby restaurants for respite. When he walked past the mulled cider cart, the smell was enough to rein him in and he watched the street seller ladle out the hot drink into the polystyrene cup, its sugar and spices snaking into the air, the taste of Christmas. It reminded him of the mulled wine Nicole had made from scratch, every year she was with them. She'd started with wine in a huge saucepan and added seasonal orange, sugar, cinnamon and nutmeg. She'd added sugar to taste, and once heated she'd stir in a little sloe gin before announcing the mixture was ready.

The mulled cider reached every extremity and warmed him through as he walked on. There was a slice of orange in the polystyrene cup to ensure the flavours stayed there, and as he reached the bottom of the drink and tipped the cup to get the dregs, it bumped into his nose. He dropped the cup into a nearby trash can and was about to cross the street when he saw Nicole on the other side. He raised a hand to wave to her, but she didn't see him. He called over but the sound of one taxi horn arguing with another drowned out his voice.

He looked up at the building she'd gone into, knowing it wasn't where she lived. It looked like an old office block, but there was no signage to indicate what it was. He watched her go inside and when the street was clear he crossed over.

His father was worried, and so was he. It was time for answers. He took the steps at the front, two at a time, and went inside.

Chapter Twelve

Evie

As the evening drew in and darkness blanketed Manhattan, Bonnie switched on the extra spot lamp on the table. She carefully unrolled the Chantilly lace. 'You did wash your hands after you had the toast, didn't you?' She checked with Evie.

Evie smiled for the first time since the confrontation with her uncle outside her apartment last night. 'Of course I did. I always do.' She reached out and touched the edge of the lace, perfect, soft, gentle and flowing. 'This is gorgeous, hats off to the new supplier.'

Bonnie nodded. 'I'm really pleased with them so far.'

'What time are the Henleys due in?'

'They'll be here in …' Bonnie checked her watch, 'fifteen minutes.'

'I'll set up the living room.'

'Are you sure you're happy to stay? I know you're off to the shelter this evening.'

'It's fine,' Evie replied. 'I'll be able to get everything ready, greet the Henleys, and then if it's okay I'll leave the details to you.'

'Perfect.' Bonnie smiled. 'Make sure you open those magazines to show our feature on the business. We're famous!'

Evie's smile lasted until she was out of view. In the living room she plumped up cushions on the two couches sitting at right angles from each other, the armchair in the corner. She arranged the magazines, opening them out as Bonnie had asked, and when she saw the feature again, she wondered whether this was how her uncle had found her. Had he somehow seen it, on a street corner, in a store, over someone's shoulder as they planned their dream wedding? He'd probably thought all of his Christmases had come at once when he found out her place of work and somehow her address, all the details that wouldn't be too difficult to find once you had a starting point.

She stared at the picture of her in the magazine, sitting at the long table, sewing a lace trim to an ice-pink veil, and she thought about last night.

He'd been lurking in the shadows, and she hadn't seen him until she put her key in the lock.

'Hello, Evie. Long time, no see.'

Her breath held in her throat.

'Cat got your tongue?' He moved towards her and she tried to step back, but she was already as close to the door as she could be.

He pulled something from the pocket of his coat, presumably a new one that had replaced the coat he'd dumped at Nicole's apartment a few days ago. 'We've got some unfinished business, young lady.' He towered threateningly over her. Even in the dark she could see every detail of his face, the clean-shaven jaw, the cut by his bottom lip, the pockmark in his cheek that'd always been there.

He showed her what he was holding: another photograph from the collection she'd wished were never taken, the hold he had over her and always would. 'I assume you found the photo in the coat.' She didn't answer. 'Plenty more where they came from.'

'Lizzy!' She shrieked, as loudly as she could. She hoped her friend hadn't been able to find her keys in her bag. They'd joked in the past that her designer Louis

Vuitton was like a black hole. Please let it be the case tonight.

'Lizzy!' She screamed again.

Her uncle leant closer when they heard footsteps, his breath hot and stale on her face. 'Scream all you like. This isn't over. You'll be seeing me again.'

'Everything okay?' Lizzy appeared like an apparition and Evie had never been so grateful in her life.

Her uncle said, 'Good evening,' to her friend as though he was a welcome acquaintance, and then he was gone, into the Manhattan streets, swallowed up again by the metropolis where Evie knew he'd lurk quietly like a lion until he was ready to pounce on his prey again.

'What was that all about?' Lizzy carefully came down the icy steps, keys in hand. She'd caught her just in time.

'Nothing.'

'Oh, bullshit!' Lizzy always was one to tell it how it was. 'Now we're going inside,' she nodded to the keys still on the ground, 'and you're going to tell me everything.'

And as painful as it had been, Evie had told Lizzy every last detail. And it had felt better than she'd ever anticipated. Lizzy had earned her stripes as a lifelong friend last night when she'd listened to Evie's story. Lizzy hadn't judged her, she hadn't even commented as Evie got her words out, one after the other. And when Evie had finished, Lizzy ran upstairs to her apartment and came back with a bottle of store-bought mulled wine and they drank the lot.

Now, as Evie surveyed the living room at The Perfect Fit Couture to ensure she was ready to greet the Henleys for their appointment, she knew that last night she'd taken another step into her new life by letting a friend know about her past. It was another step forwards, but niggling at the back of her mind was that somehow, before long, she could very well be taking a good few steps back.

*

After work, Evie made her way to the shelter, careful on the pavements that had become icy so quickly tonight. The latest haul of coats had brought in a gorgeous, red button-down woollen swing coat with deep pockets and a soft lining, and Evie was almost tempted to claim it for herself. But she was one of the lucky ones. She'd leave it for someone else more in need than her. No, what she needed was a little different to a coat … she needed a miracle. She needed her uncle to disappear.

She negotiated the frosted pavements, past a small, gated park whose railings were tipped with frost. She couldn't deny it. She'd thought about running again. Maybe she'd been stupid to run to Manhattan in the first place, a city with so much opportunity, but one that was so obvious for a girl like her. Maybe she'd run again, head to San Francisco instead. After all, she had the work experience, she had savings to tide her over at the start. Perhaps thousands of miles would mean her uncle would finally lose interest and she'd be free. She'd never have to run again.

But she didn't want a different life. Not now she'd worked so hard to get this one on track. She wanted the life she'd carved out for herself, the life with Nicole in it, and now Lizzy. She had no idea how to get through this, but by the time she stomped up the steps to the shelter, she'd made up her mind. She couldn't, and wouldn't, run away. Not this time.

Evie smiled at Roger, one of the regulars, as she shut the door to the cold and pulled off her gloves. Roger had been coming here since Evie started helping out and would be one of the many whose heart would break if this place shut down. She patted Millie on the shoulder, a woman who had started visiting the shelter every day for the last month, and she asked how the session with the volunteer counsellor had gone that morning. Evie waved over at Dorothy, one of their rather talkative regulars who was huddled at a table with two younger people Evie didn't recognise. Evie hoped Nicole had already noticed the new faces and called their volunteer counsellors if she saw fit. It wasn't uncommon for the homeless to have mental illness, and Nicole was adamant that they wouldn't fall through any crack in any government system, but get the help they needed before it was too late. As Evie shrugged off her coat, she spoke with Simon, a kind but misunderstood man with a big heart. He'd lost his job and his way, a story all too often told within these walls, but he hadn't let it change who he was at his core. Evie smiled as she left him to sign with the deaf woman, Nancy, who'd found the shelter last week.

She hung her coat in the cupboard at the far end of the room before grabbing the broom to sweep beneath the tables Nicole was busy wiping down.

'It's busy in here tonight,' said Evie. And then more quietly she asked, 'Have you met the new recruits?' She was referring to the newcomers she didn't recognise.

'I have, and I think they're fine, but Daisy will be here in a while, so if they're still here, I'll send her over for a chat.'

Daisy was one of the counsellors and only lived three blocks away so was there on hand when they needed her.

'I think the snow has brought people inside,' said Nicole, wiping down one of the plastic chairs that had a coffee spill on its seat.

'It's far colder than last year,' Evie agreed. 'We could be in for a white Christmas.' The snow seemed to be making an appearance every day now, even if it was just a flurry to coat the black, dirty slush and restore picture-postcard status to the city.

'That sounds exciting.'

'Oh, before I forget, I'd be happy to do the shift first thing on Christmas Eve. Bonnie's shutting up shop a week before and heading off to family in Florida.'

'She'll enjoy that.'

'She works so hard. She has such a passion.'

'That's the key,' said Nicole. 'Do something you love and your days will go quickly and well. Do something you hate, they'll drag and you'll resent it.'

Evie smiled and kept sweeping.

'You've already done that spot,' Nicole observed, the cloth dangling from her hand; she rested it against her hip.

'What?'

'You've swept there already and there's nothing left.'

'Oh.' Preoccupied by her necessity to keep busy and not think about her uncle's ambush, Evie hadn't even realised she was doing it. She propped the broom against the wall in the corner. 'It's so busy without Lionel here today. How long do you think it'll be before he's back?' Lionel was another volunteer, but for the last three days he'd been stuck in bed with the flu.

'Probably not for another couple of days.'

'Can we cope?'

'We've got an extra pair of hands,' said Nicole as Evie walked over to the servery to hand out the latest meals. This time it was pumpkin soup to start, followed by roast beef with mashed potatoes, peas, cabbage and gravy.

Evie picked up a bowl and a plate as she looked up to see another volunteer as he came out of the kitchen.

She turned to Nicole. ‘What the hell is he doing here?’

Chapter Thirteen
Jack

'I hope you're not like that to everyone who comes in here.' Jack took offence at Evie's tone. Then again, he kind of liked it. The women he usually met were far too agreeable, never challenged him. He hoped that said more about them than it did about him.

'I only behave that way when people have clear attitude problems,' Evie huffed. 'And we don't get many of those types, at least not till now.'

She muttered something he chose to ignore. This was more fun than he'd thought.

When he'd followed Nicole in here tonight, she'd been surprised but welcoming. They'd chatted as she worked, and when the volunteer who'd been washing up finished their shift to rush home to family, he offered to help.

'Are you sure you don't mind?' she'd asked him.

'And how exactly are you intending to manage it?' He gestured towards her wrist.

'You know me. I saw a job, wanted to get to it.'

'Some things never change.' He smiled at her fondly. 'I'd be happy to help if you chat with me while I work.'

'That sounds lovely.'

Whatever argument she had had with his father, he was happy to know the animosity wasn't aimed at him. 'How long have you been working here?' he asked.

They fell into small talk about the shelter and Nicole's involvement as Jack stacked plates in a dishwasher and washed the enormous pans by hand.

They talked about his work and about his friends out on Hollyhock Farm.

'You'd love it out there at the farm.' He turned a cooking pot upside down and placed it onto the drainer. Nicole looked around for something to dry it with. 'Leave it to drip dry and I'll do it in a while.'

'If you insist.' She smiled. 'And I'm sure I'd love it at Hollyhock Farm too. I saw the photos, remember?' Jack had shown her plenty of snaps when Nate and Julia first took over the farm. 'It's a different life than one in the city.'

'I can't imagine *you* ever leaving the city behind.'

Nicole leant against the stainless steel countertop as Jack took a piece of steel wool to the roasting pans that had been used to roast the last round of beef. 'I was always in love with Manhattan,' she told him. 'Even as a little girl. I grew up in New Jersey, but we moved here before I reached my teens and it was a time of great excitement. I'd walk along the streets mesmerised by the skyscrapers, quite unable to believe I was suddenly living among everything I'd only ever seen pictures of. I was stunned at how, even late at night, Manhattan is so alive it feels like it's the middle of the day.'

'And now?'

'Before I began working with your family, I spent a couple of years in Europe, in Sicily near my family, and I think it's the first time I'd ever realised what space does to a person. The breathtaking landscapes, olive groves as far as the eye can see, the crystal clear waters. I felt at peace there.'

'Were you tempted to stay?'

'Of course.' She considered it for a moment. 'Life was easy, laidback, but after a while I missed the energy of Manhattan, the vibrancy of life in the fast lane. Some people hate it, others love it. I think I like the best of both worlds. Now and then it's nice to escape, go away from it all to make you realise what you're missing and where you see your home as.'

'I'd like to see more of Europe, be a tourist rather than attending events for the business.'

'You should, Jackson.'

He smiled but didn't admonish her for use of his full name, it'd felt right coming from Nicole, the only other person to use it since his mother died.

He finished washing the carving knife, removed the rubber gloves and picked up a tea towel. This is what he'd missed. Their easy rapport, the way she knew things about him without him ever having to spell it out. What she'd said to him about space and a different pace of life made perfect sense. He felt the same way each time he left the city. He was beginning to realise it was fear of the unknown as well as his mother's legacy that had stood in his way all these years.

Nicole stacked some of the pots for him as he dried.

'I know you went to see Dad,' he said.

She sighed. 'It didn't go too well, I'm afraid.'

'I heard.'

'We argued about Evie.'

'He worries about you. We both do.'

'He apologised to me.'

'He did?' This was news to Jack.

'Yes, but he still didn't explain why I lost my job, why it came to that.' She took a deep breath. 'And I think I need to know to help me accept the apology.'

Jack nodded. 'You know, sometimes I can't understand him myself.'

‘You’re a good man.’ She smiled at him, her eyes kind and warm. ‘Now keep being a good man and take out a pot of coffee.’

‘Certainly, ma’am.’ He mock saluted and when he emerged from the kitchen with the piping hot pot of coffee, Evie was looking at him. And she didn’t look pleased at all.

‘Attitude problem?’ he asked now, after she’d demanded to know why he was here. ‘You’ve got one, not me. I’m here helping.’ He cleared another table, the plates gratefully cleaned of all food. ‘Excuse me,’ he said when she got in his way.

When Evie grabbed the broom and took her frustration out on the floor beneath the most recently vacated table, Nicole scurried out from the kitchen. ‘Jackson, be nice.’

‘I am. It’s her who has the problem.’

‘Jackson.’

‘Okay, okay. Now what can I do to help next?’ Now he was here he was relaxing and, dare he say it, enjoying it. A few of the regulars had chatted with him. They hadn’t shared woeful stories, they hadn’t moaned. They’d chatted about inconsequential things: the weather, the traffic chaos at rush hour, politics even. Who knew?

They spent the next hour doing more of the same—clearing plates, washing up, pouring coffees, loading the dishwasher, mopping up spills. Nicole showed him the haul of coats folded and placed on shelves at the back of the shelter when the latest newcomer turned up in shirtsleeves and a blanket around his shoulders. Jack had taken him to the cupboard and pulled out one in his size, a bright orange puffer jacket that’d be sure to stave off the winter chill, and the simple act of kindness had given him a strange sensation, much like when he helped the homeless man on the corner. He wondered what his father would make of all this.

'Where did this come from?' Jack stooped down to pick up a necklace, a delicate gold heart pendant hanging onto a chain that was broken.

'Oh, no.' Nicole took it from him as Evie appeared. 'Your necklace is broken, Evie.'

'Damn it.' Evie looked crestfallen as she held the gold chain in her hand, the heart cupped in her palm.

'It was my gift to her on our first Christmas together.' Nicole told Jack. She gave Evie a hug.

'How about I take it to the store to have it fixed and give it back to you tomorrow?' Jack suggested.

Evie was about to hand it over to him when a clatter behind them caused Jack to turn and run over as quickly as he could.

'It's Barry again.' Nicole leapt into action and followed him.

'He's drunk,' Evie whispered to Jack, as she pocketed the necklace while Jack had his hands full lifting Barry up off the ground, perching him at a table. He was heavy and the dead weight of a drunk was hard to bear on his own.

They gave Barry some food, lots of water, black coffee and he stayed there for an hour before staggering out into the night again. And by the end of their shift, and after Nicole and Evie had directed people to shelters where they'd be able to find a bed for the night, it was time to go.

'I'm meeting an old friend from school tonight.' Nicole eased on her coat and wrapped her scarf around her neck.

'That sounds nice.' Evie pulled on her gloves. 'Have a lovely time.'

'I will. We're going to be tourists in my own city,' she smiled. 'And Jackson?'

He looked at her as he fastened the buttons on his long business coat.

'Thank you for helping out tonight. I'm glad you came.'

'Me too.' He hugged her tightly. 'I can walk you to wherever you're going.'

'No need.' She smiled at them both. 'But I'll see you again?' It was a question rather than a statement.

'You'll see me again.'

'Evie, I'll see you tomorrow evening for our trip to the movies.'

Jack tried to let the exchange allay his fears that Evie had anything but good intentions with Nicole, and from what he'd seen he had to concede they were even closer than he'd thought. And Nicole was an excellent judge of character, unafraid to stand up for herself.

'Could I walk you home, Evie?' Once Nicole went on her way, it seemed logical and it'd be a good opportunity to really put his fears to rest. He rubbed gloved hands together as the icy bite of the cold continued its quest to penetrate any material tonight.

'I don't *need* you to walk me home.' She grinned. 'But if you'd like me to walk *you* home, I'm going that way.' She pointed in the opposite direction from where Nicole had turned. 'I'm a few blocks shy of the New York Public Library.'

He whistled and returned her smile, glad they could be civil. 'That's quite a way. Will you take the subway?'

'I like to walk.'

'Even at night?'

The look she gave him suggested he should stop implying she was anything but capable. 'Walking it is, then.' He held out his arm for her to take the lead on a walk that'd be at least forty minutes.

Evie pulled her bobble hat over her head covering her honey-blonde hair, and they walked the Manhattan streets that hadn't calmed much at all in the last couple of hours. A row of taxis lined the street, honking their horns, all trying to get to their destination first.

'Can I ask you a question?' She looked up at him from beneath her scarf. Her lips and chin were buried beneath the soft wool.

'Go on.'

'What made you come to the shelter tonight?'

She was as suspicious as he was, questioning motives, wanting to know what was what. 'I saw Nicole go in and I wanted to speak with her.'

'What about?'

'You're very nosey, aren't you?'

'I'm just looking out for my friend, that's all. Surely you understand that.'

She had a point. 'I wanted to talk to her about my father.' He didn't mention the real reason was to get some idea about Evie's relationship with their mutual friend. He knew she'd only argue with him. 'My father tried to apologise the other day, but they ended up having another fight.'

Evie looked up at him now, soft blue eyes suddenly curious. 'Let me guess, it was about me?'

'Not everything revolves around you,' he said, but smiled. 'But in this case, yes, it was about you. My father thinks a lot of Nicole—' He held up a hand before she could say the obvious. 'I know his past behaviour doesn't exactly support the claim, but he does.' He gulped, on the precipice of divulging his mother's death and how Nicole had filled a void, stepping in almost like a second mother even though it wasn't her official role. But he hadn't stopped himself because Evie wouldn't understand—she of all people would most likely get it—but because he didn't want to reveal too much of himself. It made him sound weak, and if it's one thing the Churchill men weren't allowed to be, it was that.

What Evie said next surprised him. 'Nicole can be pretty stubborn when she wants to be.'

His laughter caused white puffs of air to come from his mouth as they rounded another corner and ran across the road between parked cars. 'She's a strong woman.'

'She likes to get her own way.' Evie giggled.

He liked the sound of her laugh, the easy chatter they'd found with one another tonight. 'Is that what she did with you?'

'The night she first found me and tried to take me under her wing, it took all my willpower to turn her away.' Evie's face finally emerged from beneath the scarf. Whether it was because she'd warmed up or because she felt more comfortable, he had no idea. 'She helped me a few times, and it was only after the night she lost her job that I gave in. I guess I felt bad I'd caused it to happen. I think part of me had always wanted to let her help since I met her at the shelter the month before Thanksgiving, but at the same time I wanted to fight my own fight.'

He could relate to that. His father had given him a business on a platter, encouraged him all the way. He was financially secure for life but felt trapped inside a maze that had no exit for him, following paths that didn't lead to his own happiness.

They came to a stop outside a classic New York brownstone. 'This is me,' said Evie with a smile he'd not seen much since they'd first met. Her lips were pink from being buried beneath the scarf, heart-shaped at the top with a fuller lip on the bottom.

'Well, it was nice to see you again.' He cleared his throat and dragged his gaze away from her mouth.

'Thanks for walking me home.'

'It was my pleasure.' He waited for her to take the steps up to the main door and let herself in to the brownstone that had gold doorbells lined up to indicate it had been converted, like plenty of others, into apartments. But instead she took the flight down to a basement.

He gave her a nod and a wave and went on his way. When Nicole had told him Evie had found her own apartment, he'd immediately jumped to the perhaps unfair conclusion that Nicole was helping her financially. How else would she be able to afford to live in such a salubrious area? But now he'd seen the basement, the window below street level, already anticipating the lack of space inside, and after talking to Evie tonight and recognising the independent streak he wished he could conjure up for himself, he had no doubt she was paying her own way.

Reassured, Jack walked on a block. Over the last couple of weeks, he'd felt a change within himself, and it had all happened since he'd seen Nicole. Bumping into her had made him step back and assess his own life. He knew he was in danger of being just as insular as his father, only seeing things one way, never questioning before judging, and he didn't like the way it made him feel. He'd always been able to talk to her over the years when he'd finished school, gone to college, graduated and started work. He often wondered whether, had Nicole stayed, she'd be able to help him start on a new direction in his life. God knows he didn't seem to be able to do it himself.

He was about to cross the next block when he realised he hadn't taken Evie's necklace home as promised. It was probably way past fixing and needed a new chain, but he'd take care of it, no charge. He turned back into the flurry of snow just beginning to tumble from the skies above and dodged pedestrians who had their eyes glued ahead, the only way to walk without being bustled out the way, and made his way back to the brownstone to collect the necklace.

He crossed over the road, but as he approached the brownstone, some thirty feet away, he stopped. Evie was outside again, and she wasn't alone.

Jack stepped onto the second step of an earlier apartment block so she wouldn't see him. The man she was with was older than her, probably in his fifties, a tall reed-thin man with thinning hair and a menacing way about him, and Evie didn't look at all happy to see him. They were clearly arguing, but in the New York mayhem with a truck, a motorcycle and then a taxi passing by, Jack couldn't hear anything at all.

He let the conversation go on. The man was showing her something, waving it in her face. It looked like photographs. She tried to snatch them, but he had held them way out of her reach, sneering at her from what Jack could make out beneath the yellow blast of a nearby streetlamp. Evie was backed up against the railings and the man seemed about to leave, but then he moved closer, pressed himself against her and that was when Jack made his presence known.

He walked towards her and wasn't sure whether she looked more frightened or relieved. 'Everything okay here, Evie?'

'Who the fuck are you?' the man snapped, but backed away from Evie. 'This is none of your business.'

'Evie's a friend, it's my business. It looks like she doesn't want you around her. Am I right, Evie?' He didn't take his eyes off the man for a second.

'So you have a friend, Evie.' The man's smugness made Jack want to punch him. He balled his fists in case the man tried anything, but he was all words, no action. 'I wonder if your friend would like to know a bit more about you, Evie Jefferson.'

'I think you'd better go.' Jack stepped forward, fists ready.

'Oh, don't worry, I'm going. But here.' He pushed a photograph against Jack's chest, holding it face down against his coat, his hand still against it. 'Take this. And Evie, I'll be seeing you.'

Jack held the photo as the man left; but before he could look at it, Evie's hand covered his own against his chest.

'I'm begging you, Jack …' Tears sprang to her eyes, showing her well-hidden vulnerability. 'I'm begging you not to look at that photograph. Please.'

His voice softened. 'Are you in some kind of trouble?' The photograph was pinned in place against his chest, her slender fingers still covering his gloved hand over his beating heart as he decided what to do for the best. Evie looked to the ground, but still she didn't move her hand. Jack looked at the pom-pom on top of her hat, smelt the fresh laundry detergent it had been washed in last.

'Are you in trouble?' he asked her again.

Her head snapped up, and she yanked the photograph from him before he had a chance to stop her. 'That's all that matters to you, isn't it? You're worried I'll bring trouble Nicole's way.'

'It's a fair question. And maybe I'm worried about you too.'

'As if,' she huffed. 'You're just the same as him.'

'Who?'

'As bad as the man I saw at the hospital.'

'Braydon? What's he got to do with anything?'

'Because he judged me just as you're doing now. To someone like you, I'll always be the person you saw first … the homeless woman begging for food and handouts. You'll never see me any differently. People like you never do.'

'People like me?'

'Rich. Judgemental. People like you.' She shook her head, clutched the photograph as though her life depended on it.

Jack's voice hardened defensively. 'Who was he, Evie?'

'I can't tell you.'

'Can't or won't?'

She didn't answer. 'He's a part of my past, and I need to sort this out on my own.'

'And can you do that?'

She fixed him with a glare.

'You can't blame me for asking. He didn't look like he was about to give up any time soon.'

Evie looked into the distance, into the night and the hubbub of the city that never slept. 'He'll be back, but I'll deal with it.' She took a deep breath. 'Why are you here? Why did you come back?'

He looked at her for the longest time, and then said, 'I came to get the necklace. I thought I'd get it fixed.'

'Oh.' She took off a glove and fumbled in the front pocket of her jeans until she pulled out the chain and the heart pendant. She dropped it into his hand, and he opened his coat and slipped it into the inside pocket for safekeeping.

'Goodnight, Jack.' Evie started down the steps to her basement apartment, and without looking back, shut the door behind her.

Jack stood there for a time, watched the yellow glow from behind the curtains turn to black. He'd done his best to trust Evie and thought he'd made progress, but seeing her with that man made it difficult to give her the benefit of the doubt, impossible to trust she knew what she was doing. Who knew what she was involved in. Was it drugs? Prostitution? If it wasn't sinister, then why wouldn't she tell him?

Exasperated, he realised he probably didn't know this young woman at all. And worse still, Nicole didn't seem to either.

Chapter Fourteen

Evie

'You need to take out a restraining order.' Lizzy handed Evie a glass of wine.

After Jack had seen off Uncle Brett, Evie had dumped her bag in her apartment, turned out the light and waited for Jack to disappear, and then gone up to see her friend, someone who knew the whole truth.

'I wish it was that easy, Lizzy.'

'Why isn't it?'

Evie pulled a face. 'You know why. If I do that, the truth will come out and where will that leave me?' She allowed a little giggle to escape, but it was more from nerves than anything else. 'You know, I've never actually seen him look so scared.'

'Yeah? Well I hope there were brown stains in his underpants when your friend told him where to go. And speaking of this friend?' She arched a well-plucked eyebrow.

'He's a friend of Nicole's, not mine.'

Lizzy sipped her own wine and collapsed on the couch next to Evie. Her apartment on the second floor was modest, but it still could've fitted Evie's own in four times over. Lizzy had two bedrooms, albeit one tiny one that was more like a cupboard, a kitchen that was suspiciously clean and a brand new bathroom that Evie envied each time she went in it. It must be a cinch to clean, with its modern chrome fittings and bright lighting, unlike her own with its old gold taps and tiles with so much build-up in the grout that it looked no different after she'd scrubbed it.

'It sounds as though this Jack might be warming to you,' Lizzy suggested. 'Why else would he walk you home?'

'He was going the same way. What?'

Lizzy couldn't stop smiling. 'Nothing, it's just I know men, probably better than you do, at least Manhattan men anyway, and he's interested for sure. So what made him come back on his white horse and rescue you?'

'He came back to get my necklace that broke and he's going to get fixed. The family owns a jewellery business, remember?' She knocked back the red wine that relaxed her body from head to toe.

'Which jewellery business?'

'The Diamond Touch.'

Lizzy whistled through her teeth. 'Nice. Pricey, but oh so elegant.'

Evie smiled at the line of questioning. It was far better than talking about Uncle Brett. 'His father owns it so he runs it with him, I think. But I really don't know, I haven't asked him too many questions.'

Lizzy's eyebrows knitted together. She held up her index finger on one hand and then put down her wine glass. 'Hang on a minute …' Evie watched her pull a magazine from her bag and quickly flick through the pages. She opened them out to reveal a feature on The Diamond Touch with Jack in the main photograph. 'Is this him?' When Evie nodded, Lizzy's eyes lit up as she flipped another page to show Jack Churchill shaking hands with a man in front of Bloomingdales. The photograph sat at the side of a page discussing a new range of jewellery to be released by the store this Christmas.

'I saw the article this morning, Evie. The man is gorgeous! And he's rich! I can't believe your knight in shining armour is Jack Churchill!'

'Okay, I don't think the man on the top floor heard you.' Evie winced at the squeals her friend was emitting. 'Anyway, I don't care how good looking he is, or how rich—'

'Ah, so you admit he's gorgeous then.'

Evie kept quiet.

'Well if you're not interested, Evie, send him up to my apartment next time he stops by.'

'Lizzy!'

'Relax, I'm kidding … sort of.' She giggled and tilted the bottle of red towards Evie, who nodded.

They discussed Jack some more and they laughed about rich men and their trophy wives who'd married the men for their money rather than anything else. They joked about women with husbands four times their age, claiming to be in love.

'It's like you going out with my grandad,' Lizzy shuddered, picking up a family photo from the mantelpiece and thrusting it in Evie's face.

'Oh, don't!'

'Exactly. It's all about the size of their wallet.'

'Must be. I doubt it's about the size of anything else.' They moved on to discussing the latest billionaire to marry someone a quarter of his age. 'He'd be too old to even do it, wouldn't he? At least not without a hefty dose of Viagra!'

The two girls giggled the night away, and by the time Evie left Lizzy's apartment, she felt better. Even Nicole didn't know everything about her and sometimes it'd been hard to bear, but tonight she'd turned to a friend, something she hadn't genuinely done in years. And now, the only cloud hanging over her was how she was going to prevent her uncle from ruining everything she'd worked for. He seemed intent on doing that and wasn't going away, and it was going to take a lot more than a chat, a giggle and a bottle of wine to get rid of him.

Jack

In Hazelbrook, bundled up in their coats, Jack and Nate stood in front of the town clock where they'd set up their Christmas tree sales area. Nate had insisted he'd be fine alone, but this was Jack's escape, and it was a welcome one. Last night he'd gone down to the shelter again and given Nicole Evie's necklace—he'd replaced the chain but assured her it was a simple fix. He hadn't quizzed her any more, but he'd kept an eye out for the man he'd seen last night, even walking past Evie's apartment on more than one occasion to see if anything was amiss.

Jack nudged Nate as a man came towards them. 'Looks like we have our first customer.' He let his friend handle the sales side while he unloaded another couple of trees from the back of the pickup, lugging them over to the concrete base of the clock where he leaned them against the structure. It was all they could fit in for now, but when he turned around another family had flocked to Nate and the tree collection, all anxious to select the perfect specimen.

By mid-morning, all the trees were gone and they headed back to Hollyhock Farm to relieve Julia, who had another dress fitting scheduled. Two local boys, Johnny and Devlin, had been on hand this morning, as they were regularly during the festive season, to help families chop trees and lift onto car roofs. According to Julia, they'd had one of their busiest mornings yet, with families coming from New Haven, Manhattan, and others as far as Hartford and Burlington.

'You've built up quite the empire here,' said Jack when they finally stopped for a break. 'I'm exhausted.'

'Coffee?' Nate pulled two cups from the kitchen cupboard.

'Black and strong, please.'

While Nate made the coffees, Jack turned his attention to building up the fire. He buried a firelighter between logs and kindling and lit it with a match, but it would take a while before a decent amount of heat was produced.

'Use the bellows.' Nate set Jack's coffee cup on the table and then pointed to an ornate wooden, almost heart-shaped contraption hanging beside the fire.

'They're for decoration, surely.'

'We use them all the time.' He shrugged. 'I promise you, they work.'

With a smile and a shake of his head, Jack took the oak bellows down from the hook. He pointed them towards the heart of the fire where the kindling was beginning to burn and tiny flames crackled away, and he opened and shut them, blowing the air out the pointy end in the same way a concertina would move. The fire didn't take long to move quickly across the kindling, and soon the flames were licking around the larger logs and they had the roaring winter fire they'd wanted.

'Told you.' Nate smiled. 'After Julia singed her hair on more than one occasion, trying to blow onto the flames to encourage them, we ordered those online; much safer.'

Jack picked up his coffee. 'What time's she back from the city?'

Nate sank back into his armchair. 'You know women and Manhattan. They'll be going to the dress shop and then somewhere for lunch, and that'll take them well into the afternoon.'

'And your job is to leave them to it, no doubt?'

'Got it in one.'

Jack let the black coffee and the heat of the fire warm him through. Even wrapped up outside in his coat and gloves, the cold had got at him from every angle. 'I saw Nicole last night.' He'd confided in Nate about his concerns with regard to her relationship with Evie.

'And how is she? Still taking in strays?'

'She works at a homeless shelter in the city.'

Nate nodded. 'Sounds like Nicole. She's one of those people who seems lost without somebody to spoil. And I mean that in a good way.'

'I'm still concerned about her.'

'Whatever for? It sounds as though she knows what she's doing with this young woman.'

Jack's face said otherwise, and he told Nate all about the man he'd seen hassling Evie outside her apartment.

'He sounds like bad news.'

'That's why I'm worried. Whatever Evie's involved in, I don't want Nicole dragged into it. She doesn't deserve it.'

'And you didn't look at the photograph?' Nate shook his head. 'Could've given you a few clues, dude.'

'She begged me not to.'

'And you didn't argue with her?' Nate asked wryly.

'I should've looked, shouldn't I?' He looked up at the ceiling, shook his head and then he sat forwards, put his empty cup on to the table and rested his arms along his thighs. 'I've got a niggling feeling she won't be able to handle the situation and whatever is going on will come crashing down on her head.'

'There's nothing you can do about it, Jack.'

Nate was right, but it didn't make it any easier to hear. As the fire crackled and the flames climbed higher, Jack pulled the fireguard across in case it started to spit onto the rug.

'You've built a beast there,' Nate assured him.

'I like to aim high.'

'Not laughing at my bellows now, are you?'

'I did think they were a little wimpy.' Jack laughed. 'But you proved me wrong.'

'So …' Nate waited for Jack to sit down again. 'What's this Evie like?'

'What do you mean?'

'I mean … what's she like? Old/young, blonde/brunette, polite/rude. Any of the above, because so far all you've done is told me she worries you, but I know you, Jack. Nobody gets under your skin unless there's a reason and that reason can't be all because of Nicole.'

Jack thought for a moment. 'Actually, she seems nice.'

'Nice?' Nate pulled a face. 'Natasha Lyons was *nice*,' he referred back to the shy girl who sat at the back of class each day in high school, not uttering a word, handing Oreos around each break time to anyone, just to make friends.

'She *was* nice. Jeez … wonder what happened to her.'

'Don't know and don't change the subject.'

Jack exhaled. 'I don't know, Evie's just … well, she's blonde.' He ignored the approving eyebrow raise. 'At first, I thought the same way as my father did, that she was a street kid, probably a junkie.'

'And you don't now?'

Jack still had his doubts about what Evie was exactly, but slowly he was seeing the world differently and he was realising how dangerous it could be to make assumptions about someone you knew nothing about. 'I believe she genuinely cares about Nicole. At first I thought she was faking it and it was all part of an elaborate act, but now I'm not so sure.'

'Well then, there's your answer,' Nate concluded. 'Nicole and Evie have a genuine friendship so I think it's time to let them be. Whoever that man was, perhaps Evie will tell Nicole everything in her own time.'

Jack ran a hand across his chin, scratching at the stubble. He'd been too eager to leave the city behind this morning to shave. 'Maybe you're right.'

'Another cup?' Nate picked up the empties and Jack nodded as their conversation turned to school days and people they remembered, those they'd disliked, those they genuinely wished well in life.

'I gave a homeless man sitting on the street corner a meal too,' Jack admitted after talk moved on to the shelter he'd helped out at.

'You did a good thing.'

'I felt really pleased with myself afterwards.'

'You say it like it's a bad thing.'

'That's because I don't even think about buying drinks and dinners out, flying here there and everywhere on business, and for me, a burger and a coffee was nothing. I saw the look in his eyes, Nate. To him it was a whole lot more.'

Nate nodded, understanding.

'I wasn't so kind to someone else I found living on the streets,' Jack admitted. He hadn't touched his second coffee. 'When I went to check on my house, there was a boy on the porch huddled beneath blankets. I told him to leave. He couldn't have been more than late teens, and I was a real ass. I swore at him, told him to get lost. And then it was almost like I'd risen out of my body and was looking down at myself from up above. And all I saw was my father, three years ago, throwing Evie off his property and showing Nicole the door.'

'Julia mentioned you'd had a homeless kid at the house, but you did the right thing telling him to move on. You should be staying there instead of pestering us, so what's stopping you fixing it up?'

Jack grinned. 'It's time, mostly, but also a bit of inclination. I have visions about how the place will look when it's renovated, but I know I need people with time, energy and enthusiasm to make it that way.'

'So hire someone. You're loaded, shouldn't be a problem.' Nate said it in the nicest possible way.

'Yeah, maybe you're right. I could arrange for someone to come out and look at the place. Got any recommendations?'

Nate's laughter echoed against the crackling of the fire. 'Only Johnny and Devlin.'

'I'm not sure they'd know one end of a paintbrush from the other, would they?'

'You're probably right there, but they're hard workers, they'll help with the heavy stuff.'

Jack picked up his coffee cup. 'I'll think about it.'

Devlin and Johnny were certainly a possibility if they could help him with the heavier tasks—ripping out the old bathrooms and kitchens, dumping everything in a skip so he could make a fresh start on the place.

But there was someone else Jack had in mind. Someone he had to find first.

Chapter Fifteen
Jack

'I don't think you should be here.' In the offices of The Diamond Touch, Jack looked across the oak desk at his father.

'Nonsense. The fresh air and the walk did me good. The doctor says I need to incorporate physical exercise into my life more. It's something I've neglected, I do believe.'

Jack returned his father's smile. His father never walked anywhere unless it was around the golf course, to a fancy restaurant nearby to meet clients, or to a taxi at the kerb to take him to the next meeting. It was a wonder he always looked as good as he did.

'So,' Kent continued, 'this morning was a start. I walked from home to here. I was going crazy, out of my mind with boredom being stuck in the house recuperating. Do you know what I did last night?'

'What?'

'I sat and wrote Christmas cards and discussed the food shopping with Maggie.'

Jack's head tipped back as he laughed. 'You must've been bored.'

'Going out of my mind, most likely. The tedium of every day spent taking it easy will be what kills me, forget anything else.'

Jack checked his schedule, happy his father did in fact seem ready to get back to normality. 'Why don't you join us at our lunch meeting today, get right back into the swing of things.'

Kent leaned forwards, arms on the desk and alert. He'd never been a man to sit around and let things happen in front of him. 'Who's it with?'

Jack filled him in on the buyers they were meeting, who'd flown in from Chicago. 'You'll need to avoid the alcohol,' he instructed.

Kent winced. 'What if they offer me the finest champagne?'

'You don't take it!'

'I suppose I don't. And I've got to give up the cigars.'

Jack grinned. That'd be hard, especially when it came to gatherings at the house, a tradition Kent enjoyed. He buzzed reception and asked Penny to amend their booking to include one more and then shooed his father out of his office for an hour or so until it was time to go. It'd give him a chance to get through the paperwork, polish up his pitch. He'd already briefed Braydon that he'd take the lead on this one and his colleague hadn't been too happy. Braydon hated sitting there and letting anyone else do the talking, but Jack owed it to his father to get his head back in the game.

Out on the New York streets at lunchtime, the slush collected in the gutters, blackened by the filth from traffic. Jack flagged down a cab. 'Braydon will meet us there. He's held up downtown. Corner of East 29th and 1st Avenue,' he told the driver as Kent climbed in behind him.

'Christmas shopping most likely.' Kent laughed as the taxi set off through the city streets. 'He's probably picking out something expensive for Fern.'

Wow, his father had relaxed since his health scare. Before, he would've frowned upon time out in the day for anyone. The old saying 'time is money' didn't need to be spoken by Kent, it usually oozed from his pores.

‘Hey, is Linda still around?’ Jack asked, referring to the woman his father had seen on and off for the last few months. ‘You haven’t mentioned her since she came to see you in the hospital. Don’t tell me she dumped you.’

Kent shook his head and laughed. ‘We’re just friends now. It was never going to work.’

Jack didn’t ask why, but he wondered whether his father would ever meet someone who’d be long-term, rather than a quick flutter in his life.

‘Talking of Christmas shopping,’ Kent added. ‘I ordered the gifts for Cameron and the kids online.’

‘Well done, I’m impressed.’

‘I’m getting organised in my old age.’

Last year Jack had reminded him over and over again to send the gifts. With Cameron living in Toronto, you couldn’t leave it to the last minute, but his father had and the kids had had to wait until the day after Boxing Day for their new toys. They probably hadn’t noticed with all the other presents they’d received, but Cameron had been a woman scorned. She’d been on the phone bitching about it to Jack and dropped hints this year whenever they spoke to one another. Although she’d eased off with Kent since his stint in the hospital, she’d kept going with Jack and he’d had enough. Ever since his mother died, it was as though Cameron had taken over as mother hen. He loved his sister dearly, but when she’d married a Canadian whose job as a CIO at a prestigious insurance company had meant they’d move to Toronto, Jack had thought it a bit of an unintentional blessing.

‘How are we getting on looking for new premises?’ Jack asked as they made their way to the restaurant on a garden plaza with a view of the East River.

'Actually, I did a bit of online research while I was away from work, and I may well have found us something.'

'Really?'

'It's not used for retail space right now, but it's in a prime position.'

'Is it big enough for what you want?'

'It's the perfect size.'

At the restaurant they fell easily into business talk and the lunch flew by, even for Jack who finished the meeting happy he could still look interested and professional when he had to.

'So tell me more about the building,' said Jack as they waited for Braydon to escort the clients outside to the awaiting cab before rejoining them for coffees to debrief the meeting.

Kent told him of the building's location near a shopping precinct that would be sure to attract the right clientele, his plans to gut the building and make it as upmarket as the rest of the company premises, the legalities of purchasing a building.

'It sounds ideal,' said Jack, when a scuffle at the revolving door to the restaurant had both his and Kent's attention.

'Oh my God, is that …' Kent was out of his seat first, with Jack following soon after.

'What the hell is going on?' Jack pulled Braydon back from Evie and Kent moved to Nicole's side.

The waiter looked questioningly at the party congregated outside the doors, at the businessmen who hadn't yet paid for their meal. Jack handed the business credit card through the door and requested the bill. The waiter hurried off, seemingly glad the confrontation was taking place on the opposite side of the door.

‘Tell your Rottweiler to back off!’ Evie shrieked at Jack, but not before she’d stepped forwards and given Braydon a shove in the chest that almost caused him to lose his footing. Jack almost laughed at this delicate blonde pushing his stocky colleague.

‘Back off?’ he asked. ‘Why?’

‘You know why!’ Evie had her hands on her hips now. Blue eyes glared up at him. Her anger came out in white cloudy puffs of air from her mouth. God, it was freezing. Jack had left his jacket and coat inside and it was only a couple of degrees outside at most, the city glistening with a layer of frost beneath the early afternoon sun. ‘He’s making unfounded accusations, same as he made at the hospital.’

Braydon spoke up although didn’t step any closer. He glared at Evie. ‘People like you are all the same.’

‘There’s no need for that,’ Nicole came to Evie’s defence. ‘What has this young lady ever done to you?’

‘Oh, there’s plenty she probably could do to me, like she’s done to other men before me. How else would she be swanning around in fancy clothes, coming into restaurants like this?’

When Braydon smirked at them, Jack grabbed Evie’s arm with one hand and Nicole’s with the other. Kent looked on, gobsmacked, and only moved when he turned to settle the bill with the waiter who’d braved the confrontation to get a signature for the company credit card.

‘For your information,’ Nicole began, ‘this is my treat. It’s my birthday today and I wanted to take Evie out for a nice lunch. Not that it’s any of your business.’

‘Let’s get a cab back to the office,’ Kent suggested to Braydon.

Braydon harrumphed. 'Whatever you say, boss.' Jack ignored the snipe. 'I'll get the coats from inside.' Braydon went back through the revolving door, and the four remaining took a deep collective breath.

'I'm so sorry about that, Nicole.' Kent was first to speak. 'And I think we need to talk.'

'Kent,' Nicole said confidently, although if Jack wasn't mistaken, he detected nerves underlying her speech. 'I'd like you to meet Evie.'

Kent didn't move, but he at least had the good grace to look at the girl and greet her. 'Hello, Evie.'

Evie was as quiet as the first time they'd met, all of the fight gone out of her for the time being. She nodded to Kent and gave a small smile.

'Can we talk again, soon?' Kent's eyes searched Nicole's until she agreed to his request. 'And happy birthday,' he smiled. 'Did you buy a poinsettia?'

Nicole's shoulders relaxed, her gaze held Kent's and something passed between them as she nodded.

'You know I still think of them as the Christmas flowers,' Kent went on.

Jack was about to ask the significance of the plant, but Braydon pushed through the revolving door and came back to them before he had a chance.

'Well, well, isn't this cosy?' Braydon smirked, handing jackets and coats to the other two men. Evidently the time inside the restaurant hadn't improved his mood.

'What's it to you?' Evie snapped.

'Oh, shut up.'

'Braydon,' Kent admonished. 'I won't have you talking to a lady like that.'

Braydon, evidently embarrassed by the public reprimand, took a step back, eyes wide in surprise. 'I expected more from you, Kent. How can you give either of them the time of day? Especially her!' He pointed at Evie as though she was a pile of dog's mess on the ground. 'Especially given what she represents! Cynthia would be turning in her grave.'

At the mention of his late wife, Kent stopped, one arm only part way through the sleeve of his coat. 'Shut up,' he told his colleague. 'I mean it. Shut up.'

'What's he talking about?' Jack still had his jacket and coat over his arm but he no longer cared about the cold. He looked at Kent, at Braydon and back again.

'Nothing,' Kent said firmly and then to Braydon with a look of ferocity Jack had never seen before, 'If you know what's good for you, you'll keep your mouth shut.'

Jack stepped forwards. 'What's going on?'

'Taxi!' Kent yelled, then whistled and raised a hand to the passing yellow cab, which screeched to a halt at the kerb. 'Let's go.'

Jack touched Nicole briefly on the arm. 'I'll see you soon.' And he managed a smile for Evie before he left them both standing there looking as dazed and confused as he was. Why was Braydon so riled up by these two anyway? And why the hell had he mentioned his mother?

In the back of the cab, none of them spoke. They pulled up outside the office and Kent remained in the cab, claiming he needed to head home, he was tired and the doctor had told him he shouldn't overdo things. Braydon had taken off in one direction down the street without so much as a word to either of them, and Jack had been left to go back up to the office and carry on with the day-to-day running of the business, wondering what the hell was going on.

The house still seemed too quiet, even after all these years. First, Cynthia died, then Cameron moved out, Jack went off to college, and then he'd been stupid enough to fire Nicole. It was a time of immense change and you'd think by now he'd be used to it. But he wasn't; it still hurt. Coming home to the walls of this house that didn't echo laughter or sibling rivalry, or even love anymore, hurt as though part of his insides had been ripped out. And he knew some of it was his own fault. This house had begun to be a stark reminder of how he had failed his family. Not in a financial sense, he'd managed to get that right at least, but in every other facet of life. He'd failed to keep his wife safe, to have genuine friends by his side, and his relationship with his kids had an underlying strain he felt keenly.

He undid his tie, pulled it from his shirt collar and loosened his top button. He reached for the bottle of whiskey, took off the top and pulled out a glass from the kitchen cabinet. He poured a measure and cupped the wide glass in the palm of his hand, then swilled the mixture round and round, staring into the murky depths. He was so angry with Braydon he hadn't been able to look at him in the cab on the way back from the restaurant, let alone talk to him. He'd been about to open his big mouth, Kent was sure of it, and Jack knew nothing of the real cause of his mother's death. Kent had protected him for over twenty years and that was the way he wanted it to stay.

Jack had cried over his mother's death. They'd pulled together as a family for a while and tried to remember what a beautiful woman Cynthia was both in heart and soul. But neither Jack nor Cameron had ever been told the truth about what happened. As far as they knew, Cynthia Churchill died of heart failure, something Kent was sure would've haunted Jack when he'd collapsed at the office and been taken to the hospital. Jack was only eleven when his mother died and he hadn't probed any further about it, he'd taken the lie and dealt with it in the best way he could. Of course the internet hadn't been around back then either, something Kent was thankful for. Jack could've easily found out the truth if it had been. Nothing stayed secret for long with the digital age.

Still holding the glass, Kent drifted into memories of how he'd met Cynthia for the first time. It'd been at a hot dog stand in Manhattan one summer's day in July. He'd not long been out of college and was on his way to an interview in a sharp suit, white shirt and ice-blue silk tie when he'd stopped at the street vendor for a can of soda. The humidity was in levels his body didn't tolerate too well and his mouth was dry, he was nervous and desperate to hydrate. He was running through interview questions in his mind when a girl in a scarlet and white polka-dot cotton dress had turned around from paying the vendor, hot dog in hand, and bumped into him. The hot dog had the works: mustard, onions, sauce. And all of that had ended up down his shirt, his tie. The only saving grace was that his suit jacket was hanging from the tips of his fingers, slung over one shoulder in the oppressive heat.

'Oh … my … God!' She'd dumped the hot dog behind her on the serving rack, grabbed napkins from the dispenser and rubbed at Kent's shirt.

'I don't think that'll work!' He'd shouted, a knee-jerk reaction at the disaster.

‘I’m sorry, I really don’t know what to say.’ She’d looked upset. ‘Can you change when you get back to the office?’

He’d been about to shout at her that he didn’t have an office, he had a goddamn interview! But the look in her eyes had captured him and never let him go. The chocolate brown eyes looking up to him, searching his, had melted his anger away. She’d forgotten all about her hot dog and he’d ended up running to the nearest department store with her hand in his and choosing a new shirt and tie from the racks. She’d waited outside the office block where he was interviewing for a job as a trainee manager. He’d gotten the job, and something he hadn’t set out to find that day. He’d found the love of his life.

Now, in the kitchen, he tipped the glass back until the whiskey met his lips. But he couldn’t do it. At three o’clock in the afternoon, in this house with all its memories, he couldn’t risk adding to Jack and Cameron’s pain by turning to the bottle. He put the glass down when he realised he was squeezing it so hard it threatened to break. Braydon had almost opened his mouth this afternoon, and because of what? His frustration about a homeless girl and his former housekeeper who’d helped her? Kent didn’t understand it. But Braydon knew the whole truth about Cynthia’s death. One of the reasons Kent put up with the man was because he worried that if he ever got rid of him, Braydon held a hand he could deal and blow apart the worlds of those Kent held dearest. The truth would destroy Jack. It had already almost destroyed him. And if the truth came out, Nicole’s life would fall apart for a second time. She had no idea who the Churchills really were, nor how inextricably linked they would always be in the most shocking way possible.

Chapter Sixteen
Jack

Jack had run a loop around the upper section of Central Park this morning before most people had been rudely awakened by their alarm clocks. He'd been unable to sleep last night, partly because of the hailstorm lashing against the windows of the condo, but also following the confrontation outside the restaurant yesterday and his father's subsequent refusal to answer any questions. He hadn't been to the townhouse, but he'd called his father, twice, both times on the pretence it was to do with the accounts. Whether his father saw through those excuses he had no idea, but whatever was going on, it preoccupied Kent so much he'd agreed to Jack leaving early from the office today, something he usually didn't take too kindly to.

Back at his condo after a morning at the office, Jack changed out of his suit and shirt and pulled on jeans and an ink-blue woollen sweater. He lifted the bouquet of flowers he'd bought, out of the water in the sink, shook off the drips from the stems and wrapped them in the same paper the florist had used earlier.

Down in the parking garage Jack lay the flowers carefully on the passenger seat. The garage was next to his building and he paid a fortune to rent the space each month, but as he followed the ramps down to the exit, he knew without it these trips away from the city would be few and far between. He pulled the visor down and slipped on a pair of shades and then turned out of the garage and onto the New York City streets, facing the winter sun in full force, lifting the season from the dreariness of the cold and damp.

Jack wound his way out of the city and towards his destination of New Haven and the floral scent filling the car reminded him of the important stop he had to make first. Turning off the highway, he followed the signs through a small town, past houses in streets lined with maple trees that had long since shed their red leaves but come spring would sprout striking red flowers, giving the landscape an entirely different edge. Eventually he reached the cemetery. He took a deep breath. It hadn't been intentional, but he hadn't been here for some time. Not because he'd forgotten his mother, but because sometimes life got in the way until it reminded him, with a jolt, of what he'd once had.

He pulled in and drove through the gates slowly, following the paths he'd come to know only too well over the years. He parked between two cedar trees he'd seen in their infancy, trees that towered above him now, yet pulled him in as though this place was an odd extension of home. The cemetery was well kept. Gardeners discreetly tended to flowerbeds, floated from one gravestone to another clearing up stray twigs or dirt blown in from the season, a tree further down was being trimmed and cut presumably to keep it manageable, its gnarly deep brown bark a sign of its age and its place in the cemetery oddly appropriate. Jack smiled at one of the gardeners who returned a compassionate nod as he made his way over to the plot where Cynthia Churchill was buried.

He bent down and picked up the pin type vase on his mother's gravestone. It was empty and he wondered whether it was his violets, months ago, that had last been here or whether his father had visited and left his own tribute.

When the fresh violets were neatly slotted in to the vase and Jack had placed it down on the grave, he sat back on his heels and ran a hand over the curved top of the headstone that perched on a rectangular piece of concrete surrounded by grass. His fingers traced his mother's name, the phrase 'In Our Hearts Forever', the date she was born, the date she died.

He adjusted the vase so the violets caught some of the winter sunlight. They were his mother's favourite flower. One particularly hot summer's day in New York City, as his mother had been pouring two glasses of homemade lemonade, the flower from her hair had fallen into the jug of liquid. Jack had leapt forwards to rescue it before it'd sunk further and they'd giggled and drank the entire jug anyway. His mother had gone right back outside, picked another violet from the pot she'd nurtured for months and slotted it back into the dark curls of her hair that swished about her shoulders. She'd shown no signs of ill health then, and Jack had never thought their days together would come to such an abrupt end. Even an entire lifetime would never have been enough to tell her how special she was to him, but he tried so hard, every day, to remember how lucky he was to have had the years that they'd had.

The week after they'd buried his mother, Jack had come to the cemetery, a posy of violets clutched in his hand. His father had cried alongside him, each of them wondering where their lives went from there, and as they'd climbed back into the car, Jack had seen a lady, about his mother's age, with a teenage boy. He'd wondered whether the boy had lost his father and Jack wanted to run over, tell him how much the world sucked, how unfair this all was. But when they'd walked away, Jack had seen the tombstone they'd been standing in front of. It was for a child, a girl: a daughter and a sister, and the dates had spanned a mere five years. From that moment, Jack had never looked at another epitaph again and made a point of reminding himself of the beautiful life his mother had enjoyed up until her final day. Not everyone got to enjoy being mother and child in the way they had.

'I miss you, Mom,' Jack said now, his words imperceptible to anyone around. Neither the gardeners, nor the man humming softly in front of a white gravestone two rows down, could hear him. 'I miss you every day.' His fingers brushed the tombstone as he wished she was here now, wished he could ask her to let him in on what his father was keeping from him and why.

Jack drove sedately out of the cemetery, following the curved roads, and made his way back out of the gates. He stopped the car at the end of the drive before the main road, pinched the top of his nose in the space between his eyes to stop any tears threatening to fall. It didn't often happen these days, but now and again something pressed on a bruise that was there for life and would never go away entirely.

'Pull yourself together, Jack,' he scolded himself. He pulled onto the main road that would lead him to New Haven, and within half an hour he parked in the driveway of his house ready to start his search, his search for a face he'd not been able to put out of his mind.

*

Back in Manhattan, Jack knocked at the door of Nicole's apartment. After a fruitless search that afternoon, he'd been forced to give up and drive home, and as he'd grabbed takeout menus from the kitchen drawer while the answering machine delivered his messages, he'd heard Nicole's voice.

Nicole pulled open the door to her apartment now. 'Jackson, I'm so glad you could make it.' She pulled him into a hug.

'How did you know my home number?' he asked, taking off his coat.

'I may not have contacted you in some time, but I always knew where you were.'

The moment sat between them, until Nicole remembered what she was doing and took his coat to hang up.

'You rescued me from another night of takeout,' he confessed, following her into the kitchen and meeting the aroma that'd already snaked its way to the hallway when he'd arrived.

'Don't tell me you survive on takeout! Not after I spent so many years trying to educate you on the importance of eating right.'

'I remember.' He laughed. 'I think I was one of the few kids who started college with basic culinary skills. Most of the guys I knew couldn't even boil an egg.' Nicole had had him helping in the kitchen from early on, especially with his father working such long hours. Tonight he'd intended to go to the supermarket and whip up a quick stir-fry, but he'd spent so long walking the streets of New Haven that he'd run out of time and energy. 'What are we having tonight?'

Nicole smiled. 'Chilli.'

His eyes lit up. 'And garlic bread?'

'Of course! With cheese on top.'

One of the first dishes Nicole had cooked Jack and his father was her legendary chilli. It seemed so simple, but she'd added a few extras: a pinch of sugar, some ketchup, baked beans as well as other pulses, a rich beef stock and a touch of dark chocolate. Instead of eating the dish with cornbread or tortilla chips, she'd made cheesy garlic bread as an accompaniment, and Jack swore it was one of the first times in a long while he'd seen the creases in his father's face appear from delight rather than sadness and worry. They'd dipped the cheesy garlic bread, cut into long finger wedges, into the sumptuous meaty dish and eaten until they were fit to burst.

'I hope you'll cut the garlic bread into fingers,' he told her now.

'Jackson,' Nicole admonished playfully. She lifted the lid from the pot on the stove and stirred the mixture. If Jack remembered right, it would have been simmering gently for almost two hours by now to allow the flavours to really come out.

'How on earth did you manage to cook this with your wrist out of action?' he asked.

'Ah, Mrs Mack from downstairs chopped everything for me so all I needed to do was put everything into the pan at the appropriate time and stir. There's one thing I forgot to ask her to do though.'

'And what was that?'

'Grate some cheese.' She took out the block of cheese from the refrigerator and the grater from the cupboard and handed both to Jack.

'Consider it done.' He smiled, unwrapped the cheese and began the process. 'So, why invite me tonight, all of a sudden?'

'It was horrible seeing you both the other day, what Braydon said to Evie. To a lot of people, it's probably black and white: Evie is the bad, I'm supposedly the good. But don't you think everyone deserves a second chance?'

Jack was careful with what he said. 'I do.'

'But?'

'Well, are you sure you know everything there is to know about Evie? You said yourself that she's never shared her history with you.'

Nicole thought for a moment. 'Jackson, have you ever trusted someone enough that you don't need all the details? Have you ever had so much faith in them that you're willing to let them prove themselves in their own time?' He couldn't say that he had. 'Well, that's what it's like with me and Evie. I pushed for her to let me take care of her, and believe me it wasn't an easy job. I hope one day she will tell me what happened to her, what she's still so scared of. But what I don't want to do is push her, before she's ready.'

He felt a sense of satisfaction that even though Nicole and Evie were close, Nicole was still on the ball. She suspected Evie had secrets too.

'Now, what can I get you to drink?' Nicole had a glass of red already poured. 'I can offer you red wine, white wine, or a beer. I got the beers in especially.' She opened one side of the French door refrigerator and presented the contents with a flourish of her hand.

'You've twisted my arm.' He grinned and took the beer from her. He sat on the bar stool on the opposite side of the kitchen countertop, warmed at the thought of her buying the beers for him, most likely before she even knew whether he'd turn up.

'So, how have you been?' Nicole asked. 'You know, since …'

'Since our run-in at the restaurant you mean?'

Nicole pulled a face. 'I don't know what that was about. Your friend—'

'Wait a minute. He's no friend of mine. He's a colleague. And believe me, I wish he wasn't even that.'

'He certainly has his opinions.' She cradled her glass in her hand as she leaned against the counter.

'That's all they are. But I do need to ask you something.'

'Go on.'

'I get the impression he and my father know something they don't want to share. About my mother.'

'I'd say that's a certainty. But I'm sorry. I have no idea what's going on either.'

'Sorry, I just thought … well, I thought with you and my father being close over the years, you may have been able to shed some light on it.'

'We were close.' She stepped forward and put her wine glass down on the countertop next to Jack. 'But he never confided in me, not about your mother. Oh, we had some laughs and I was there through your teenage years and when you went off to college, but I'm afraid I can't tell you anything.'

Jack sighed and took another swig of beer. 'For years I've wondered why Braydon is still working at the company. I always thought it was his work ethic, his performance, his ability to design and work in any area he was assigned to. I knew it wasn't his dazzling personality. But now I realise it's because he has some kind of a hold over my father.'

'You think Braydon is blackmailing Kent?'

'No, not blackmailing, at least not directly. But whatever my father wants kept quiet, I'd put money on that being the reason he doesn't get rid of Braydon.'

'You're probably right. But remember we fought the last time we saw one another. I don't think me talking to your father will help one bit. Tell me, Jackson. I know Kent apologised to me for what happened that night with Evie, with me losing my job, but has he ever shown any kind of remorse?'

Jack thought about it. 'He has, in his own way. He's never said anything to me, but as I've said before, I know he regrets what happened.'

'No, I don't mean with me and my job. I mean with Evie.'

'I'm not sure I follow.'

'I wondered whether he sees the situation any differently; whether he sees her as a person, not just someone on the streets. You know, I think that's the hardest thing for these people to do. They get stuck in a rut, a hopeless rut they can't climb out of, and when they do, if they don't have support they'll slip right back down again.'

'I guess you're right.'

'Can I ask how *you* feel about Evie?'

'Me? I don't know her.'

Nicole took a sip of wine and he got the impression he'd kind of proved her point, but before they could discuss the matter any further, the doorbell chimed again.

'Could you give the chilli a stir please, Jackson?'

'Of course.' He got down from his stool and went around to the other side of the counter, lifted off the lid of the pan and stirred the rich mixture, more than a little tempted to try some. 'It's looking good,' he called out. 'And I didn't sneak any of it,' he assured Nicole as she returned to the kitchen.

'Jackson, you remember Evie, don't you?'

He'd been blindsided.

'Hello, Jack.' By the tone of her voice and the look on her face, Evie had had no idea he would be here tonight either. Knowing that, made him less angry with Nicole at least.

'Nice to see you, Evie.' He would keep this civilised, not like the confrontation in the street the other day. He replaced the lid on top of the pan and stood out of the way as Nicole took garlic butter from the fridge and spread it along the cut pieces of baguette before adding a generous sprinkling of cheese across the tops.

Evie said nothing in return but he couldn't blame her. Instead she smiled, presumably to keep the peace also, and carried on telling Nicole all about her day at work. Surreptitiously he watched this woman who'd come into Nicole's life right before he exited it. Her honey-blonde hair hung in large, loose ringlets tonight, and blue eyes sat beneath textured lashes that fluttered as she spoke. It was the first time he'd noticed, but she had a faint beauty spot below her left eye, right above her cheekbone.

'How are things at the shelter?' he asked when Nicole shooed him out of the cooking area so she had the space to open the wall oven and put the prepared garlic baguettes inside. They moved over to the table area, Evie with a glass of red, Jack with the beer he'd almost finished.

'They're fine. Thanks again for your help the other day.'

'No problem at all. I enjoyed it.'

Evie raised a quizzical eyebrow.

'You don't look convinced,' he said.

'Do you blame me?'

He knocked back the rest of his beer. 'Don't base your opinion of me on my asshole of a colleague.' He lowered his voice at his colourful description of Braydon. Nicole had never been one for bad language. 'He was wrong the other day, completely out of order, and he knows it.'

'I bet he still has a job though, doesn't he?'

'Yes, he does.' He wished he could say that he didn't.

'Just goes to show,' said Evie.

'Goes to show what?'

'You lot are all the same.'

'What?'

'You prejudge people based on your own opinions, your own assumptions. We're from two very different worlds, Jack. No, correction. We exist, now, in two very different worlds. One is genuine, the other …'

'Wait a minute.' He wasn't going to let her have the upper hand all night.

But he didn't get a chance to argue back because Nicole came over to the table and set down the hot tray filled with cheesy garlic bread fingers onto the flower-shaped silicon table mat. 'Could you grab the pot of chilli for me please, Jackson, and put it on the other table mat? I managed the tray one-handed but the pot's too heavy.'

'I'll get it.' Evie jumped in before he even had a chance to move.

He wasn't about to argue with her, and he didn't miss Nicole stifling a laugh. Clearly she knew Evie well enough to know this girl didn't give up anything without a fight.

Jack spooned out bowls of chilli and grabbed another beer before they tucked in heartily to their meal. Evie had had this dish before too, even made it herself from time to time, she told him, and they dunked cheesy garlic bread into the mixture happily, the conversation on safe topics including ice-skating, Christmas shopping, Christmas food choices and the memories of snowy festive seasons gone by.

'Mom hated the snow,' Jack told them both. 'She was a summer New Yorker through and through. Oh, she loved to watch the scene unfold outside the window when the fire was lit and she didn't have to go anywhere, but boy did she make a fuss when she'd have to go out in it. I think she waved a banner the day I started taking myself off to school and she stayed at home. She'd do a lot of the jewellery designs sitting at the kitchen table, or beside the fire.' He smiled at the memory.

'I love the snow,' said Nicole, 'but by the time February comes around I've had enough and I want spring to appear.'

Jack tore off another piece of cheesy garlic bread to dip into his chilli. 'What about you, Evie?'

'What about me?'

It was the first time he'd heard her defensive since they'd started eating. He thought she'd softened with a bit of food inside her, but apparently he was wrong.

'I wondered whether you like the snow or prefer the summer heat,' he said tactfully.

'I do like the snow.' Her shoulders relaxed. 'I like the summer too.'

'And what's your favourite memory of the snow?' Nicole asked.

Evie dragged a piece of cheesy garlic bread through her chilli. 'I don't really have many.'

'Come on, you must have some. I remember we'd have the biggest snowball fights when I was a teenager. But the boys would get too rough, send the girls crying half the time.'

Evie finished the piece of chilli-dipped garlic bread. 'We never had as much snow as you get in New York, but I did build my fair share of snowmen, had snowball fights.'

'Where are you from?' Jack asked.

'The south coast of England.'

'I didn't realise. You sound American to me. How long have you been living here?'

'I've been here twenty years almost to the day, so my accent has all but gone.'

Jack poured another glass of water from the carafe. He wondered again what this woman's story was. 'Did your entire family move here?'

Evie nodded, but she didn't elaborate. 'Can I get you another drink, Nicole? I'm assuming you're okay.' She nodded towards Jack's beer next to his water glass.

'Let me,' Nicole jumped up and went to fetch the bottle of wine from the kitchen. The atmosphere was tense at the reference to Evie's past and Jack didn't know where to look. He knew Nicole wasn't comfortable either. It was rare for her to run out on a situation, but perhaps she was at last beginning to realise how little she really knew about Evie.

The conversation turned to destinations in Europe that any of them had visited or would like to see one day. They talked about the shelter, and Nicole asked about Nate out at Hollyhock Farm, about the Christmas tree side of the business, the fruit picking that would start with the changing seasons.

'They're doing really well,' said Jack. 'Nate has taken to it like a duck to water. It feels as though he's been doing it his whole life.'

'He never struck me as the office type,' said Nicole. 'Right back when he started taking ice hockey seriously or when you two would go off on your hiking trips or skiing trips, I always pictured him doing something outdoorsy.'

Jack laughed. 'You make it sound as though we're a couple. We were attached at the hip,' he explained to Evie.

'How long have you known him?' Evie cleared the dishes from the table and brought over a lemon meringue pie she'd picked up from the bakery a block away. Jack recognised the name in the swirly writing on the side of the box, a bakery Nicole had frequented even back when she'd worked as a housekeeper for the Churchills.

'We went to school together, and we've been best friends ever since.'

The look Evie gave him was one of curiosity, one he hadn't seen before, like she wanted to know more, as though she was confused about this side of Jack she didn't know. He took it as a good sign.

They devoured a generous slice of the lemon meringue pie each, the lemon tang refreshing after the chilli. Jack cleared away this time, and washed up in the kitchen while the women chatted some more, and at his insistence went through to the living room. This evening was going well, better than expected. When he'd seen Evie show up tonight, he'd thought the evening would drag until he could get the hell out of there, but then he'd relaxed, deciding it might be a chance to try to find out more, really see how she was with Nicole.

He went through to join the women. The fire cast its orange glow over the room and he sat on the rug in front of the fireplace as they chatted about anything and everything: the jewellery for sale at The Diamond Touch, Nicole's Christmas feast and her plans to get around any of the trickier jobs with just one arm. They talked about a few characters from the shelter and they talked about the forecast for extra heavy snowfalls at Christmas. And by the time the evening came to a close, Jack realised that, actually, they'd all had a pretty good time.

'Thank you for inviting me tonight.' He pulled on his jacket.

'It was my pleasure,' said Nicole. 'I'm glad you came.'

Evie wound her scarf around her neck and pulled the matching sky-blue bobble hat over her blonde hair. 'Dinner was lovely, Nicole. I'll be full until next week. I'll enjoy the walk home tonight.'

Evie pulled open the door to the apartment and picked up a stray envelope on the mat right outside. 'Oh, someone's left you this.'

Nicole's outstretched hand hovered mid-air, but Evie didn't seem to want to hand over the envelope all of a sudden. Jack peered closer, but he couldn't tell what it was. The envelope looked normal enough to him.

'You know what,' said Evie. 'It's just junk mail. They were dropping these by our building earlier today.' She shoved it into her pocket. 'I'll bin it.'

Nicole laughed and held out her hand again. 'My bin's closer, give it to me and I'll get rid of it.'

But Evie was already on her way to the elevator. 'I'll see you tomorrow at the shelter.'

'I'll see you soon,' said Jack to Nicole, and then almost ran to dive into the same elevator before Evie shot down to the ground floor and escaped into the night.

They stood side by side as the elevator moved slowly down. 'So, what's in the envelope?' he asked, eyes ahead, watching the numbers of the floors change.

'I told you. It's junk mail.'

‘Let me see it then.’ The elevator reached the ground floor and the doors slid open.

‘Goodnight, Jackson.’

His full name on her lips made him grin. She was doing it to wind him up and it was fun to know he was getting to her. As much as he hadn’t liked her at first, and still suspected she had ulterior motives when it came to Nicole, they’d had fun tonight. And she was a pretty woman. He couldn’t help the flirt and the enjoyment of it all.

‘Hold on a minute.’ When they reached the bottom of the steps outside the apartment building, he grabbed her arm before she shot off into the night. ‘What’s the rush?’

‘It’s late. I need to get home.’

‘I’ll walk you.’

Her blue eyes looked up at him, and he was reminded again of the night she was out on the back patio at his father’s townhouse, terrified and unprepared for what life had to throw at her next. She still hadn’t taken her hands out of her pockets and he knew the envelope was inside.

Jack held out his hand and Evie stared at it. ‘Don’t worry, I don’t want to hold your hand. It’s just there’s a trash can, right over there. I’ll drop the junk mail into it.’

Hands defiantly in her pockets she said, ‘Just leave it, would you?’ She tried to go on her way again.

‘Oh no, you don’t.’ He held her arm tighter this time.

Evie spoke through gritted teeth. ‘If you don’t let go of me right now, I’ll scream and have you arrested for sexual harassment.’

He let go and held up both hands and let her go on her way. But after she’d turned around at the end of the block to make sure he wasn’t following her into the night, he went the same way as her, hanging back enough and ducking into shop doorways whenever he thought she might turn around. She didn't live all that far from Nicole, and by his reckoning he only had another few minutes before she dumped the envelope and he wouldn't be able to find out what it contained.

She came to a stop next to a trash can and Jack noticed she'd opened the envelope and was going through its contents right now, ready to toss away whatever it was that had changed her friendly demeanour tonight. He took a step closer, and another still, but froze. He could hear her, softly, against the sounds of the New York streets, the gaggle from a group of girls across the street, cars swishing across the blackened slush in the gutters, and she was crying.

When her hand moved to toss away whatever it was that had upset her, he stepped forwards. 'Evie.'

She froze on the spot, but before she could do anything else, like throw the evidence into the depths of the trash, the wind whipped up around them and a selection of photographs launched into the air and then fell to the ground.

And when Jack bent down to retrieve them at the same time as Evie, his mouth fell open.

Chapter Seventeen

Evie

Jack was almost a foot taller than her and strong too, so when he held the photographs in his hands high in the air, Evie tried in vain to snatch them back.

'What the hell is this?' Jack demanded.

The look of disgust on his face right now was exactly what Evie had wanted to avoid, from anyone. From Nicole mainly, from her boss, Bonnie, and from anyone else who knew her. Her uncle wasn't going away. He was lurking in the shadows ready to ruin her life.

'Give them to me!' she yelled as passers-by paused momentarily at their altercation, but not enough to stop and take an interest. New York was like that. People were too afraid to get involved in case they came off worst.

Jack had flicked through a couple of the photographs and she was mortified. All of them showed her in various states of undress, and in one of them she was completely nude.

'So this is how you make your money, is it?' he asked. 'And I'm assuming Nicole doesn't know anything about it.'

'Please, don't tell her. I'm begging you.'

'Who was the man, Evie? Does he have something to do with this?'

The tears she'd cried when she'd opened that envelope, knowing how close her world had come to blowing apart, had dried up now and determination kicked in.

'It's none of your business. Now give … them … back.'

'Who is he?'

'I don't owe you anything.' She reached again for the envelope, but he was holding it way out of her reach. It was hopeless.

'Nicole is important to me and I won't have anything ruining her life.'

'Ruining her life? You Churchills did that when you fired her! She may have walked away quietly and with dignity, but I saw how torn up she was. You'd been her life for years and she was devastated! How can you claim to be looking out for her? Where have you been for the last three years? I've been by her side. Where the hell were you?'

'I was devastated too. She was a huge part of my life! Maybe you could take some of the blame for what happened. What, just because you didn't have a place to live makes you completely innocent in all this?'

'You self-centred son of a—'

He rested his fingers lightly on her lips in the same way he'd done at the hospital that day. 'Don't finish that sentence. I buried my mother twenty years ago, but the pain is still there.'

God, that made her feel terrible.

Jack lowered his arm and slotted the photos into an inside pocket in his coat, battling away her hands as she tried to grab them.

'What are you going to do?' she asked him.

'I should show these to Nicole.'

She shook her head, willing him not to. 'You'll ruin my life if you do.'

'Then you need to tell me exactly what is going on.'

*

‘It’s cold in here,’ said Jack, jacket still on and hovering in the doorway as though he wasn’t sure whether it was safe to go in to her basement apartment.

‘I’m afraid the radiators aren’t much good.’ She crouched down and turned the dial up to full in the room that housed the living room and kitchenette in one. ‘It’ll get warmer soon. Can I get you a cup of coffee? Something stronger?’ She pulled out the bottle of gin she rarely touched save the odd occasion she and Lizzy had enjoyed a nightcap.

‘I’ll have a coffee, if it’s not too much trouble.’

‘No trouble.’ She filled the kettle and flicked the switch, cringing at how polite they were being now she’d agreed to tell him everything if he came back to her apartment with her and they didn’t discuss it on the street. ‘Do you take milk?’

‘Black is fine.’

She lined up the mugs and put coffee in each, and while she was waiting for the kettle to boil, she switched on the tree lights and the twinkle lights dotted around the apartment. She felt safer with Jack here and wasn’t worried about her uncle watching the apartment and knowing she was inside.

‘I bet your place has a closet as big as this apartment,’ she said, trying to lessen the weight that hung between them in the air. ‘Where do you live, by the way?’

‘In a condo in the East Village.’

Evie wasn’t at all surprised his place was in such a coveted location.

‘You’ve made this place homely,’ he said, although by his clipped tone she knew he was anxious to move the conversation forwards.

The kettle coming to the boil filled the silence between them. Evie’s hand shook as she poured the water onto the coffee granules. The only reason she wasn't going for the gin right now was that she was freezing and she longed to wrap her hands around a warm mug for comfort. And she had to do this. If Jack was going to keep her secret and not tell the world, she had to tell him everything.

'Here you go.' She handed him a mug.

'Thanks.' His fingers brushed against hers as he took it carefully from her hands. He set it straight down on the coffee table while she cradled hers between her palms.

'Evie, I have to ask you.'

She slurped her coffee. 'Ask away. I said I'd tell you everything.'

'That man, is he your … oh God.' He put his head in his hands. 'I'm just going to come right out with it and say … is that man your pimp?'

She almost sprayed her mouthful of coffee everywhere. If the situation wasn't so awful, she'd laugh at his ridiculous assumption. She shook her head. 'I swear to God, it's nothing like that.'

'So what's with the nude picture? Is he an old boyfriend?

The thought turned her stomach. 'He's my uncle.'

Jack had started to lift his coffee mug, clearly relieved to have asked the question and have her deny it. But now, he put the cup back down again.

'Your uncle?'

'That's right.'

'He's family, and he has those sorts of pictures of you? I didn't see all of them, but I got the gist.'

She cringed at the thought of him seeing any. The top one, she knew because she'd just seen it herself, was of her lying on top of a white fur rug wearing a black lace basque and matching knickers. But there were worse photographs than that. There were countless pictures of her in different styles of underwear, some in raunchier poses than others; but there were also photographs of her topless, wearing nothing but a thong, a handful of shots where she wore nothing but her birthday suit.

Evie looked down into the depths of the remaining black liquid in her cup.

'Come on, Evie.'

She met his gaze, pleaded with her eyes not to make her do this, but she had no choice.

'Just start from the beginning.' He took off his coat as the apartment started to heat up. The radiators may be dire, but the space was tiny after all.

Evie stared at the Christmas tree lights, the angel on top, the baubles almost iridescent in this light, the silver reindeer hanging from the bottom branch. And then she told Jack her story.

'My father emigrated from England to run a business with his brother. The business in the UK had expanded and international reach was what he'd always strived for.' She harrumphed. 'He was one of the most ambitious men I'd ever known.'

'What was his business?'

'It was a furniture business and it grew more rapidly than even my father had predicted. Dad took on Uncle Brett who, up until then, had drifted from office job to office job. We all settled into life in America, especially Mum who loved the glamour compared with her dull village life on the south coast of England, dealing with nothing but school drop-off and pickups and the only highlight a trip to the pub if Dad had time at the end of the day. She joined committees, had a wide circle of friends and for a while everything was perfect. Until she got cancer.'

'Oh God, I'm sorry.'

'Yeah, cancer's a bitch.'

'Carry on,' he urged when she'd stayed quiet for too long.

She looked at him briefly and then away again. 'The cancer was bad, but Mum had the best hospital facilities, top doctors, she was cared for so well. She went into remission after a couple of years and I thought that was it, life would get back on an even keel.'

'But it didn't?'

She shook her head. 'The world was going belly up and the business was one of the casualties. Money was tight and bills were mounting up. A couple of years later, the business was forced to shut down and my father was lost without it. He'd shut himself away, barely talking to either of us, and when he wasn't doing that he was out goodness knows where. All we did was hope he was trying to find another job so things could go back to normal. But one day …' She shook her head at how clichéd this sounded. 'He went out and never came back.

'Mum's cancer returned soon after and took its toll on us financially and emotionally. Mum had been working a part-time job that just about covered our living expenses while I was at school and then college, but when she got sick she'd had to give it up. The cancer was worse this time. Mum was crying constantly because Dad had left, her world was crumbling around her, and because this was the end. She was dying and there was nothing anyone could do to fix it.'

She paused, looked into the depths of her coffee. 'Mum was put on end-of-life care with end-stage breast cancer. We lost the house and I had no choice but to move in with Uncle Brett and my Auntie Mo. Mum had never liked my uncle much, but she was grateful there was someone there for me, a roof over my head. I always told her I was fine living there because I never wanted her to worry about me.

'I visited Mum at the hospice every spare moment I could. I should've been applying for a real job, a proper paid job rather than the pocket money I was getting at a local fast food joint, but I wanted to spend every moment with her. You know, I always wished I'd had a sibling. I wanted someone else to be in the same position as me, to know exactly how I was feeling, the pain caused by Dad's disappearance and Mum's illness. None of my friends really got it. Their lives were so normal in comparison.'

'I can understand that,' said Jack wistfully. He tipped his head back to get the dregs from his coffee cup.

'You have siblings?'

He smiled. 'A sister, Cameron. She's a giant pain in the ass sometimes, but her heart's in the right place. And when Mom died, even though we rarely talked about it, it felt good to have someone there who knew what I was going through.'

Evie smiled back at him. 'You're lucky.' It took her a minute or two to continue. 'Before Dad left and Mum died, I'd been lucky. I'd never wanted for anything, except a bit of time with my father when he wasn't working, but I'd always had food on the table, nice clothes—although designer outfits are wasted on kids, in my opinion—I was ferried around in top-of-the-range cars, taken on ski holidays in Aspen. My parents even put a pool in the backyard at the house, a tennis court that was rarely used. Mum would lie in the sun every day and we'd talk or we'd swim side-by-side, before she got sick and before the business began to fail. I loved the water, the way it made me feel free, the escape I felt when my face and ears were submerged and I could forget everything else.'

Evie took her coffee cup out to the kitchen and took out an ice-cube tray from the freezer. She emptied four cubes into the bottom of a tumbler, then half-filled it with gin and added a splash of tonic, but not so much it would take away the edge she needed. She held the gin bottle aloft to ask if Jack wanted to join her, but he shook his head.

'There's something you need to understand about Uncle Brett,' she said when she'd slumped down on the armchair again.

Jack sat forwards, intrigued.

'One day, not long after my twentieth birthday, my parents were out at a garden party. I'd been swimming and was getting changed in the outhouse. Mum had a thing about dripping through the house so had had a shower and change room built at the foot of the garden.' She grinned. 'Sometimes, in the winter when it wasn't used much, I'd hide in the outhouse and read a book. They'd have no idea where I was. And for those moments it was like an adventure. I used to pretend I was in my own place, somewhere near the beach, with nothing but bookshelves keeping me company.'

She knocked back an enormous gulp of gin. 'Anyway, this day when I was getting changed, I'd just taken off my swimming costume and went to grab my towel when I saw someone out of the corner of my eye, watching me from the garden through the window.' She looked to Jack. 'It was him, my Uncle Brett. I grabbed a towel, yelled at him but he looked like he wasn't sorry at all. And he knew I wouldn't say anything. He knew the problems with the business, he knew Mum hadn't been well, and he knew how much I hated to rock the boat. From then on, I never changed in that pool house again. I didn't even take a book out there for fear he'd show up and want more than a sneaky look at a girl a third of his age.

'After Mum died and I was living with my Uncle Brett and Auntie Mo, it was fine for a while. At least with my auntie around I knew he'd never try anything, but I still hated being near him. All I wanted to do was get away, but finding a job was next to impossible. The fast food joint I'd worked at had shut up shop like many local businesses, and my job applications hadn't hit the mark anywhere. I was lost. I'd spend hours at the library every day just to escape the house, and I'd hang around the shopping mall to pass the time.

'One day in the mall, I was approached by a man. He was in a suit, designer, and said he was a photographer with an international modelling agency. He handed me a business card, asked whether I'd ever thought about modelling. Oh, he had all the phrases down pat, telling me I had excellent bone structure, the height they needed, dewy skin—whatever that means—and I had the "look" he was after. The next week, I had a job. And despite my reservations, it was a hell of a lot of money to turn down. I started working with him at the studios; mostly it was just us, but I was comfortable. He'd take my photographs in perfectly respectable outfits and I'd get a pay cheque at the end of each week. The money I earned would be my ticket out of the rut I was in and I wanted to come to New York, get a place of my own and find a job that would mean the start of a new life.'

When she paused, he asked, 'Can I grab one of those?' nodding at the gin in her hand. He stood up. 'I'll get it myself. Glasses?'

She pointed to the cupboard above the cooktop. 'Plenty in there, ice in the freezer, gin in the bottle.'

Evie waited for Jack to fix himself a drink and took a swig of her own before she pressed on. 'The modelling was going great and all I wanted was to save money. Since the day my uncle had spied on me when I was naked, he'd looked at me differently … you know, the look that tells you someone could cause a whole lot of trouble if you put so much as a foot wrong.

'I cried myself to sleep more times than I can remember. I missed my mum more than I thought possible. You know, when it's cancer you think you're prepared, you think hearing the diagnosis is the worst part, but when you're with someone day after day watching them fade away, it haunts you for a long time after; forever even.'

'I'll bet. It was different for me,' said Jack. 'I never had to watch my mom suffer. The heart attack was quick, one minute she was there, the next she wasn't. Perhaps it was easier that way, although on the other hand, I would've liked a chance to say goodbye.' He shrugged.

Evie shook her head. 'There's no good way to lose a parent.'

They both nursed their gin and tonics before Evie continued.

'Do you know, I still remember her smell? She wore this perfume that was too strong for her kind-hearted nature, but it was her. And her hands were always so soft. I still remember what it felt like as a little girl clutching her hand when we went to the swings, when she'd take me shopping. Dad would laugh at her and her bottles of hand cream deposited around the house: in the kitchen, the downstairs bathroom, the bedroom, one in her handbag, another in the car. In the hospice I'd rub her hand cream in for her, trying to keep some semblance of who she'd once been.'

'It sounds as though you were close.'

'We were.'

'You know, it's okay to miss her. I still miss my mother too and I'm a man, I'm supposed to be okay about it.'

Evie smiled, grateful his anger and accusations had subsided at least for now.

'How long before you'd had enough?' he asked.

'I kept modelling and my savings were increasing a little, although I needed to buy any extras for myself. My uncle and auntie's care only covered the roof over my head and my share of the bills, but clothes and toiletries or a meal out with a friend, that was all for me to take care of. And I was happy with that. I liked the independence and in a way it made me more determined.

'One day, the photographer at the agency asked whether I'd be willing to pose for lingerie magazines. He said there was a demand for it. At first I said no, but he said he'd double the pay I was already getting and I couldn't pass up the opportunity. I figured it would be like wearing a swimming costume, except lacier.' She managed a laugh. 'Again, everything went well. I was taking home more money.'

Jack took a big swig of gin and coughed. 'Should've added more tonic.' He got up and did just that and at least he'd made Evie smile until it was time to continue.

'One day I showed up at work and this time the photographer wanted me topless. He offered me three times more money and again I couldn't resist.' She closed her eyes. 'God, I was so stupid. I didn't investigate him, check any credentials. All I'd thought about was the money and I had no idea where the photographs were going. I started to ask questions, but he was evasive, wouldn't tell me. I knew the photographs of me clothed were in catalogues, a couple in magazine advertisements. The lingerie photographs had gone the same way, and it was only once I'd started the nude modelling that I began to wonder. After all, there weren't any garments on me to sell!'

Jack topped up her glass with gin and added a splash of tonic.

'I decided, stupidly I guess, that it didn't matter where the photographs were going, as long as I had the money. But one day when I turned up at work, the photographer, Gary, was sheepish. He told me my work had come to an end, he had no use for me anymore. He wouldn't look at me and kept his face turned away. He said he'd pay me what I was owed and then he didn't want to see me again. I wasn't devastated. I was confused, but it was a relief not to have to model again. I had some money and knew I could build it up, albeit slowly, as long as I found any job, and fast.'

'So then what happened?'

'Uncle Brett was waiting for me when I got home. He was sitting at the kitchen table, grinning. I poured an orange juice, the last of the contents in the fridge, and that was when he leant over my shoulder and dropped a picture of me on the bench. He told me I'd been a "naughty girl" and then he passed me a job application that had been sitting on my nightstand in my bedroom. He'd told me that employers wanted the right sort of person working for them and that when these photographs were made public, I'd never get a job. I'd heard all the horror stories at school, about kids who have online profiles that are a red flag to employers and I'd always toed the line in that respect. My comments and photos were always respectful and I only friended people I knew and trusted. And he was about to blow that apart.

'In return for his silence, he wanted me to model for him. God knows, I hadn't seen that coming. He was related to me and the perving on me in the change room had been one thing, but this was disgusting. There'd always been something odd about him. I swear that was why he was the black sheep of dad's family, running away overseas the first opportunity he got.'

'Why on earth would your dad give him a job in the first place?'

'Because Dad was the peacemaker. He did it for his parents who were heartbroken Brett had left and wasn't in touch with them, save the odd occasions of birthdays and Christmas. Dad was always the son who'd shone, done well at school, gone on to better things, and he wanted to save the day, I suppose. Probably one of the most ambitious things he's ever done.'

'I still don't understand your uncle. What man does that? What man preys on a young girl, a member of his own family?'

'I don't understand it either. I heard my parents talking one night about Uncle Brett having problems. The words counselling and psychological issues were tossed around in the conversation, but they never said anything when they knew I could hear.'

Jack shook his head. 'I have two nieces and the thought of … God, it makes me sick to my stomach.'

‘I don’t get it either, but that was the way he was. He wanted pictures and the way he looked at me I knew it wouldn’t stop there. I knew I couldn’t tell Auntie Mo. She was a solicitor in the area, well respected, and this was the sort of gossip—and believe me she’d have called it that—which could destroy her reputation. No, I knew she wouldn’t be on my side. She was good to take me in and give me a home, but she was no mother. Perhaps I underestimated her, but I couldn’t take the chance.

‘He told me, right there in the kitchen, that he’d followed me and had paid Gary a little visit, promising if he came near me again he’d get more than the black eye he’d already given him. I realised then that that was why Gary refused to look at me at the studio. Uncle Brett had all the photographs, all the negatives, any digital images; and he now had a hold over me. He’d backed me into a corner and I couldn’t get out.’

‘Was that when you ran?’

She nodded, swiped a tear from her cheek as painful memories resurfaced. ‘I barricaded my bedroom door that night, packed a bag and climbed out of the window. I hitched a ride to the nearest train station where I waited for the first train, the next morning, and then I came to New York.’

Jack brought the gin bottle over and topped them both up. No extra tonic this time.

‘I had enough money to stay in a bed and breakfast for a few nights and my determination kicked in. I thought, I can do this, I can find a job, get somewhere to live and it’ll all work out. I tried to have faith. But the job didn’t come, even jobs in street cafés were impossible to get, already taken by someone else who got there five minutes before me, and as for the jobs for people with high-school qualifications, it was me and a thousand other young hopefuls.

'After a few weeks, the money started to run out and I was worried. I moved into a cheaper bed and breakfast, but a week later that was it. I had no home. I had nowhere to go, no job and knew nobody. I'd find a doorway to huddle in, cursing the fact I hadn't had the foresight to pack a blanket in the backpack, but I'd assumed by now, seven weeks after running away, I'd have a job.'

'What was it like?'

'Living on the streets?'

Jack nodded.

'As bad as you'd think.' She took a swig of gin. She didn't need any more, she felt the effects of alcohol already, but it helped her to go on. 'I consider myself one of the lucky ones. I was only homeless for nine weeks all up. After I'd slept in doorways, on park benches and anywhere I could find, I braved going to one of the shelters. I hadn't dared to before then. I'd wanted to be on my own. I felt disgusted with how I'd let my life become merely an existence. Sometimes I'd feel as though it was all my fault, as though it was the universe's revenge for my privileged upbringing. I thought hey, this is real life, finally bringing me down a peg or two.

'I lost an incredible amount of weight, so much that even I noticed my bony hips protruding through one of the two pairs of jeans I now owned. And I was permanently hungry, constantly cold. I stayed the night in one of the shelters, just the once, but in the middle of the night there'd been a man; violent, he was, and shouting and screaming at everyone. It was the stuff of nightmares and I ran from it. I felt safer on the New York streets.' She laughed at the irony. 'Crazy, huh?'

'I don't think you're crazy,' Jack assured her. 'But I do know this gin is going right to my head despite the fill we had at Nicole's.'

Evie went over to the cupboards. 'I don't have any food to soak it up, I'm afraid. I may have the crust from a loaf of bread, or some cereal.' Even though she had a job, she didn't buy much when she shopped. It still felt like an extravagance and she was frugal in what she chose. She only bought the necessities, with alcohol the exception.

Jack pulled out his phone and hit speed dial.

'What are you up to?'

'Pizza. We need pizza. Any preference?'

She shook her head and giggled. 'Actually, I am pretty hungry. Must be the gin.' She'd noticed her legs felt decidedly wobbly when she'd gone over to search the kitchen cupboards.

Jack ordered a pizza with flavours that made her mouth water but flavours she wasn't sure went together: pineapple, pepperoni, onion, sweetcorn, olives. What were they doing? They'd gone from hating one another to sharing a pizza?

Evie poured two big tumblers of water as they waited for the food and handed one to Jack.

'So how did you meet Nicole?' he asked her, first thanking her for the water.

'I went to the shelter where she works, a few times. I liked it there. I felt at ease, nobody hassled me, nobody tried to counsel me. They just let me be. And then one night when I was huddled up in a doorway, Nicole recognised me. She tried to take me home with her, but I refused.' Evie laughed. 'She wouldn't take no for an answer till I promised I'd check in at the shelter in the morning if she'd leave me alone for now.'

'But she finally convinced you?'

There was no malice in his words, no accusations. 'Every time I'd visit the shelter, Nicole would make it known to me that she was there to help, but she stopped hassling me. Then one night, huddled in a doorway, a man approached me. He offered me money to … well, you know.' She couldn't look at Jack now. 'And when I said no, he offered me more and then he tried to pull me away, towards the park. God knows what he was planning to do, but I fought him with everything I had and ran straight to the shelter. It was shut already, they don't open overnight and I didn't trust anyone else. It may seem stupid that I didn't go to another shelter for the night but I was scared, too scared to be able to relax anywhere. So I walked around.'

'All night?'

She nodded. 'All night, until seven o'clock the next morning when the shelter opened up. I was sitting on the steps and lucky for me, Nicole was there. She took one look at me and pulled me inside. That was Thanksgiving.'

'The day we first met.' The words sounded odd on his lips.

'An hour later, once everything at the shelter was sorted, Nicole took me to her apartment where I showered and had a good meal. She left me to sleep while she went to her housekeeping job at your father's house. She trusted me completely, didn't hide anything.' Evie smiled. 'I could've cleaned her out. Her jewellery wasn't hidden, and I remember she had several expensive-looking ornaments out on display. There was even a jar of small change on the kitchen bench, which must have amounted to well over fifty dollars. Maybe it was a test, I don't know, but she came home in the middle of the afternoon and I went on my way again.'

'You weren't tempted to stay?'

'Of course I was. I mean, you've seen it, her apartment is gorgeous. It was safe, warm and felt almost like it could be home, despite its unfamiliarity. And when I said I was going, she looked so sad, as though me being there had saved her rather than me. But I went on my way, begrudgingly taking twenty dollars she handed me, and she told me if I wouldn't stay in the apartment then I was to come to your father's house, about nine o'clock when she was almost finished, and she'd feed me. I knew she was saying it because she wanted to see me, check I was okay.

'So I stopped by the house as she'd said and we talked for a bit, out back. She hates food going to waste you know, said half the people at the party didn't know how bloody lucky they were.' She stopped, covered her mouth. 'Oops, I shouldn't have said that.'

Jack grinned. 'I couldn't agree more. Some of those people my father associates with are assholes.'

Evie smiled at his frankness. 'Well anyway, that's the whole story up until the moment you and I … first met. I left but I hung around a couple of hours as I wanted to make sure everything was okay for Nicole, that she hadn't made your family angry. When she walked to the next block and I stepped out from the shadows, she was crying. Proper, sobbing tears.'

'Fuck.' Jack grabbed his gin instead of the water and knocked it back.

'The first thing she said, before she even told me she'd lost her job, was that she wasn't going to argue anymore and I was coming home with her and that was that. She sorted me out with a job within a few days, and after almost a year of living in her apartment, I was able to move out into this studio. Rent in Manhattan is crazy so it's all I could afford, but it was really important I did this for myself.'

The doorbell buzzed three times, short and sharp.

'That'll be the pizza.' Evie took money from her purse, Jack took cash from his wallet and after a battle of wills they agreed to go halves. Funny, Jack seemed more shaken than Evie was, she decided. He looked as though his world had just been put on the spin cycle when she was the one confessing, not him.

It was almost midnight, but Jack and Evie were ravenous. The chilli and garlic bread had long since worn off, and the gin plus the confession time had made them so hungry neither of them spoke as they devoured a couple of slices each.

When the eating slowed, Jack asked, 'Was it long before Nicole got back on her feet? I tried to get in touch, you know.'

'I know you did, she told me. We became close, almost like mother and daughter in many ways, even though I fought it at the start. But also we became best friends. I think she thought that by cutting all ties she was doing you both a favour. That night left a lasting scar on her, and it only did that because she cared so much about you both.'

'She was like one of the family.' Jack broke the stringy cheese between two slices of pizza when he pulled one piece from the box.

'I think that's why she cut all ties. She was thinking of you as much as herself. She never got another job, just upped her hours volunteering, so I know money wasn't a problem for her. I think she comes from a wealthy family, not that I've ever asked much, it's just an impression I get. My guess is that she was your housekeeper for so long because she felt she'd found where she belonged. Something tells me she's never been so happy since. I saw it when I agreed to live there with her and then an almost despair when I was leaving.'

Jack sat back. 'She's a good woman. There's no denying it.

Evie put down the remains of her pizza. 'Okay, I can't fit another thing in.'

'Me neither. I'm officially full, and a little bit drunk.'

Evie giggled and let a moment pass between them. 'So now you know everything,' she said finally.

'Now I know everything,' he nodded. A yawn escaped and broke the silence between them. 'I also know I need to get to bed. I've got work in the morning.' He stood and picked up his jacket. 'Thanks for telling me everything, Evie.'

'If my uncle goes public with those photos, it'll be the end of my career.' She watched Jack shrug on his jacket. 'My boss, Bonnie, is understanding but she's running a business, she has an image to portray. We're exhibiting at three major expos next year, right here in New York.'

'That's fantastic.' He zipped up his jacket.

'Not if these photographs get out it won't be. Buyers, sponsors, industry professionals … they'll all see them and I'd be ruined. I'd lose my job, this apartment, not to mention putting my dreams on hold for anything else to do with my career that I've built from scratch.' She rubbed her eyes with the heels of her hands. 'You know, one of the worst things about living on the streets was the way people looked at me. They'd scramble past a bench or a doorway where I was huddled, but not before they'd glance at me with a look of pity, sometimes disgust, but always an I-hope-it-never-happens-to-me look.'

'So what are you going to do?'

'I don't know.'

'What I don't understand,' said Jack, 'is what your uncle has to gain now from putting those photographs out there. Is it just vindictive satisfaction for him?'

Evie shook her head, recounting the night her uncle had cornered her on the street, the night Jack had come to her rescue. 'He wants money. He has no job, my auntie left him, the house has been repossessed. He's at rock bottom. He says I owe him. He put a roof over my head for a long time, took me in when Dad left and Mum died.' Tears sprang to her eyes. 'He told me there were other things I could do if I didn't want to part with cash.'

Jack reached out and touched a hand to her arm. 'He's one sick bastard.'

'He wants to know where my father is too, and won't believe me when I say I have no idea.'

'Would you tell him if you knew?'

Evie shrugged. 'Kind of a moot point really. And do you want to know the worst thing?' She didn't wait for an answer. 'If these photographs get out, I'll lose Nicole's respect and that matters to me more than anything. And I know Dad left without a backwards glance, but it'd break me if he ever saw these pictures.' Her voice faltered for a second. 'He walked out on us but … I can't help wondering why I was never enough for him. Kids are supposed to be the ones who make mistakes, the ones who are forgiven no matter what. Was I really so terrible?' Her voice echoed around the walls as the lights twinkled back at her.

When Jack reached out again with his hand and gave her shoulder a reassuring squeeze, she knew she'd been just as guilty of misjudging him as he had of her. Nicole was right. Beneath the brash exterior, his heart really was in a good place.

She moved to the door and slid off the chain, unlocked it with the key. 'Thanks for listening to me, Jack.'

He stepped outside, turned back and smiled. The snow was falling onto the concrete and the steps leading up from the basement.

'The city will look beautiful in the morning,' she said, her head leaning against the doorjamb.

'It certainly will.' He zipped the collar of his jacket right up to his chin, made a face to show he felt the chill on the New York air. 'Goodnight, Evie.'

'Goodnight, Jack.'

Chapter Eighteen

Jack

Jack slept better than he'd expected the night after Evie's confession. It must've been the gin. He never usually drank the stuff, but it had hit the spot as he'd listened to the truth, the confession about her life. And this morning, it made him all the more determined to find the boy he'd been looking for.

As he drove out of the city and headed for his property in New Haven, in his mind Jack debated nature versus nurture. He was the son of Kent Churchill, an extraordinary and very successful, not to mention wealthy, businessman with a hunger Jack didn't share. On the flip side, Jack had spent thirteen years under the watchful eye of Nicole, a woman who wasn't related to him biologically yet a woman whose nurturing ways surely must have something to do with his empathy for Evie, his understanding for the boy he was looking for.

He pulled up outside his property. All the other times he'd come searching, it'd been for stints of an hour or two to no avail, but today, he wasn't leaving until he'd scoured the streets for the boy he'd found on his porch that day and told to get lost. He wanted to put right what he'd done. He wanted to give this boy a chance just like Nicole had done for Evie. Of course, the boy could end up being bad news, but for once, Jack was determined to see past any rash pre-judgements and at least give the boy a go, if he ever found him.

Armed with a flask of hot coffee in his backpack, three sandwiches to cover him for the whole day and a bottle of water, Jack was thankful it wasn't snowing now as he trudged the streets of New Haven looking in each and every doorway. He searched storefronts, looking for the face he knew he'd recognise, he caught the bus to the city wondering whether the boy would think it was better to head there. He caught a cab to a shelter where he thought he'd try his luck before he ran out of daylight, and when he asked around he realised how his description of the boy: jet-black hair, tanned complexion, blue eyes, sounded like half the boys in America. Deflated, he began to make his way back to his property.

A few blocks from home, he passed a local park. Acres upon acres of parkland with ample places to hide spread out before him, but with the day about to start drawing in, he decided it wasn't even worth starting looking there today. It'd have to be another time. He was about to leave when he saw movement at the entrance: a gait he'd seen before as a figure moved away from him.

It was the boy. Jack was sure of it.

What he didn't want was for this boy to bolt when he saw Jack coming towards him. So instead of rushing over, Jack hung back and followed the boy another two blocks until the boy crept down the side of the garage of a ramshackle property that looked even more dilapidated than his own.

Jack followed him. A twig snapped underfoot, already hardened from the frost that hadn't cleared all day. Hearing the warning, the boy swung around suddenly, but not before he'd grabbed a weapon. He faced Jack, armed with a fence panel, nails protruding at threatening angles.

'What the fuck do you want with me?' the boy yelled.

'Kenny, thank you so much.' Evie took the rose one of the visitors to the shelter handed her when he arrived for breakfast that morning.

'I didn't steal it. It fell from a bouquet as a man in a suit took the flowers away from a florist and I even waited for him to stop and pick it up, but he didn't. It was so beautiful, I had to rescue it.' Kenny's grubby face looked at her, awaiting approval.

'Kenny, you are a kind man.' Evie smiled as she went to find something from the kitchen that would serve as a vase.

'Here, try this.' Nicole handed her a tall glass, chipped at the top but suitable for the purpose.

Evie filled it with a little water, popped the rose in and leant in to smell the petals. She held it aloft behind the servery for Kenny to admire, and when he smiled she set it down near the cutlery stack where everyone coming inside could see it.

'Did Jackson see you home safely last night?' Nicole asked. Evie knew she was asking more than that.

'Thank you, he did. He was a gentleman. Can I ask why you always call him Jackson when nobody else does?'

Nicole ran a dishcloth beneath the hot tap and squeezed it out ready to wash down tables. 'I think he introduced himself as Jackson and so I kept using the name. Over the years he told me only his mother had ever called him by his full name, and I remember being really touched that he didn't seem to mind me doing it too.' She wiped the top of the servery, caught the spill of ketchup from the bacon sandwiches that had been served.

‘Have you heard from Kent since the other day?’

‘No, not a word. I think he’s as embarrassed as Jack, but he’d never admit it. That man always kept his cards close to his chest.’

Evie wondered whether Nicole, too, had more of a story to tell.

‘Two sausage sandwiches,’ Meg from the kitchen announced.

‘Thanks,’ Evie called in response. She collected the orders and delivered the first to Kenny, with a wink, the other to Mal, the man he was sitting with tonight. And when she returned to behind the servery to ask when the next round would be ready, she noticed Nicole’s face fall.

‘What’s up?’ Evie looked at Nicole and then followed her gaze, turning round to see what had got her attention. It was a man in a suit standing next to someone holding a clipboard.

‘Can I help you?’ Nicole was already on her way over.

Evie went out back to check on the upside-down puddings and helped dry the dishes while she was there. She thought about the closeness she and Jack had shared last night. When those photos had turned up at Nicole’s apartment, she’d been terrified and never would’ve predicted it would’ve led to her telling Jack everything. He’d moved from being the enemy to an ally, and again Evie felt as though her life here in New York was taking shape even more. It’d been hard to trust people for a long time before she arrived, and living on the streets she trusted nobody; but with first Nicole, then Bonnie, and now Lizzy and more recently, Jack, she was starting to realise how important friendships were. And they didn’t need to be established over a long time. Sometimes friendships simply clicked into place when you least expected.

'Here you go, three sausage sandwiches.' Meg put the plates onto the counter.

'I'll get these out there. Compliments to the chef.' Evie grinned at the volunteer chef. She went out front and took the sandwiches to the nearest table, but her mind wasn't on the banter she met with or the smiles from the regulars. She was concentrating on the men, walking around the room now, one with a tape measure measuring the doorways, the windows.

'What's going on? Who are they?' Evie asked when Nicole came to her side. She didn't look too happy.

'They're sniffing around to check the place out. They already visited last week, so I don't know why they're back.'

'Where are they from?'

Nicole shrugged. 'I don't know, but I sure as hell am going to find out.'

Evie watched as Nicole went over, hands on hips, blue and white checked tea towel swinging from one hand. The men looked startled and Evie let a giggle escape. Nicole could be quite intimidating when she was determined to get to the bottom of something.

'What's wrong?' Evie asked the second Nicole walked back over to her.

'There's someone very interested in this building.' She shook her head, looked to the floor, and if Evie wasn't mistaken her eyes filled with tears.

'Who?'

'The Diamond Touch.'

Evie's face fell.

'The Churchills are interested in taking over the lease, buying it. I don't know the ins and outs, those men wouldn't tell me much. All I know is that because of Kent Churchill, all these people who trust us and stay safe when they are under this roof will have something else snatched away from them.'

Evie stood, stunned until a ruckus dragged her attention away. But it was only Jenny, one of the regulars, falling through the door into one of the men in suits. She'd given him quite a fright by the looks of things, and Evie would have laughed in different circumstances. 'Can't you talk to Kent?' she asked. 'He might listen to you.'

Nicole hooked an eyebrow suggesting he would do nothing of the sort. She sighed. 'Oh, I guess if it wasn't him then it'd be someone else.'

'You sound like you're giving up.'

Nicole leant against the kitchen counter. Evie had never seen her so deflated. 'I'm tired of fighting, Evie. I'm tired of fighting anything. Life shouldn't be this hard.'

Evie wanted to probe. There was more to this than the loss of a building. The Nicole she knew would be talking about where to open up next, the petition they could do, how she'd tackle the Churchills. But that Nicole wasn't here now and defeat had crept in.

'Those Churchills have a lot to bloody well answer for.' Evie grabbed her coat from the cupboard, apologising as she sent a cup of tea flying from a table. She stooped down to pick it up, mopped it up with a piece of paper towel, and stormed out.

'Evie, where are you going?' Nicole called after her.

Evie spun around at the doorway. 'They think they can mess with people's lives and they don't give a shit about anyone other than themselves.' She'd thought she'd seen a glimmer of humanity in Jack last night, but this was his business too and you could bet he'd be in on it, ready to make a quick buck or thousand, or million even. He was as bad as his father. 'I won't let them do this to us.'

And with that, she stormed out.

*

She'd been right. Jack's condo building was nothing short of magnificent. Evie couldn't even fathom what it would be like to come home to this, with its limestone-clad lobby and views that would look out over neighbouring rooftops and the Empire State building.

Jack had told her the street address, but standing in front of the building now, looking in through the glass doors at the lobby, she had no idea what the next step was. These places were secure, the tenants paid for it, so she wouldn't be able to march through the doors and up to his condo to have it out with him. She hovered near the entrance. It wasn't as though she was huddled beneath a blanket now, she wasn't a scruffy homeless person as she'd been once upon a time. She was clean, respectable, and dressed in a smart wool coat, with a healthy glow to her cheeks from the cold; she felt sure she could be mistaken as any one of these residents leaving or coming home to this building. She was wondering how she could use her respectability to her advantage and gain entry, when she turned at the voice behind her.

'Evie, what brings you here?' It was Jack, a ruby red scarf hanging around the collar of a black business coat completely dissimilar to the jacket he'd worn to Nicole's the other night. It was as though there were two Jacks: the one who did business in Manhattan every day, powered by a suit and tie, and the other Jack who dressed in designer jeans hugging a pretty awesome runner's body.

She crossed her arms, dismissing any complimentary thoughts. 'I've come to see you, actually.'

'Oh?'

'We need to talk.'

He was clearly on his way out, but said, 'Let's go up to my condo. We can talk there.'

Evie took in her surroundings and was tempted by his offer, but she didn't need to take the elevator to know it would be plush, or step into his apartment to know it would have top-of-the-range appliances and views to die for. It was all money to him, but some things were more important.

'I'd rather not,' she told him. 'What I have to say won't take long.'

He cradled her elbow and led her away from the building, out of the way of another couple on their way in, a man on his way out. 'Then at least let me buy you coffee.' He saw the look on her face. 'Or you can buy me one. There's a café right across the street.'

'Fine.' And she stalked over the street without waiting for him.

They ordered two coffees and Jack brought them to the table. 'So go on then, what's given you a face like thunder, like you want to kill me?' He grinned, warily. 'I kind of thought we might be friends after last night.'

'Not after what you and your father have done, no.'

He slurped his coffee, wincing at the heat from it. 'And what are we supposed to have done?'

'The shelter.' Her voice went up at the end. Was he deliberately playing dumb?

'What about the shelter?'

'You're taking it from under us, putting new premises there.'

He spluttered now, sending the top of his coffee splashing onto the table. Evie handed him a bunch of napkins, but she didn't wipe it for him. Let him clean up his own mess.

'Don't tell me you had no idea,' she bit.

'I didn't. I honestly didn't know my father had the shelter earmarked.' He shook his head. 'I don't think he knows it's where Nicole volunteers. He's been off the ball lately, since his health scare, so he's not investigated things to the nth degree, and this perfectly illustrates my point.' He mopped up the last of the spill and sat back in his chair, uninterested in the coffee. 'If he knew Nicole was involved, I don't think he'd go near the place.'

'I want to believe you, Jack.' Evie had thought last night she'd found a friend, but now Jack seemed like one of those people who reeled you in, managed to gain your trust and then hit you the second your back was turned.

'But you don't.'

'We live in different worlds, you and I.'

'See, that doesn't help, because we both live in the same one … Manhattan.' He smiled hopefully as he looked back at her.

Evie wished his dark brown hair didn't look so good she wanted to run her fingers through it, and that his toffee-coloured eyes would shift their focus to something or someone else.

'I'm in a world where friendship and trust trumps all else,' she said, 'whereas you're in a world where the mighty dollar is the be all and end all. I think you try to have genuine friendships, I saw that last night, but at the end of the day Jack Churchill does what he wants as long as he makes a profit. I thought more of you, Jack. I thought you were strong, stood up for what you believed in the way you stood up for Nicole when you thought I was trying to take advantage of her. But you'll never be any different to your father.'

Her chair scraped back as she got up to leave, but Jack's hand shot out and covered hers. She looked down at it.

'Evie …' His voice was soft, but she didn't want to look at him.

Tears sprang to her eyes, her hand still beneath his. 'The lease is up and we have no money to renew it anyway, so I guess you've won the battle.' She tried to move, but his hand gripped hers again and pulled her back.

Jack stood up and abandoned his coffee. 'I didn't know anything about this, I swear. And furthermore, I kept my promise last night and I've told nobody what you told me. I've kept the secret and I'll continue to do so. How can you not trust me?'

She looked at the ground.

'Come on.' He tipped his head to the door. 'Follow me, I want to show you something. Give me one chance to prove myself to you, that's all I ask.'

*

Evie sat in the passenger seat in Jack's fancy car that wasn't only clean but smelled so fresh it was as though it had just been driven off a factory forecourt. It smelt like the Mercedes her father had bought brand new, ebony black, slick as the life he'd led for a while.

The car weaved through the streets, the traffic, the smog of Manhattan until they reached wider roads, and buildings faded away to be replaced by greenery speckled white by the snow, by trees, by the feeling of space. Every now and then Jack moved his head to check his rear-view mirror or his wing mirror. Evie had agreed to give him a chance, but she still had no idea where they were going. All she knew was that they'd started to follow the signs to New Haven.

'I love it out here.' Jack indicated to overtake a lorry and then pulled back into the lane again.

'Do you come here often?' As soon as she'd said it she giggled. 'Sorry, that sounded like a bad chat-up line.'

He grinned as he turned off the main road and followed a street with a canopy of trees above them, lacking the spring splendour they would surely have in a few months. They came to a quieter area with maple trees lining the streets.

'You know, I always wanted to own a maple tree farm,' Evie said, gazing out the window. 'I blame my Mum. She would make pancakes every weekend and I'd always eat mine with lashings of maple syrup. We did a class project on it once, at school, learning about how it's made.'

'I must admit, I buy the bottles but never think about it.'

'Now why doesn't that surprise me?' she teased.

He indicated left into another road, this time lined with houses; some large, some small, some grand, others modest.

'I had visions of planting the trees,' Evie continued, 'and then spending my days tapping the bark to let the sap run into a bucket.'

'It sounds like a nice dream. So what happened? What made you exchange maple trees for wedding dresses?'

Evie smiled. 'I was only a kid when I dreamed of the maple syrup. As I grew up, I made a few of my own clothes and found I loved it and did it well. My dream changed from the sticky stuff to the magical dreams of couples tying the knot.' She shrugged, the change of career direction a fait accompli.

They pulled into the driveway of a property where a young lad was hauling sticks, stones and other debris into a heavy-duty garden waste bag. 'Whose place is this?' She unclicked her seat belt when Jack did the same and they got out the car, pulling their coats on to meet the December chill.

'It's mine.' He kept walking towards the boy, leaving Evie to turn around in circles taking in the neighbourhood, the family area it seemed to be and the contrast to a place where she'd ever put Jack.

'Evie,' said Jack, 'I'd like you to meet Todd.'

Jet-black hair fell into duck-egg blue eyes as the boy wiped a hand on filthy jeans. 'Pleased to meet you,' he said.

Evie held out her hand. 'Pleased to meet you too.' She wondered who he was and what he had to do with Jack.

'How's it going?' Jack asked Todd. 'You look like you're making some headway.'

Evie let them talk about the garden, the old fence panels, a cut-down tree and the remains of an old shed. All of it needed to be cleared. She heard Jack ask Todd discreetly whether he'd eaten. She didn't catch the response, but Jack seemed happy with whatever he'd said because he beckoned to her to follow him inside.

Evie left the view of the neighbourhood around the front of the property. The houses either side of it were well kept, neat hedges bordering their gardens, one with a white picket fence standing at the front, the other with low black railings running in front of the garden bed.

She wondered how long it would be before Jack's house fitted in neatly with the others.

Jack leant in to Evie as they walked up the porch steps. 'I'm afraid it's not much warmer inside. But we can make coffees to warm us up and replace the two we left sitting on the table in the café.'

She blushed all of a sudden, remembering the heat from his hand as it had touched hers to stop her storming off.

She followed him through the front door, the first thing on the property to look new and secure. 'At least now I can see the reason you come out here.' She walked behind him until they reached what must have been a kitchen once upon a time, but now had only a very old, rickety table, a small bar fridge and a cardboard box filled with essentials including teabags, coffee supplies and a tub of sugar. 'It needs a lot of work.' She hesitated and then said, 'I never expected you to want to set foot outside the hustle and bustle of Manhattan, let alone buy a place. Unless you're doing it up to sell?'

'It'd fetch top dollar if I did, especially with the enormous porch out front.' He pulled out the coffee jar and placed it on the table, then filled the kettle at the sink that still stood, just about. The tap groaned when he switched it on, and it spat the water out before the flow improved. 'But it's for me.'

Evie tried not to let her utter surprise show. 'I assumed you'd sell,' she said, almost to herself.

'Exactly,' he said, his voice playful. 'You assumed. You've got a lot to learn about me, Evie.'

She nodded to the offer of coffee, shook her head to the suggestion of sugar and took the cup when he'd filled it. 'It's enormous, this place.'

‘Come, let me show you around. You don’t even need to worry about spills, as I’ve not tackled the floors. In fact, this has been the first week I’ve done anything with the place since I bought it.’

He showed her the laundry room behind the kitchen, then the dining room, another room that he suggested he may use as an office, and finally an enormous living room with a bay window at the front to one side of the porch. The ceiling in this room had damage, but the cornicing was fancy enough that, once painted, would give the room character.

‘That’s a gorgeous fireplace,’ she said. ‘Tell me you’re keeping it.’

He joined her where she was standing looking at the mahogany mantelpiece and surround with tapered columns. It had a tiled insert of sea green and cream tiles, dirty now, and a couple of them chipped, but nothing a good restoration wouldn’t fix.

‘Don’t worry, I’m keeping it. It’s a feature of the room.’ He took a sip of coffee, and when he looked around him, Evie wondered if he was doing as she was and furnishing it in soft cream to blend in with the darker floorboards, hanging chocolate drapes at the windows, a rug in front of the fireplace.

They moved to the wide staircase to take them one floor up, and both avoided the broken step halfway. He showed her no less than five bedrooms, two with ornate fireplaces. The house was so old, and Evie could see opportunity at every turn to make it into something so beautiful, rescue it from its demise.

When she passed the farthest bedroom from the top of the stairs, she noticed a pillow, a sleeping bag and a few blankets. ‘Do you stay here sometimes?’ She nodded to the bedding.

He shook his head as they moved along to the window in the front bedroom. He nodded down to where they could see Todd working away. 'I don't, he does.'

'Who is he?'

'He's Todd.'

Evie adjusted the mug in her hands. 'Yes, and who is Todd? Is he a friend?'

'I suppose you could call him that, yes.'

'Jack, stop being so cagey, would you.'

'Sorry, I was having a bit of fun.' He laughed, but then his face turned serious. 'I came out here a few weeks ago and Todd was a boy I found on the front porch, beneath a dirty old blanket. He was homeless.'

Evie looked at Jack, then at Todd. 'You didn't tell him to go?'

'I did, yes. I yelled at him, scared him half to death apparently, and I would've called the cops if he hadn't left right away.'

'So why didn't you?'

'I thought I'd seen the last of him, and I had, he never came near the place again. But when I thought about it later, I realised I was no different to my father. You see, Evie, my father isn't a bad man, and I still haven't gotten to the bottom of his absolute overreaction that night he fired Nicole, but it doesn't mean I want to follow in his footsteps. The business, my involvement with jewellery, is all for my mother. She was the brains behind the designs in the first place and the reason the business began, but it's never been my passion.'

They both watched Todd, this time dragging the bag of garden debris to the end of the driveway to line up with another before he grabbed the next bag and disappeared down the side of the house, presumably to the back garden.

‘This is as far as I’ve gotten to leaving behind a life that isn’t really me,’ Jack confessed. ‘My father knows I bought a property, but as far as he knows it’s an investment, not a home.’ He shrugged. ‘I see it differently.’

‘And why don’t you tell him?’

‘I will, one day.’

‘So how did you find Todd again?’

‘It wasn’t easy. He’d long since scarpered from this house.’ He told her all about his day looking in the city, at shelters, at local hangouts, the park where he’d eventually spotted the kid. ‘I guess it’s Nicole’s influence that did it. I saw what she’d done by giving you a chance and I began to realise that second chances don’t come along that often for people like …’

‘People like me?’

He hesitated. ‘I don’t mean any offence, Evie.’

She smiled at him, sat down on the windowsill. ‘Is this safe?’

He pulled a face but then laughed. ‘I’ve sat there enough times myself. See, this is the master bedroom so I’ve been planning what to do.’ He pointed to the wall on the left that separated the master from the box room where the sleeping bag was. ‘I’m going to knock that wall through and put in another bathroom. Then I’ll put in another staircase going up to the attic, which will make a nice retreat. It’s nothing now. I can’t even take you to see it, but it’ll be great when I’ve finished. The roof is pointed, characterful. Todd and I have discussed it at length.’

‘You must trust him.’

Jack shrugged. ‘Not really, I don’t know him. But I took a chance, as Nicole did with you. I don’t know how he came to be homeless, I didn’t ask, but instead of telling him to stop sneaking into gardens or hiding out on other people's porches, I thought I'd see if he could prove himself. I needed someone to get clearing this place while I'm at work—there's too much to do for me to only work at it at the weekends, and in return I give him a bed—only an old mattress, granted—and I buy him enough food. I'm paying him a wage too, but I said I'll keep it safely tucked away in the bank for now. He didn't question me on that.'

'I guess the trust works both ways.'

Evie's comment hung between them until she said, 'So this is the reason you come all the way out here, away from the city.'

'There's another reason too.'

'Oh?'

He stood up. 'Finish your coffee and I'll show you.'

Evie couldn't help smiling as she followed him out of the room and back down the stairs.

*

They drove away from New Haven and towards a town called Hazelbrook, and when they turned into Hollyhock Farm, a blond-haired guy who was strapping a Christmas tree to the roof of a family sedan waved over to them.

When the family was good to go, the man came over and introduced himself. He shook Jack's hand and turned to Evie. 'You've brought a friend.'

Evie grinned back at him and extended her hand. 'I'm Evie.' He'd disguised it well, but not well enough, because she detected the note of pleasant surprise and knew then that Jack had already told Nate about her. She hoped that was a good thing.

With nightfall not too far away, they left Nate to finish up with another customer, and Jack led Evie further down the land, to a section filled with bushes.

'What's this?' she asked.

'It's a maze.'

'Really?' She moved to step inside, but he held her back.

'It's not quite ready yet, but it's been an ongoing project of mine.'

Her fingers stretched out to feel the trees, and she kept her hand against them before stepping back and onto the bank of grass behind. Standing on tiptoes, she tried to see inside.

'I'd love to walk through it,' she enthused.

'You can, another time.' Jack smiled at her.

'Did you do all this by yourself?'

He nodded. 'It's been a labour of love and I've enjoyed every minute.'

Evie didn't know what to say, first the house and his kindness with Todd and now this. He was surprising her more and more, but she guessed that had been the point of the visit after she'd judged him and given him a piece of her mind at the coffee shop.

After Jack had talked some more about the process of resurrecting the maze, he said, 'Come on, it's getting dark, but if we go back to the house, I'll show you the photographs of the original maze I was trying to recreate.'

She followed him up to the house, and as the sky darkened, Nate joined them.

'Have you been busy today?' Jack asked his friend once they were ensconced in the warmth of the house. Nate had left one of the local boys down at the shed to help any customers before they closed up at 5 pm.

'It's less than a week to Christmas,' Nate winked at Evie. 'What do you think?'

'Silly question,' Evie chided, although her tone was mocking.

Jack led Evie to the hallway where he showed her the photographs of the original maze. She was warmed by its story, by the task Jack had taken on in the name of friendship.

Their next port of call was the fireplace where Jack lit the firelighters, arranged the logs and kindling and then reached for the bellows to get the first flames going. Evie only just stopped herself giggling. It was like watching a peacock opening its feathers to attract a mate—he was going to great lengths today to prove to her that he was a gentleman, capable, completely different to the image she'd built up in her mind.

Nate, having taken a shower and changed out of his muddy work clothes, came through to join them. 'Evie, can I interest you in a hot chocolate?'

'I would,' Jack recommended. 'Julia only drinks this Belgian stuff, top of the range, ridiculous in its price and calorie content.'

'Then how can I refuse?' Evie watched as the flames grew higher, taking with them the log that would burn long into the evening. She took delight in Jack's childlike face at having got it right.

As Nate went over to the kitchen, Evie excused herself to use the bathroom. When she'd gone over to Jack's condo earlier, she'd never have guessed this was how the day would pan out. Here she was, actually enjoying the man's company, meeting his friends and seeing a different way of life to the one she'd already placed him in. By the time she rejoined the men, a woman in a chocolate-coloured woolly hat was hugging

Jack. Nate shut the door behind her and when Jack let her go, kissed her cheek.

'Evie, this is Julia,' said Jack.

Julia's blonde hair escaped when she tugged off her hat and Evie grinned. 'I do believe we've met.'

'You two know each other?' Jack looked from one woman to the other.

'Julia's a client,' Evie explained.

Nate took out another mug to make Julia a hot chocolate too. 'So you're the one who's had my fiancée so excited about "the dreamiest dress you could possibly imagine"?' He feigned a female accent, did a small pirouette on the spot, completely out of character for his alpha male appearance.

'Guilty,' Evie admitted. To know Jack was a friend of someone as down to earth and genuine as Julia convinced Evie all the more that he was very different to the man she'd assumed he was.

Julia waxed lyrical about Evie's prowess with making wedding gowns and accessories, careful not to let the men know specific details, and when she took over the hot chocolate making in the kitchen, she asked Evie to help her as the men went through to the living room and collapsed into the couches in front of the fire.

'What's going on between you and Jack?' Julia leant in conspiratorially. 'Are you together?'

'No! Not at all. We know each other through a mutual friend.'

'Who?'

'Nicole.'

Julia snapped chocolate into pieces and divided the bits between two awaiting mugs as Evie stirred the pan of milk on the stove. 'She's a lovely lady. How do you know each other?'

'Evie worked with Nicole when she was at the agency,' Jack interrupted. Evie wondered how much of the conversation he'd overheard before he'd sneaked up on them.

'Thank you,' Evie mouthed when Julia's back was turned. Julia seemed to accept the explanation although Evie wondered, given how close Jack was to Nate, how much this woman knew about her past already. But if she knew, she wasn't giving anything away and Evie was grateful.

The hot chocolates were as decadent as Nate and Jack had promised, and Evie sat in the chair closest to the fire as they chatted and laughed and the night fell over Hollyhock Farm, a comforting blanket of a life so different to the one Evie had assumed Jack led. This juxtaposition was filled with integrity, genuine friendships, and in the last seven hours her opinions had made a complete U-turn.

'Both of you must stay for dinner,' Julia insisted. If Evie wasn't mistaken, both she and Nate seemed to be thriving on Jack having company. 'Unless you need to get back to the city.'

'Dinner would be great,' Jack answered.

Evie cleared her throat. 'I'd love to, it's very kind of you to offer.' Tonight was a rare night off from the shelter, and instead of going back to her apartment alone, she felt excited that she got to spend the evening in such great company.

Nate and Julia insisted they didn't need any help when it came to preparing the beef stroganoff and as they chopped, peeled and diced, they left Jack and Evie to talk over a beer each beside the fire.

'They're really nice people,' said Evie.

'Nate's my best friend. He's been with Julia for years, and I can't imagine a couple I like more.'

Evie jumped as the fire crackled and spat out a piece onto the hearth.

'We'd better move away.' Jack laughed.

'You need to stop blowing it with those bellows!' She smiled at him, reminded of the way he'd taken charge today and how she hadn't minded one bit.

The orange glow of the fire highlighted Jack's neck as he tilted his head back to get more of his beer. 'I'd better savour this. You, on the other hand, can get completely wasted and I'll ferry you home.'

'I don't think that'll be necessary, but thank you for the offer.'

'What do you think of it out here at the farm?'

She didn't hesitate. 'It's a different world entirely.' Without thinking she added, 'I hope I get to go through the maze soon.' As soon as she'd spoken, she realised she was implying another visit, but before she had a chance to feel too awkward, Jack put her at ease.

'I'm sure that could be arranged.'

Right now, with the easy conversation, the fire crackling and the enticing smell of dinner snaking towards them, Evie couldn't imagine a happier place.

When dinner was served, they sat around the oak table talking weddings, Christmas trees, holiday markets, jewellery. They chatted away about all the tasks on the farm that Evie had never thought about, they discussed fruit picking and Evie promised to come up here again in the spring. And by the time Jack and Evie drove away from the farm that evening they'd already promised an exchange visit, with dinner in the city in the New Year after the rush of the season had calmed for Nate and Julia.

Driving away from Hollyhock farm, Evie realised these people, friends as they had become after only a few hours, had treated her as an equal, and more frighteningly they'd treated them as a couple.

'They do know we're not dating, don't they?' She looked across at Jack as the car slowed to the town's speed limit when they arrived at one end of the main street of Hazelbrook, the big clock watching over the shops, some of which were lit up with their own arrangement of lights. The place held that small town feel, as though even strangers would be drawn into its embrace.

Jack grinned. 'They know we're friends, yes. Oh, they'll be matchmaking like hell, but let them. It gives them something to do.'

Evie's heart skipped a beat. She'd found Jack attractive at the start, but good looks alone had never been enough for her to fall hook, line and sinker for anyone. Then again, she was beginning to realise Jack Churchill was a whole lot more than the handsome, almost arrogant businessman she'd first met.

'Why are we stopping?'

Jack had pulled up into the forty-five-degree angled car park space in front of a row of shops, the town clock to one side.

'I love this town,' he said, pulling his jacket from the back seat and indicating for her to do the same. 'It feels free. Even the air is different here somehow.' His eyes glistened when he looked at her. 'Let's walk.'

'You're crazy,' she giggled. 'It's so cold!'

With the time close on eleven at night, the temperature had dropped. The pavements twinkled with a frost that ran all the way along to the opposite end of the street, up the side of the clock tower. Evie pulled on her gloves and scarf and they walked along, past a bakery that come morning would most likely have pastries galore, loaves of bread shaped different ways, cut or ready to be sliced however you chose. A liquor store had closed for the night, a flower shop had ruby-red poinsettias in the window along with a Santa on a sleigh pulled by reindeer and filled with more flowers, gorgeous ice pink roses. An archway led to a circular set of wooden benches and they passed beneath it. It too was lit up with lights that had been wound around its entire shape.

Evie sat on a bench and jumped up again.

'Cold?' Jack asked.

'Just a bit. My butt will turn to an ice block if I sit there.'

Jack sat down himself as Evie looked around them, and then he moved along the bench a little and nodded to the space where he'd been. 'I warmed it for you.'

'With your ass?'

His laughter echoed across the empty street. 'Now that you put it like that …'

Evie smiled and sat down anyway. 'Thank you.' She wondered what Lizzy would say if she could see her now. Presumably she'd go on about Jack, how gorgeous he was, how he always came to her rescue. The thought warmed her right through rather than making her want to run for the hills, which was definitely a first.

Jack nodded up towards the moon, tonight a crescent shape, clear-cut and surrounded by a cluster of stars. 'There's something magical about looking at it, don't you think?'

'There is.' Her words sounded small against the night air, the weirdness of the situation.

'When I was a kid it was a real family thing to do, to go out and look at the moon. All four of us would gaze at it for ages, not caring if it was getting cold, or still too warm from a summer's day. We were always there. It was as though by looking at it everything in the world just settled around us, we knew where we were, who we were.'

'And you don't now?'

He looked down at his hands encased in woollen gloves. 'Sometimes I wonder if things could be different.'

'You mean if you left the city behind?'

He turned and looked at her. 'You're very perceptive.'

She looked from him, to the moon, to the stars. 'You're a completely different person out here.'

He let her comment settle before he said, 'My mother had a real passion for astrology, you know.' His breath met the cold air. 'She believed that even when our lives were chaotic, or didn't make any sense, the universe and the stars would see to it that everything worked out in the end.'

'And you don't believe that?'

He shrugged. 'I wish she was right. I wish I had that much faith in the world.'

'I think your mother's way of thinking about the world is nice, but I'm not sure I agree.' Was she speaking out of turn? 'I believe part of the universe and the stars is in us already and so the best person to take charge of your life is you.' She may as well keep going now. 'Only you have the power to change your life, Jack. You need to let go of whatever is preventing you from making changes and instead of trusting in the stars, learn to trust yourself.'

Jack took a deep breath of the winter air. 'You're lucky, you know.'

'Oh, I know. I'm lucky Nicole found me when she did.'

'Is she very angry with me and my father?'

'About The Diamond Touch being after the shelter premises you mean?'

He winced at the clarification.

'You know Nicole,' said Evie. 'She's taking it personally.'

'I'm sure she is.' He hesitated. 'But I didn't mean you were lucky to have found Nicole.'

'Then what did you mean?'

'I was trying to say you're lucky to have the guts, the strength to do something about it when your life took a wrong turn. Guts are something I seriously lack.'

'But why?' She looked across at him. 'The business will run without you, and I might not know your family, but I can imagine if your mother was anything like mine she'd want you to follow your own dreams, whatever they were. You know, Mum and Dad lived the high life before the business went down the pan. They wanted for nothing. Dad in his expensive suits, Mum with pricey make-up, more clothes than Harvey Nicks.' She laughed and then turned serious. 'But I hated that. I didn't want to wear delicate dresses, designer tops. I soon learned to make clothes and that was what made me an individual. It was part of me. It was never part of them, but Mum knew it was *my* way.

'It's hard, damn hard to start again, but it's better than living your whole life running scared or in someone else's vision, someone else's map of what they want you to have, what they want you to be. From what I saw today, you should be proud, and that's what would've made your mother proud, not staying in a business you have no interest or passion for. And I know I'm lucky in so many ways, but I will never forget where I once was. Just because you reinvent yourself and move forward doesn't mean you ever forget where you once were. It's what shapes you into the person you become. You had a different life once, but that doesn't mean you have to pretend it never existed.'

'Do you ever pretend your days on the streets didn't exist?'

She gulped. 'You know, I really don't. I can't. Those days were hellish and a lot of the time I was at rock bottom. But those days were a part of me and who I became.'

He smiled at her. 'Come on, even my ass is freezing now. Let's go home.'

And when they stood and walked back to the car, and the moon hung above them in the sky as though guiding them back towards their everyday lives, Evie felt more stable and settled than she ever had before. Not just because of how she was physically and what she'd achieved, but the way her heart was beginning to open out like a flower, taking in more friendships than she'd realised it was possible to have.

Chapter Nineteen

Jack

'We need to get the deal sewn up before Christmas,' said Braydon, pacing the room now things weren't going his way. 'Then in the New Year it'll be all systems go to start gutting the place, make it into another of The Diamond Touch's finest premises.'

Jack watched his father loosen his shirt collar. He'd had every intention of coming in here today and telling his father everything about how he'd felt over the years since he'd started working at the company. Last night Evie had instilled a sense of confidence in him he'd never known he'd had, and when he woke this morning it was the first time he had truly believed he could change his life. But now, since Braydon had frogmarched him straight to an emergency meeting, the tension was running so high he didn't know what to do for the best.

'I'm sorry,' said Jack to Braydon. 'But why are we in such a rush?' He wanted to take his father aside and tell him what the building was currently used for, how by buying this he'd alienate Nicole, possibly for good this time.

Braydon stopped pacing and fixed his glare on the youngest Churchill. 'The Diamond Touch needs to move forward, the whole reason we looked for premises in the first place. I think we should instruct the lawyers to push the sale through.'

Jack looked to his father, who sighed long and hard.

'Maybe Braydon's right,' Kent conceded. 'Maybe we should get the legalities sewn up and we can all move forward with the next phase.'

'Dad, there's something you should know first.' Jack cleared his throat, but before he had a chance to say anything else, he heard voices down the corridor, increasing in volume until the door to the office burst open and in marched Nicole.

Kent stood. 'Nicole? What's going on?'

'I need to talk to you.' She didn't acknowledge Jack or Braydon.

'Let's go to my office.' Kent moved past the table, but Nicole's feet were firmly glued to the floor.

'No need. I'll say what I've got to say and then I'll leave.'

Kent sat down again. Jack attempted a smile of acknowledgment to Nicole, but she was focused on the purpose of her visit.

'If this is personal,' Braydon whispered to Kent, 'I'll leave you to it.' He moved to leave, but stopped as soon as Nicole began yelling at Kent.

'How dare you! How dare you take away the shelter from us!'

Kent looked bemused. 'I'm not sure I follow.'

'The building you've been sniffing around. I don't suppose you've bothered to think about who you'll be affecting!'

'Now wait a minute. What has the building got to do with you?'

'I volunteer there. Have done for years. And now everything we've worked for will be taken away just like that, just so you can dazzle the city with the finest jewellery, add some more zeroes to your bank account.'

Braydon shut the door to the office and stayed to hear more.

'You took my job once before,' she shouted, 'and now you're determined to take my life again!'

'I'm not trying to do anything of the sort.' His father's voice was softer than it'd ever been during a confrontation of this magnitude. 'I heard something about it being used as a shelter, an overspill from the city shelters in the daytime, but I had no idea you were involved.'

'Well, I am. And those people need another place to go. Do you know how many homeless people there are in New York City?'

She'd asked the same question to Jack once, and he cringed when Braydon grunted as though he spoke for all of them with his inability to care.

Nicole took Kent's silence as his answer. 'No, I don't suppose you do. You're up here in a cosy office, going home to that big house you have all to yourself, and you wouldn't give two hoots about anyone in need.'

'Nicole, that's simply not true.'

'Come on, then, let's hear about your concern for other people, the charitable work you do to make a difference.'

'Hang on a minute.' Kent stood, hands on hips.

'Dad … take it easy.' Jack motioned for him to sit down. The last thing they wanted was for his blood pressure to skyrocket and land him back in the hospital.

'I object to you talking to me like this,' Kent argued, his anger mounting. 'I'd be happy to talk about this rationally, but I won't be yelled at in my office.'

Nicole and Kent stared at one another, and Jack wondered which of them was going to pounce first.

Eventually Nicole's shoulders dropped and she pulled out a chair. 'May I?'

Kent held out his hand and gestured for her to sit. Without looking away from Nicole, he said, 'If you could excuse us please, Jack, Braydon. I'd like to talk to Nicole alone.'

Braydon showed no signs of shifting until Jack took the lead.

Shutting the door behind him, Jack knew that at least one thing he'd wanted to talk to his father about had been taken out of his hands.

'Do you think your old man is going to let her keep her precious building?' Braydon asked.

Jack rolled his eyes and walked away, calling over his shoulder, 'No idea.' What he really wanted to add was that he didn't care about some stupid building. He didn't actually give a damn about anything much to do with this company right now.

Kent

'I'm sorry. It wasn't professional of me to barge in on you like this.' Nicole's corkscrew curls were pinned back in an updo that certainly gave her a business edge. Deep brown eyes looked at him for the answers she wanted to hear.

Kent rested his elbows on the table, fingers steepled in front of him, fingertips resting against his lips. 'You know, once upon a time,' he began, 'I had the edge. I was a businessman with no margin for error. No corners were cut, not until now. I'd have known exactly who had the lease on that building. And I wouldn't have cared. It wouldn't have caused me anything more than a fleeting concern that my plans could be delayed.'

'And what about now?' she asked.

'Like I said, I'm losing my touch, my hunger for success. The heart attack scared me to death, the thought of leaving Jack to pick up the pieces.'

'He doesn't deserve that.'

'No, he most certainly does not.' When Nicole reached out and touched a hand to his arm, his bicep tensed beneath his shirt. The feel of her touch was like a hug that brought him home.

He shook away the feeling, the feeling he couldn't allow to grow, and sat back in his chair so the distance between them was marginally bigger. 'Tell me about the shelter,' he said.

'I started volunteering after I finished working at the house.' She didn't meet his gaze yet. 'I needed something to occupy my time, but I had plenty of money since I inherited a hefty sum when my godmother died the year before.'

'I remember when it happened,' said Kent. She'd confided in him about the loss of her godmother, but not about her inheritance because she'd wanted to keep working with the Churchills even though there was absolutely no need.

'I didn't need to generate an income,' she continued, 'and when I saw the ad for people to help out, everything fell into place. I like to help people. It's why I became a housekeeper, but this was so much more.'

'So much more than working for snooty rich people,' he finished for her, and when she looked about to protest he held up a hand. 'I'm not offended.'

'Meeting Evie affected me deeply, Kent. And it's good of you and Jack to worry about me, but our relationship is deeper than you could ever know. She's like family to me and the help isn't all one-sided. I know that if I ever needed her, she'd be there in a heartbeat and vice versa. Don't you think everyone deserves somebody like that in their life?'

He held her gaze but avoided the question by asking one of his own. 'Tell me about some of the other people you met at the shelter.'

'Do you really want to know?'

'I asked, didn't I?' He'd probably surprised himself much more than her.

Nicole took off her coat, put her bag down on the floor beside her, and over coffee and cookies that Kent requested Penny bring in, Kent got to know the shelter and its regular residents, but more than that, he got to know Nicole all over again. They talked about the other shelters in the city, how Nicole saw her shelter taking the overspill and offering something extra, and by the time they'd finished talking, Kent had no doubt in his mind about what he wanted to do. She'd said it herself when she'd arrived and accused him of not thinking about anyone outside his immediate cushy world, and it was true. It hadn't always been that way, but since Cynthia died and Jack had pulled away from him, he'd never felt so empty.

'Perhaps we can work together on this, Nicole.' Without any further explanation, he finished his cup of coffee—decaf on doctor's orders—and pulled open the door to the meeting room to ask Penny to let Jack and Braydon know they should come back in.

'I'll go.' Nicole lifted her bag. 'I don't much like your colleague, I'm afraid, and I'm sure the feeling is mutual.'

Kent put a hand on her arm. 'Sit, please. You need to hear what I have to say. And so does Braydon.' He leant closer. 'And I don't like him much either,' he whispered as the man in question re-entered the room. He returned her relieved smile.

'What's going on?' Braydon demanded.

'Sit,' Kent instructed. 'Let's wait for Jack and then we'll start.' He didn't miss Braydon scrutinising Nicole, but this wouldn't take long. He knew how Braydon would react, but right now he was past the point of caring. It was time he got his priorities straight.

Jack came in and shut the door behind him. He winked at Nicole. 'I see you've been treated to the finest cookies we have.' He noted the gold tubular tin of Fortnum's Chocolossus biscuits.

'All right, let's get started.' Kent took charge and stood at the head of the room as though chairing an official meeting. The only difference was he had no visuals to back up his presentation and Nicole was sitting five feet away from him. He started with a spiel about The Diamond Touch's need to expand, the benefits of opening another premises, and for a while Braydon looked pretty smug, as though he knew exactly where this was heading.

'It has come to my attention,' said Kent, 'that The Diamond Touch opening up in the intended premises could hurt the company rather than build it up.'

'What?' Braydon was out of his seat.

'Sit, please.' Kent's voice didn't invite argument. 'I feel that in light of what I now know, we would be doing the city a great disservice by taking away a resource relied on by many. What I propose is—'

'This is bullshit!' A line of sweat streaked across Braydon's top lip. 'The public want the shelter shut down. There's a petition to get rid of it!'

Kent ignored the protest. 'I propose we back the shelter. I propose we lease the building with our company money—my company money,' he directed at Braydon. 'Plenty of major companies make similar moves. As yet, our business hasn't done anything to fundraise for those in need, and it shames me to admit it. I'm a New Yorker, always have been, and perhaps it's high time we gave something back.' He looked to Jack, then Nicole. 'Are we all on board?'

Nicole's eyes filled with tears. 'So we can operate as usual, for the foreseeable future?'

Kent nodded, surprised at the buzz he felt. 'You can keep going as you are, yes. And you'll have the financial backing from The Diamond Touch.' He turned to Jack. 'Son? Are you happy with all of this?' He wasn't sure. Had he done the wrong thing, again?

Jack shook his head and puffed out his cheeks before he spoke. 'Dad … I am so on board with this.' He stood up, came over to his father, shook his hand and with the other patted his shoulder. 'This makes The Diamond Touch a company I'm proud to be a part of. And Mom would be proud too.'

Kent felt his eyes glisten with tears. 'Thanks, son.' He looked at Braydon now. 'And I'm not saying no to expansion. All I'm suggesting is that we put a hold on the development. In the New Year, we'll keep a look out for alternative premises.'

Braydon was leaning against the back of a chair, now unable to look at any of them. 'This is fucking bullshit,' he spat. 'Of all the ludicrous, hare-brained, stupid schemes …'

'I'm sorry you feel that way, Braydon.' Kent pulled off the top of the tin of Fortnum's biscuits and offered them around.

'You've lost your edge!' Braydon hollered. 'You're a fucking pushover.'

Kent bit into a cookie, enjoying taking a stand with his own business, something he should've done before today.

'I expected more from you,' Braydon hissed.

Kent looked at him, held his stare. 'Watch it, okay. I'm still the boss.'

Braydon went to leave the room but stopped and turned back. 'You're a joke, Kent Churchill.'

'Now hang on—' Jack moved forward, but Kent stopped him.

Braydon pressed on and directed his ferocity at Kent. 'And how can you even consider helping the homeless after what they did to your family?' He pointed to Nicole. 'She's no better than that slut, Evie.'

'Enough, Braydon.' Kent rose to his feet. 'I won't tolerate you talking like that in my office.'

'Your own wife died at the hands of a homeless person.' Braydon's voice silenced everyone in the room. 'And here you are supporting them.'

'Get out!' Kent roared. 'Get your things, and get out!'

'Don't worry, I'm gone. I'm tired of keeping your secret.'

Kent launched at him before he could get out of the door or utter another word. He punched him squarely in the jaw, sending him stumbling back. Jack pinned his father's arms behind him, Nicole stood with her hand across her mouth.

Braydon spat in Nicole's direction and Kent went for him again. This time Jack let him punch him twice, once in the stomach, another across the eye, before he held him back again.

Braydon scrambled to his feet and didn't say another word. He'd already said enough and when Kent turned,

Nicole and Jack were looking at him, searching for answers he knew he'd finally have to give.

Chapter Twenty

Evie

Evie finished backstitching the seam of a gold flower girl dress. 'There, what do you think?' She held it up for Bonnie's inspection.

'I think the little girl will love it.' Bonnie smiled at Evie's handiwork. 'I see you made a matching drawstring purse too.'

'I thought she could keep a tissue in there, some lipstick if she's allowed.' She took the dress over to the rack to hang it with the two matching dresses for the older bridesmaids in the wedding party. 'You know what little girls are like.'

'We have a new commission already for the New Year,' Bonnie announced. 'The family saw our feature in the magazine.'

'Well, I'm impressed.' Evie took the pins from her pincushion wristband and dropped them into the tub on the table before screwing on the lid and returning it to the drawer in the sideboard.

'Evie, I'd like you to take the lead when they come to see us in January.'

'Sure, I'm happy to look after them.'

Bonnie stopped her before she could drop the strewn threads into the bin at the side of the room, the reel of thread into the drawer beside the pins. 'No, I want you to manage this one. I want you to take it from discussion to design.'

'Oh.' Evie leant against the table. 'I'm not sure I'm ready. I—'

'Nonsense. You're more than ready. I've seen the sketching you do after talking with brides and bridesmaids, and your vision for what they want is never far off. Sure, I'm the one who draws up the formal designs and patterns, but it's nothing you're not capable of. Relax.' She smiled. 'I'll oversee it without interfering unless you're completely off the mark.'

'Thank you, Bonnie. You don't know what this means to me.'

Bonnie put a hand on Evie's shoulder. 'I do and I'm happy to give you the chance to prove yourself. Granted, when Nicole brought you along the first day, I was doing her a very big favour, but that's no longer the case. You've earned this with your natural ability, a talent that can't be taught.'

Evie gulped at the high praise. 'I won't let you down.' She brimmed with delight, barely able to think about the wait between now and mid-January when she could meet the bride and put her dreams onto paper and into fabric.

'Right, time for a break.' Bonnie pinned white tulle together around the mannequin she was using so it couldn't slip off. 'Coffee? I'm parched.'

'Let me make them,' Evie insisted, and as Bonnie went to get the post that had dropped through the letterbox onto the mat, Evie whistled her way through to the kitchen. She wanted to explain to Jack what it felt like to do a job you were so enraptured by that every day you appreciated being there. It wasn't that every day was without stress or problems, but rather the hassles you faced were always worth it in the end. He needed a job where he felt that.

She took out two lilac and cream mugs and reached for the coffee pot.

'What's this?' Bonnie asked from behind her.

Evie turned as she poured the second mug of coffee. 'What's what?' When she saw the photographs Bonnie was holding in her hands, she yelped. She'd missed the cup entirely and instead poured the scalding hot liquid across her hand. Staring at the photograph on top, it was as though the naked Evie in that picture was laughing back at her: silly little Evie, thinking she could have a job, an apartment, make a fresh start. What a silly girl.

'I think you've got some explaining to do, young lady.' Bonnie dropped the photographs onto the table.

Chapter Twenty-One
Kent

'What's going on?' Jack demanded. 'What the hell was Braydon talking about? What does he know that I don't?'

Nicole sat stunned, and Kent knew she'd sewn together the pieces for herself. When she stood and made for the door, he blocked it. 'Don't leave.'

'I think we both know I need to.'

'No,' he said adamantly. 'This is coming out, once and for all, and you both need to be here. It's been kept quiet for long enough.'

Her pleading eyes almost saw him relent, but he had to go through with this now.

'Jack, please sit down. Both of you. I want you to promise you'll stay here in this room until I've finished everything I have to say.'

He didn't wait for confirmation but popped his head around the door and checked that Braydon had left. He'd deal with those ramifications later. Right now he cared about his family first and foremost. He told Penny under no circumstances were they to be disturbed.

'I'm trying to put two and two together, Dad,' said Jack, pacing the floor, 'but I keep coming up with nothing.'

Kent sat in the chair nearest the door, almost as though he didn't trust either of them not to run off.

'When your mother died, I wanted to protect you, Jack. It's what a father does. I never wanted you hurt. You'd been through so much.' He clasped his hands together, the skin white around his knuckles with the tension. 'I lied to you about how your mother died.' He looked at Jack, then away again. 'Your mother was stabbed, killed on the street, outside the first shop we set up together.'

Jack's whole body stiffened.

'You'd been through a lot. I wanted to protect you.'

'But she was dead. How was it protecting me to not know how she died?' His voice was laced with bewilderment. 'I don't understand any of this.'

Kent looked at Nicole who refused to meet his gaze. He still wasn't convinced she wouldn't bolt.

'Do you remember the night she died?' Kent asked Jack. Although he had hoped this moment would never come, over the years he had thought about the words he'd choose if he ever had to tell his son the truth.

'Of course I do. We'd been at the game, and what was one of the best nights of my life turned into the worst.'

Kent nodded. 'That's right.' And he watched Jack's face as realisation suddenly dawned.

'Oh God, *you* always closed the shop, always. We never let Mom do it because you said it wasn't safe, but I'd begged you and begged you to take me to that game.'

Kent had always known this would be impossible for Jack to comprehend.

Jack paled. 'She insisted she could close up herself late at night. That's when it happened, isn't it?'

Kent nodded. 'A couple of homeless guys leapt on her as soon as she left the shop. They wanted her jewellery—her wedding ring, engagement ring, the watch I'd had made for her birthday. She'd given them everything. She wasn't stupid, your mother. She knew everything could be replaced, everything except her life.'

‘So why did they hurt her if she gave them everything?’

‘They panicked. Maybe they thought she’d chase them, identify them to the police. All it took was one stab wound, and it was fatal. She bled to death outside the shop that night and Braydon took the call from the police. He’s known ever since then.’

Jack sat back in his chair, scraped his fingers through his hair. ‘If we hadn’t gone to the game, if I hadn’t been so spoiled and gotten my own way, if I’d—’

‘No,’ Kent told him, his voice firm as pain bore down on his son. ‘You will not blame yourself. This was not your fault, none of it. I don’t ever want to hear you imply that it was.’

‘Yeah, so whose fault was it then?’

A small voice from across the room cut through the silence. ‘Mine,’ said Nicole.

Jack shifted his focus from his father to Nicole. ‘What? We didn’t even know you back then. How can any of this possibly be your fault?’

Kent and Nicole exchanged glances, and Jack looked from one to the other.

‘Because,’ said Nicole, ‘I gave birth to the boy who killed your mother. So if anyone is to blame, it’s me.’

Chapter Twenty-Two

Evie

'How's the hand?' After she'd spilt the coffee, Bonnie had leapt forward and turned the cold tap on, thrusting Evie's skin beneath it before the burn settled. And then she'd given her an ice pack wrapped in a tea towel, which by now had started to warm through in the heat of the kitchen.

'It's fine, which is more than can be said for my pride.' Evie gestured to the photographs now turned face down on the table. It'd been harder to tell Bonnie the truth than Lizzy, or Jack. Nicole and Bonnie both trusted her, and Evie had lived in constant fear of revealing her true self; she'd been petrified of how anyone close to her would react. She felt it was a level of betrayal to keep this from them, but when the truth had poured out, Bonnie had locked up the front entrance and they'd hidden out in the kitchen as Evie told her the whole sorry story: everything from her teenage years, to caring for her mother and her father disappearing, to the reappearance of Uncle Brett in her life.

'I don't understand what he has to gain by publishing those pictures of you.' Bonnie shook her head. 'He'll ruin your reputation, but there's nothing much in that for him.'

'Except he gains the upper hand,' said Evie glumly.

'And he could ruin my business in the process.'

'I'm so sorry, Bonnie. I always thought I'd leave, run to New York and that would be the end of it. I never thought he'd pursue me like this.'

Bonnie looked into the space between Evie and the kitchen door. 'All those expos, all that media coverage. If he wants to, he could ruin everything.'

'I'm so sorry.' Evie exhaled. 'I threatened to go to the police once, but I was so scared, I didn't dare. All I wanted to do was make a go of things on my own, away from him. And now, all I want is to keep everything I've found, everything I've worked for.' She felt tears threaten again and bit down on her lip.

Bonnie handed her a tissue. 'I'm sorry, Evie. I'm not angry at you.'

'You're not?'

'How could I be?' She tilted her head to one side, understanding. 'You were a child when this all started, and that man is a predator. No child deserves to live in fear as you did. Uncle or not, he should be punished.'

'I don't want to go to the police now.'

'Why? I'll vouch for you.'

'Don't you see?' Tears fell freely down her cheeks. 'If I shop his own brother, no matter what he has done, Dad will never come home. I'll never know why he left me. I wasn't good enough then for him to stay, so ruining his brother's life will only push him further away.'

'Oh, Evie.' Bonnie's hand covered hers. 'If he's the sort of father worth having, he'd do everything in his power to support you.'

'So why did he leave me? I look at Jack Churchill and he doesn't get on with his father, but they're there for each other. His father has kept a business going so Jack has a future. Jack was by his father's side when he had a heart scare. Whatever has happened in their lives, their family has stuck together. What do I have to do to have the same in my life?'

Evie fell against Bonnie, and Bonnie let her cry on her shoulder. She soothed her with her words. 'You've done nothing wrong, you hear me? Nothing.'

After Evie's tears subsided, Bonnie said, 'I understand why you did it.' She took out a block of chocolate from the kitchen cabinet, winking at Evie as she passed her a few squares. 'You were fighting for survival in the only way you saw how. What I don't understand is why you didn't tell me. We're friends now, more than employer and employee.'

'When my uncle threatened to put the images onto social media, I knew his goal. It was to embarrass me, and anyone who'd ever helped me get out of the life he had for me in Connecticut. He would've made sure your reputation was tarnished for taking on a street girl, someone who made her money taking her clothes off. Who wants to be featured in a bridal couture magazine in a dress designed by a girl off the streets, a glamour model who bared all? And bringing any disrepute to you and The Perfect Fit Couture was more than I could bear. Without this chance you gave me, I don't know where I would've ended up. In this business, reputation is everything.'

'Oh, Evie.' Bonnie shook her head, but she didn't deny Evie was right. She'd taken years to build up a reputation, and the thought of losing it in an instant couldn't be thrilling at all.

'I didn't ever want Nicole to know either. She gave me a chance when she found me living on the streets and I didn't want to lose her respect. There are certain things you do and certain things you don't do in society, and taking your clothes off isn't something I see many people approving of.'

'Listen, take the afternoon off, Evie. Go to Nicole's, tell her everything.'

Evie shook her head.

'It's not a request, it's an order. It's time you were honest with her, and if I know Nicole, which I think I do, she'll admire you for that, never mind anything else.'

Evie collected her coat and her bag, and knowing what she had to do, emerged into the crisp autumn air on the New York City streets, wondering whether she was taking the final steps in her existing life and whether if, in a few hours' time, she'd still be able to hold her head high in this new version of herself.

She was so consumed with her thoughts she didn't notice the man stepping out of the shadows as she arrived at Nicole's apartment building; the man who slipped into the elevator as Evie laughed with Reggie the doorman when Mrs Aberman's poodle pooped in the foyer; the man who grabbed her the second the elevator doors closed, covered her mouth to stop her screams.

Chapter Twenty-Three

Jack

'Your son killed my mother.' Jack said it over and over again wondering whether, if he said it enough times, someone would laugh and they'd all realise it was a joke. But it didn't happen that way.

'Let me get this straight.' Jack looked at Kent, then Nicole, then back again. 'You've known about this all along, and yet you *hired* her and had her work in our house every day for years, knowing the truth.'

'Jack, I—'

'No, Dad. Don't you see how incomprehensible that is to me? Not telling me the truth, I can take. But letting me get close to her!' He couldn't look at Nicole now, not anymore. 'Why would you ever do that?'

Kent

'I owe both of you an explanation,' Kent began, eyes begging Jack to give him a chance. 'When Cynthia was killed, I lost interest in everything apart from the business and the minute details of her death. I hoarded newspaper reports, I read everything over and over again, hoping somewhere along the line I'd find a sort of peace. I wanted to know about him, the boy who'd taken her away from me and changed my life.' He looked at Nicole now, and her red-rimmed eyes looked up from the tissue she'd pulled apart with her hands. 'So I searched more and found out everything I could. I found out about Noah.'

Nicole gasped and shot up from her chair. Kent stopped her at the door. 'Please, Nicole.' Reluctantly she sat down.

'I found out about Noah and his mother, Nicole.' He looked at the woman in question. 'I discovered they'd struggled as a single parent family until one day Noah Capra ran away from home after an argument.'

Nicole sniffed, stared out the window as she spoke. 'I remember it. He wouldn't put out the trashcans at the kerb, and I made a stand, saying he was old enough to pull his weight. God, it was so ridiculous, but we'd been fighting for a long time. He was in trouble at school, struggling with the homework and I didn't see his unhappiness. I didn't know how low he felt.'

Jack stayed silent throughout and Kent knew he had to continue. They weren't leaving this room until he'd said everything, and he knew he wouldn't breathe properly until this was done.

'I read about the gang Noah had become involved in,' said Kent, 'and I read about how his mother had spent every last cent she had, trying to find him and bring him home.'

Nicole's tears fell, along with a guttural groan that spoke of the pain she'd been in for so long.

Still Kent pressed on. 'I found out that after Noah and his friends, or the gang, whatever you'd like to call them, had robbed and killed Cynthia, the boy had written a note confessing everything to his mother.'

Nicole's sobs filled the room, and Jack's eyes swam with tears.

'Noah wrote how sorry he was,' Kent told Jack. 'He wrote to his mother to tell her it wasn't her fault, none of it was, that he couldn't live with what he'd done. Noah killed himself that summer.'

Jack's head shot up. He looked first at Kent, then across at Nicole. He rammed the heels of his hands into his eye sockets, pushing away tears.

'I don't understand why you had me in your house, your life,' Nicole said, bewildered, dazed almost. She'd spent the last ten minutes crying, crying for the son she'd lost, crying out with confusion at what Kent was telling her. 'This all sounds like some kind of sick joke.'

'It wasn't like that at all.'

'Yeah, then what was it like, Dad?' Jack's anger was in danger of boiling over. There were two people in this room who needed to know everything, but the story had to start from the beginning.

'I was grieving for Cynthia, and at first I wanted to find out as much as I could about the person who'd killed her. It was my way of dealing with it, I guess. But then, the more I delved, the more I wanted to know. I wanted answers, damn it. So I found out where Nicole was working, the agency she was with, and I arranged to interview her as a housekeeper. I had no intention of hiring her. I wanted to see the woman who'd borne the son who turned into a killer.' He heard Nicole gasp, but she didn't move. 'And the woman I met that day, the woman I fully intended to tell exactly what I thought of the boy she'd brought into the world, turned out to be more normal than I'd ever expected.'

He pulled a hand through his hair. 'I hated you, on paper, on the computer screen,' he directed to Nicole, 'and I hated what your son had done. I hated that he wasn't around to pay for it anymore, to be brought to justice. But when you sat there that day, hands clasped in your lap, talking away with a sense of pride for your work, vulnerable and alone just like I was, I saw another side. I saw another victim of the crime, a woman who'd had her entire world pulled out from under her, just like me. And I saw a woman who was no more to blame for what happened than I was.'

'I don't understand how you kept all of it quiet,' said Jack. 'How could you keep the secret so long?'

'It was one of those things where it had gone on for so long that it was easier to keep up with the lie than tell the truth. The fact of the matter was I enjoyed Nicole's company. I'd been lonely, so focused on getting answers that would never have taken away the pain, that I'd shut myself off. I even distanced myself from you, Jack, as much as anyone else. And I'll never stop regretting that.'

'All you cared about was your work,' said Jack, unable to meet his father's gaze.

'It must have seemed that way, but deep down it never was, I promise you.'

Jack nodded.

Kent turned to Nicole now. 'Do you understand why I did what I did?'

Tears in her eyes she looked back at him. 'Noah wasn't all bad, you know.' Kent reached out and touched her shoulder and she covered his hand with her own. 'He was such a gentle child. When he was eight years old, he brought home a kitten he'd found on the street. The poor thing had been hit by a car or a bike; its foot was all squished and Noah had gone to the nearest store, asked for a box and he'd lined it with his school sweater to wrap the cat in and keep it warm. He was distraught, made me call a vet to take a look at him. We took care of him. Noah made Missing Cat posters he plastered all around the city even though he wasn't supposed to, leaflets to drop through people's doors. He told me, "Mom, this cat has a home, it must come from somewhere. And I have to help him find his way back."

'Four days later, the couple who owned the cat turned up and took him home. Noah put on a brave face and said goodbye, but he was devastated, I could tell. He was kind, caring, considerate.' Her voice faltered. 'But he lost his way.'

Tears flowed freely down her cheeks now. 'I should've done more. I should've found him, nurtured him back to the boy he once was, shown him the way. It was my job,' she cried, 'as a mother. And I failed him!'

'I need to get out of here.' Jack held up his hands to tell his father to back off when he tried to reach out for him. 'I need to leave here, now. I can't do this.'

'Jack, wait!' Kent called after him but let him go, let him storm from the office. This was a lot to take in, far too much, and Jack needed to cool off before he'd listen to reason. If he ever would.

Kent knelt down in front of Nicole, holding her hands as she sobbed.

'Is this why you told Evie to get away, when she showed up on your property that night?' Nicole asked now.

Kent sighed, pushed himself to standing and pulled over a chair opposite. 'I hated you as much as I hated Noah, until that day you came to the house,' Kent explained. 'But from that day, you became a friend, the closest one I'd ever had, as it turned out. I didn't plan it that way, not at all, but you slotted right in to our lives, and with every day that passed, it became harder and harder to tell you who I was. I'd long since hidden away all the photographs of Cynthia—something Jack despised and which didn't help our relationship—because they were too painful. Who knows, if I hadn't hired you, maybe I would've put them on display again. But I knew I couldn't risk you finding out who I really was. I knew it would scare you, it would break the friendship, and your friendship was something I found myself clinging onto almost as soon as I'd found it.

'The night I saw Evie outside my property and realised you were helping her, two things happened. All I could see was a homeless person just like the figure who'd killed my wife. She was of the same mould and I wanted her gone.'

'You said two things happened.'

Kent hesitated. Despite the winter outside, the heat in the office was working overtime and he removed his cufflinks, dropped them in his breast pocket and rolled up his shirtsleeves. 'You'd been with us for thirteen years, a lifetime, and the other thing that happened to me that night when I found you with Evie was that the fear inside me that you could be snatched away reared its ugly head. I realised how scared I was of ever losing you, like I lost Cynthia.'

Nicole's hand reached out and covered his forearm and he stared down at it. All the years she'd been in the house their skin had never been so close, their minds had never intertwined as they were now. 'You were always a good man to me, a real friend.'

Kent stood up, faced the wall. 'That's just it, you see. I realised I wanted to be more than a friend. I was falling in love with you and that night I realised just how much. It felt like the ultimate betrayal. Falling in love with the mother of your wife's killer. It's the stuff of chat shows! It's almost laughable. And the guilt I felt. I hadn't breathed a word of the truth to Jack over the years. I wanted to protect him from the cruel world and what had really happened. How could I ever explain my feelings to him?'

Nicole didn't say anything, but he heard her get up and walk over to him. He felt her by his side, where she'd been for thirteen years without realising it.

'You think I'm some kind of sick bastard, don't you?' He still didn't look at her. Her body was inches away from his own.

'No, I don't.' Her voice conveyed her understanding, her relief. 'Oh, but I wish you'd told me all of this.'

'You'd have run a mile.'

'You're right.' She sighed. 'Kent, please look at me.'

He turned slowly. 'Are you telling me we could've ever been together, knowing my wife died at the hands of your son? Are you telling me it wouldn't have driven an impossible wedge between us?'

Nicole reached a hand up to his cheek, brushed her fingers slowly down towards his mouth, grazing the faint stubble that couldn't yet be seen unless she took a step closer. 'Is that why you fired me? Because the situation was impossible?'

His hand covered hers. 'I was scared. Scared of what would happen when you knew the truth, frightened of how Jack would change his view of you. And I could never have told you I loved you without explaining who you were, who we were. That would've magnified the lie, and I couldn't have lived with it. A lie like that is no way to start a relationship. But I'm so sorry I did that to you.'

'I left New York, you know. When it happened, when Noah … I went to Sicily, travelled around. I was trying to make sense of everything, or at least something. I wanted to get away from the news, the horrible things that go on in a big city. It was a couple of years until I felt ready to return to New York, and that was when I found work with a housekeeping agency and found you.'

She put her hand against his chest and his heart beat beneath her palm. 'I always knew there was more to you than you revealed. I knew you had something you were keeping from me, from Jackson. I knew you had an inner kindness that most people never saw, but the night Evie showed up you were like a different person entirely. I think if you hadn't fired me, I'd have had to walk away anyway. I couldn't be with a man who didn't believe in second chances, with a man who didn't believe in the greater good.'

He reached out and hooked a corkscrew curl behind her ear, looked deep into chestnut eyes he'd missed since she'd stopped coming to the house every day. 'Do you believe in second chances?'

Nicole leant her head against his chest, her arms snaking around his waist. 'I do now,' she said.

Chapter Twenty-Four

Jack

At Hollyhock Farm, the rain came down harder. Any snow on the ground had turned to slush as Jack wacked nails into the wooden structure that would become a pay booth for the maze when it was up and running for the public.

'Jack, get inside!' Nate hollered. 'Leave that till tomorrow, you've done enough!'

He didn't look at his friend. After the showdown with Nicole and Kent at the office, he'd driven out to the farm and without explanation had started work. Nate had found him, hammer in hand, nails at the ready and hadn't asked him anything, until now.

'Jack, what the hell is going on?' Nate cowered beneath the tiny pointed roof of the shed, trying to stay dry.

Jack didn't care how wet he was getting, and without looking at Nate, he said, 'Mom didn't have anything wrong with her heart. She was murdered.' He attacked the wood with another nail. 'Oh, and by the way, it was Nicole's son who murdered her.'

Put like that, he had the upper hand. His friend was too shocked to ask questions. Jack was too confused to answer any. They simply stood there, side by side, getting soaked through, a hammer each, banging in the rest of the nails to secure the front panel.

An hour later, Jack left the farm and returned to Manhattan. The only sounds filling the car were the slicing of dirt and slush on the roads as his wheels cut through them, and instead of going home he ventured to his father's townhouse, the home his mother had lived in, the home she'd brought him to as a baby, the four walls where they'd harboured her killer's mother for thirteen years.

There was a rare space to park out front and Jack left the car, plodded up the front steps, and before he could knock, the door opened. Kent stood behind it, no sign of the housekeeper, old or new.

'You're soaked.' Kent waited for Jack to slip his shoes from his feet. 'There are spare clothes upstairs in your old room. You must've left them here once before, some sweatpants, an old hoodie. You'll find fresh towels in the linen cupboard. Take a shower, warm up, then we'll meet down here and we'll talk.'

For once, Jack did as he was told without challenge, without comeback. He took the stairs one at a time towards his old room, passing by the smaller room that had once been the nursery for Cameron, then for him, but now housed folders and paperwork to do with the business, the overspill from the office.

After he'd showered and pulled on the dry clothes, Jack returned downstairs and into the living room where his father was tending to the fire with a poker. He added one more log, and as the flames licked around it and he saw Jack, he said, 'Scotch?'

'Neat,' Jack confirmed.

Kent took the lid from the crystal decanter and poured two measures, handing one glass to Jack. Whatever health measures his father was on, tonight they could be forgotten. Both of them needed this.

'I'm trying to work this all out in my mind.' Jack looked into the deep-golden liquid.

'I know this has all come as a shock, but I didn't intend to hire Nicole. I—'

'No, not just with hiring Nicole, but ever since Mom died. What the hell has been going on with us?'

Neither of them spoke for a while.

'Dad, I've been working my ass off in this business Mom started, the legacy she left, and you've been doing the same. But it feels as though we pull in different directions. You're able to focus completely on work, see the bigger picture, but I'm not sure I ever could or ever will. I want out, Dad.'

Kent looked up at him, his hand stilled on his glass.

'That's right. It's taken me years to say it, but today, the day of truths, I can't wait any longer. I can't wait for you to tell me why you brought a relative of my mother's killer into our house. I don't need to know right now why you lied to me and couldn't trust me with the truth. All I want is to be free. I want my life, a life that I choose for myself.'

Kent knocked back his Scotch in one. 'I had no idea you felt that way, son.' The leather couch groaned when he sat down. 'Why didn't you say anything?'

'Because all these years, I've wanted to make you proud. I wanted to make Mom proud. And I know that sounds stupid when she isn't here anymore, but she didn't get to see me graduate high school, she wasn't there to watch me go off to college, she's never welcomed a girlfriend into her home, she won't ever see the man I've become. And working my butt off in the business always made me feel as though I could hold onto the last pieces of her, that I hadn't let her go.'

Kent's hand scratched across the stubble on his chin. 'What a mess I've made of everything.'

'It's not only your fault. I could've spoken up.'

‘I doubt I would’ve listened.’

Jack smiled ruefully.

‘Your mother had a real passion for jewellery making and I wanted to give her the world, so I turned her designs into reality. We built a multi-million dollar company on the back of that dream. But you know, a few weeks before she died, she’d had the flu and been cooped up in bed all day for over a week.’ He sat down next to his son. ‘I’d looked after her the best I could even though I’d been flying across the country to meet buyers, build the business even further. Anyway, one day after I’d returned from Seattle, I sat on the edge of her bed, insisting she sipped from a glass of water and keep her fluids up. She’d told me that lying there all week, she’d had a chance to think about the life we led. She said how thankful she was to be so lucky as to have me, to have you and Cameron, to never have to worry about where the next dollar was coming from.

‘But then she told me that being married to me was like being married to two different people. There was the husband who sat on the edge of her bed and looked after her, rubbed her head to soothe her, brought her a bowl of grapes because she was too sick to go downstairs for herself. He was the same husband who went to every one of their son’s soccer matches at school, their daughter’s swim meets, and sat through every parent-teacher meeting, nurturing his children to become fine grown-ups. The other man, she told me, was the man who strived to give her more than she would ever need. The man who wanted to make more money, throw lavish parties, to be a New York success story. She told me she was proud of what we’d achieved, but she was content if it never became more.

'I thought about that conversation, after she died. I turned her words over and over in my head to make sense of them, and I knew she was right. And had she lived, I think I would've pulled back, let the business run itself a little bit and focused on the family life I had the luxury of having provided for. But when she died, some days I felt as though it was all I had left. I convinced myself that you needed something to fill the void and so I worked myself into the ground making the business even bigger, seizing every opportunity to grow, taking every chance. And it took away my pain most days, gave me a focus. I think I was terrified that if I stopped, the pain would consume me, and I wouldn't be able to function.'

Jack swigged his Scotch, allowing the liquid to sharpen his senses. 'So you're saying Mom didn't want the business either.'

Kent shook his head. 'It wasn't that simple. She wanted the business. She loved designing jewellery, but she was a woman who was content with her lot in life. She was a lot like Nicole.' He smiled, tentatively. 'They're the same Zodiac sign you know.'

'Kind-hearted then,' Jack smiled. Both Cynthia and he shared the Aquarius sign, and his mother had often reeled off the good and bad characteristics of an Aquarian. 'It's the sign of a progressive thinker, someone who respects the differences between people. I'm still not sure I fit that mould, but Mom and Nicole sure do.'

'I think you're underestimating yourself. I'm Aries. Your mother always told me I was a go-getter, someone who led the way.'

'Very apt.'

'What else was it?' He pulled a face as he recalled his wife's words. 'Ah … I have a magnetic personality, apparently, and I bring excitement to peoples' lives.'

Jack shook his head, laughed. 'She loved her astrology.'

'She did. It's the first section she'd find in a newspaper. Never mind the catastrophes of the world or the state of the economy. She'd go straight to the horoscopes, reading them out to me almost daily.'

'She loved looking at the stars. We'd go out and find the best location. We'd wait for the sky to change to pink, deepen to purple and then I'd watch her looking up at the stars. A few times we were lucky enough to spot the Winter Circle. Not a constellation but an asterism, she told me. It was a circular pattern consisting of stars that I can't remember the name of now, but I was more interested in watching her than the sky anyway. Beneath the stars was what Cynthia was about, she looked her most beautiful, her most at peace.'

Jack didn't miss the catch in his voice. 'I miss her.'

'Me too, son.'

'Can I ask why you packed away all the photographs of us as a family?' It was candid, but he'd never really understood his father's reasoning.

'I didn't put them away and forget about them, I promise you. I put them all away one day in a fit of rage, angry she was gone, that our lives had been ripped apart. And then I got them out again, positioned them all around the house. The day Nicole was due to come over of course I hid them again, just until I'd talked with her. And when she began working here, of course I couldn't get the photographs out again. But I always kept one in the office. And you always kept the same one in your room. And Nicole never once went in there. I think she was afraid of encroaching in a teenage boy's territory, afraid she'd meet the stench of filthy socks and goodness knows what else.'

'I find it hard to believe she never once went in my room in thirteen years, smelly socks or not.'

Kent shrugged. 'I wonder if she'd even recognise Cynthia anyway. Perhaps she'd never really looked at the photograph of the woman her son killed. Perhaps it was too painful for her.'

'She must've been through hell,' said Jack.

'I'm sure she has.'

The conversation settled until a crackle from the fireplace reminded Jack to speak again. 'Where is she, anyway?'

'She went home to her apartment. She said something about cooking supper for Evie tonight.'

Dear God, what was Evie going to make of all this? Nicole's son was a murderer; Kent Churchill had lied to everyone, all these years.

'I'm not angry with Nicole,' he told his father. 'I can't be. Somehow she's detached from my mother. Whether it's because I've always thought natural causes were to blame, I don't know, but I don't see her as the mother of a killer. When you first told me, of course I did, but not anymore. Is she angry with you for lying to us all?'

Kent shook his head. 'No, she's not angry.'

Jack thought back to the night Nicole had brought Evie into their world. 'All of this, is this why you reacted so strongly to Nicole helping Evie?'

Kent nodded shamefully. 'It was wrong of me, I know, but that night I didn't see a young woman in desperate need of help. In that moment I wasn't a parent,

I was a grieving widower and a man who was scared this person could take away everything I held dear.'

'Can I ask whether Braydon knowing the whole truth is why you've allowed him to stay with the company for so long?'

Kent took a deep breath. 'Oh, he was good at his job first and foremost, but slowly I began to dislike the man more and more, and then of course I was petrified he'd open his big mouth and blow everything apart with the truth. Lord knows what he'll do now. I've got visions of him exposing the whole story to the press, telling everyone how Kent Churchill fell for the woman whose son killed his first wife.'

'What will you do about Braydon to ensure he doesn't take this to the newspapers?'

Kent shook his head. 'Do you know what? I don't think I really care if he does. Not now. Not now the truth is out. I always thought this business was what saved me from myself, but really it's been like a noose around my neck, threatening to tighten and snap me, break my relationship with my own son. I should've given it away years ago and focused on you and Cameron.'

'What's done is done.' Jack tried his best to sound philosophical. 'Talking of Cameron, does she know anything about this yet?'

'No. And she won't, until I go to Toronto and tell her everything. I won't do this over the telephone.'

'No,' Jack agreed. 'Hang on a minute, wind back.' Using his index finger, he drew a small circular motion in the air. 'You said something about falling for the woman whose son …'

Kent nodded. 'I've been in love with Nicole for years, but I knew nothing could or would ever happen.'

‘My God.’ Jack poured a double shot of whiskey, unlikely to be driving anywhere now tonight. ‘I never saw it.’

Kent finally sat down on the opposite end of the couch. ‘Neither did I, not for a long time, but I felt it when Evie showed up and I saw her threatened. I know now that wasn’t the case, but to me it was very real that Nicole could be taken away. It was that night I realised how strong my feelings were and I felt like a traitor. To my wife, to my children.’

‘But Dad, you’ve never been short of a woman or two.’

‘I know, but it was this particular woman that was the problem. All the women over the years have been fun, pleasant, but never anything more.’

‘Like father like son, eh?’ Jack lifted his glass, took another glug. ‘I never let a woman get close. After I saw what losing Mom did to you, I didn’t ever want to be that hurt again. I figured if I could keep all women at arm’s length, just have a little fun, I could never have my life snatched away from me like that.’

‘It’s a sad way to be, son.’

Jack nodded. It was sad, and it was lonely too. ‘You know, despite the circumstances, I’m pleased about your feelings for Nicole.’

‘Really?’

He nodded. ‘Don’t get me wrong. If you’d told me right after I’d found out about Noah, I would’ve called you crazy, but I’ve calmed down since then. Nicole is a wonderful person, and like you say, she’s just as much of a victim as we were with what happened. God, all this time and she never told us she’d lost a son to suicide. Noah paid the ultimate price with his life, Nicole has paid the price of losing a son and living with the guilt.

Perhaps now, enough is enough.' It was as though a weight had been lifted off his shoulders rather than being added to with the new knowledge.

'I can't imagine the pain she's gone through. Losing a child …' Kent shook his head. 'The thought is unbearable. It's what drove me on to provide you and your sister with a family business, a future. But really all I ended up doing was taking a world away from you.'

'Dad, you didn't do that. You did everything for me. It could've been worse, you didn't do so badly.'

'Do you know what I'd really like, Jack?' He looked at his son. 'I'd like to keep the business but scale back on my ambition for it, let it run, grow, tail off, whatever. There are more important things in life.'

'There are.'

'But this is your inheritance we're talking about. If the business fails—'

'Then it fails. Worse things have happened to us, Dad.'

'Yes, I suppose they have.' They sat in contemplative silence. 'What will you do?'

'I'm not sure.' Jack smiled now. 'I may stay in the jewellery business, get a smaller store, be more hands on and less global. There's an empty store in Hazelbrook, right in the little town. I could set up a small outlet there. Who knows, but I'm excited at the possibility of doing something on a smaller scale, focused on the love of design.'

Kent sat forward, forearms on his thighs. 'So tell me. What's going on with young Evie?'

'The homeless woman?'

'No,' Kent shook his head, 'Evie.'

Jack smiled. It hadn't been said, but he guessed it was his father's way of admitting that sometimes he was too quick to judge, sometimes he assumed people from certain walks of life were all the same.

'She's an amazing woman,' said Jack. 'Very wise as it turns out.'

They talked some more. They talked about Evie, about how over the years she and Nicole had nurtured a trusting relationship that rivalled any mother and daughter bond either of them had even seen. They made coffees, opened a bag of roasted peanuts and ate nearly all of them. But most of all they laughed and bonded as father and son, relaxed in one another's company. They understood each other better than they had before. Jack told his father all about taking Evie out to Hollyhock Farm, how he'd helped at the homeless shelter and how he had helped Todd, a boy who needed to be given a second chance,

'I'd like to see the house sometime,' said Kent.

'I'd like that too.'

Kent washed the last handful of peanuts down with a glass of iced water. 'So, do you think anything will happen with Evie?'

'I don't know. I think I'd like it to.' Jack had never discussed a woman with his father before and he smiled at the new experience. 'And what are you going to do about Nicole?'

His father shook his head. 'I'm not sure.'

'Well, don't waste time. You're not getting any younger.'

Kent picked up a peanut, lobbed it at his son's head. Jack opened his mouth just in time and deftly caught the morsel. He winked at his father, delighted to see this other man emerge at last, a man he respected wholeheartedly.

Kent got to his feet. 'Come on.'

‘Where are we going?’ Jack followed suit as his father left the room, picked up his coat from the coat stand in the hallway.

‘We’re going to go get our women!’

Chapter Twenty-Five

Evie

'Are you okay?' Evie asked Nicole, both of them sitting side by side on the kitchen chairs Uncle Brett had lined up along the wall, out of reach of anything that could help their plight.

'Shut up!' he yelled at them. 'Right, this is how this is going to work. You,' he shoved Nicole's shoulder with the hand that wasn't holding the knife, a dirty old knife with a blade that looked rusty, but Evie suspected wasn't at all. 'You are going to go to the nearest ATM and withdraw as much cash as you can, from every account.'

'There's a limit of—' Nicole tried.

'Shut up!' The blade wiggled in his hand and Evie knew he was nervous. She was pretty sure he'd never have the guts to use the weapon, but she couldn't chance it. 'You will get as much cash as you can and bring it back here. I'll keep young Evie as my insurance policy, so if you try anything, involve the police, tell that fat doorman downstairs, do *anything*, then what happens to her is your fault. Do you understand?'

Nicole nodded, genuine terror etched across her face. Her uncle had already raided Nicole's jewellery box, made her open a safe Evie didn't even know she had, taken Nicole's gold watch, and a charm bracelet she'd been collecting pieces for since the day she met Evie, to give to her when she thought she would accept it.

What had she done bringing this man into Nicole's life? Jack had been right. With her came trouble, and that meant trouble for Nicole.

Evie had arrived at the apartment ready to tell Nicole all about the photographs, all about the nude modelling. She'd joked with Reggie when a dog had done its business in the foyer and the stench had sent her running for the elevator. She hadn't seen her Uncle Brett until she'd stepped in and he'd grabbed her from behind, a hand covering her mouth to silence her as the elevator crawled up to Nicole's floor. And then, rather than hear everything from her, Nicole had heard the sorry story from him, his words twisting Evie's insides as they echoed around the apartment, all her secrets out at last.

Nicole picked up her purse from the counter and made her way to the door.

'And don't try anything.' Uncle Brett came over and yanked Evie from her chair, to her feet. He held a knife against her throat, a move she hadn't expected. She froze, the cool metal against her skin a threat if she so much as squirmed.

When the door shut behind a terrified Nicole, he ordered her to sit down. It was a welcome relief to be away from that knife.

'There could've been an easier way round this, you know.' He came up to her now, his face so close she felt the spittle escape from between his lips.

'Well, when you've got your money, you can go.'

'That's just the thing. I'm not sure if I can.'

'You've got what you came for,' she said, doing her best to look as though she wasn't scared.

'Have I? I'll always have those photos, but there's something else you can do for me.'

Evie didn't like where this was heading, not one bit. Her body tensed up as he moved around her like an animal sizing up its prey. She wanted to stall him, keep him talking until Nicole got back with the money, then hopefully he'd forget all about wanting her for anything else.

'What happened to family loyalty?' she asked him. It seemed to work. His facial expression went from leering at her to actually thinking about what she said, but it didn't last long.

'All the family I've ever known have walked away, including you. I don't give a crap about family loyalty. To me, it doesn't exist.'

She had to keep him talking. Come on, Nicole. Evie counted in her head how many steps it would take to reach the ATM at the end of the street. She imagined Nicole's hands shaking as she put in her PIN, withdrew the cash, pushed it into her purse and made her way back through the darkened streets.

Uncle Brett went over to the kitchen and scooped up a pile of photographs, flicking through each of them. Evie looked at the door. It was only her to get through it now, Nicole was out. If she ran, past the kitchen area, while he was perving at those photographs, she could get out. She could escape.

Her legs twitched, she almost left her seat, but he was sharp enough and looked up before her feet even moved.

'Plenty more where these came from.' He taunted her with the photographs.

'They don't matter to me now, Nicole knows everything, and you've told my employer. I've got nothing to lose.'

'Oh, so confident aren't we, Evie? You're so sure of yourself. That was always your problem.'

She shrugged. She was anything but.

'Just remember how small the world is with technology. I could see these go viral, pop up everywhere. You'd be a global sensation. I might even

Photoshop a few of them, get you doing something else. Maybe when your friend comes back, I could take some more shots.'

'My God, you're sick.'

He lunged at her, the knife stopping before it reached her throat. 'Careful now, don't tempt me.'

His breath was hot on her face until he backed off, laughing. 'I need a drink.' Without turning his back on Evie, he opened the fridge and took out a beer, put down the knife and cracked the bottle open against the bench. He snatched up the knife again, and when he'd taken a few glugs of beer he heard the door go and was there like a shot.

'I got it.' Nicole came in and walked confidently past him and over to the kitchen table. Evie tried to read her face but couldn't.

'You stay there,' he ordered Evie, and waved the knife at her before following Nicole over to the table where she upended her purse. Notes flew out across the glass top.

'There, it's as much as I could get.'

'It's not enough,' he growled, roughly estimating how much was there when he put down the knife and flicked through the notes. It only looked to be a few hundred. He grabbed a fistful of Nicole's hair, tipping her head back, exposing her neck. Evie could see the knife beneath the money, but she knew if she tried to get to the weapon, he could snatch it up and hurt Nicole, and she couldn't risk that. She'd brought enough hurt into her home already when all Nicole had ever done was to go out of her way to help her.

'I'll get more,' Nicole pleaded.

'Too bloody right you will.' He pushed Nicole's head away and she screamed. Evie rushed to her side and held her. Her body was shaking. Evie's wasn't, almost as though she was numb to the damage he could do now.

'It was all I could get from the one account,' said Nicole. 'I need to take my other ATM cards.'

'Why didn't you take them in the first place?'

'I thought they were already in my purse.' Her voice shook. 'They're in the kitchen drawer. The top one,' she explained as he began pulling each drawer open. 'They're right at the back.'

He pocketed the extra three cards. 'This time, we'll all go together.' He scooped up the money from the table, shoved it into the sports bag he'd used to stash the jewellery he'd already taken, a silver-plated photo frame with a picture of a young boy and Nicole.

Evie saw the moment Nicole spotted the photograph. 'You don't need the picture,' she said. 'Leave the picture, keep the frame. Do something half decent for once in your sorry life.'

'I'm the one with the knife, remember. So you'd be better off shutting the fuck up!'

Nicole pulled at Evie's arm. 'Leave it, it doesn't matter.'

But Evie could tell it did.

Uncle Brett opened the door and pushed them into the corridor, but as Evie reached to hold Nicole's arm, she saw two men swoop on her uncle. It was Jack and Kent, one coming from the left, the other from the right.

'He's got a knife!' Nicole shrieked.

Evie screamed, stumbled back in the commotion, falling to the carpet. Kent held the arm with the knife firm, Jack had Uncle Brett in a headlock and they disarmed him within seconds. Evie scurried forwards on her hands and knees and retrieved the knife out of harm's way. And then everything happened in fast forward. The elevator opened again and three police officers stepped out in front of Reggie, who rushed to Nicole's side. Uncle Brett was cuffed by one officer, restrained by another and the third took both women inside the apartment where Nicole leant against Evie, sobbing in relief. And then she fell to her knees and unzipped the holdall, took out the photograph and clutched it to her chest.

It was a good hour or so until the women, Kent, and Jack were left in peace at the apartment. The worst was over, Uncle Brett had been taken away and Evie had no choice now but to tell the police everything and hope that they could stop the photographs from ever appearing and robbing her of the life and friends she couldn't imagine being without.

Nicole and Kent had sat and told Evie everything too, all about how their lives were linked. Nicole had gripped hold of the photo of Noah that Evie's uncle had almost taken away from her, and when they'd finished their tale, Evie had hugged Nicole tightly. 'You should've told me,' she'd said over and over, wishing she could've absorbed some of the pain for her friend.

*

As the atmosphere in the apartment returned to normal, as least as much as it possibly could, Nicole and Kent went into the kitchen to fix up food and drinks. Nicole had offered her homemade coffee cake and a fresh pot of coffee, and Jack took Evie through to the living room.

'Sit in front of the fire, warm up,' he told her. 'You're shaking.'

'I'm not cold,' she insisted.

'It's probably the shock. Please, sit.'

She did as she was told and plonked herself down on the edge of the couch. 'Those photographs will never go away, you know. It's not like the olden days with negatives and only one or two copies. In the digital age it'll never be over. He will do his time in jail, whatever that is, then he's free to do exactly what he said he'd do. He'll end up ruining me as soon as he can.'

Jack sat next to her, and she was surprised at the feel of his skin on hers as his hand covered her own. 'Evie, I don't know enough about the law to know what he can get away with when he's out of jail, but I do know I have enough money to help you out.' He raised the hand not holding hers when she began to protest. 'No, money doesn't make you happy, I realise that.' He beamed a smile at her, eyes melting her like hot fudge. 'Will you let me help you?'

She nodded.

When his phone bleeped, he took it from his pocket and read an awaiting text. 'Sorry, it's Todd checking when I'll next be at the house.' He tapped out a reply. 'I'd told him I'd be there tonight, but I'll tell him I can't make it.'

'How's he getting on?' Evie asked as Jack finished and put his phone away. Even though she'd told Jack not to judge all homeless people as one, she felt an affinity with the boy, knowing what it felt like to be in his situation.

'He's working really hard. Too hard some days, but I appreciate it. I believe in him, I really do. I'm going to let him use the address as his own once the renovations are finished, see if we can get him some work.'

'That's good.' Evie nodded.

'So are you ever going to admit it?' he asked.

'Admit what?'

'That you were wrong about me?' He didn't sound as confident as the words implied he should.

She smiled. 'Jack, there's something else I need to tell you.'

'There's more?' He pulled a face of disbelief.

Evie didn't want to look at him, but she made herself. It was nothing but the truth from now on. 'I'd met Braydon once before, before that day at the hospital.'

Bewildered, he said, 'I know, he was at the house the night my father went mental and threw you off the property.'

'No, before that.'

'When?'

'It was about four weeks before that night. I was sleeping rough in the doorway of a house not far from your father's place. I'd found a house with a basement entrance that was pretty concealed. It was out of the wind, out of the cold, had a small overhead shelter if I huddled in close to the step. Anyway, one night, I came back there after I'd had a good meal at the hostel and I settled in for the duration, at least until the sun came up the next morning and the streets got busier again.

'I woke up to someone pushing my leg with their foot. This big brown shoe was pushing at my leg beneath the blanket, and I looked up to find a man in a suit looking down at me.'

'Braydon?'

'At first I thought it was the owner come home and ready to have me arrested, so I stood up, apologised, I was ready to move on. But he was kind to me, talking softly, understanding almost.'

From the look on Jack's face, he'd already worked out where this was going.

'He asked my name, asked if I'd eaten. He was perfectly nice. Until I tried to move on. That was when I realised he was interested in more than being friendly.'

'Oh God, did he …'

Evie held up her hands. 'I can fend for myself quite well. I listened to him go on about money he'd pay if I went home with him, how we could make this a regular thing, how I'd be off the streets in no time with the money he could give me. He kept running his fingers through my hair, lifting it to his face. That was when I tried to walk away. His grip tightened, but he didn't have a chance to do anything because I kneed him so hard, exactly where it hurts, and he could barely stand, let alone get me.

'I never went back to that doorway again, let me tell you. I found somewhere else, a few streets away, and that was when Nicole found me.'

Jack shook his head, his hands steepled in front of him, with his elbows rested on his knees. He closed his eyes and leant against his hands. 'That bastard.'

'I don't think he appreciated the rejection.'

'Braydon never did do well with the word "no".'

They sat contemplating this new snippet of information, nothing compared to the drama of tonight but enough to have shaped Evie's life and opinion of men, especially the rich, until this moment. Until Jack had proven they weren't all the same.

Jack turned and put his hand back on hers. 'Evie, there's something I want to ask you.'

'Go on.'

'Would you have dinner with me one night?'

She grinned. 'Are you asking me on a date, Jackson Churchill?'

'I think I might be.'

'On one condition,' she said.

'Okay …'

'No fancy restaurants. You'll have a budget. I'm not saying I don't want to ever be wined and dined, treated once in a while, but I want us to start with basics. Think you can do it?'

He grinned. 'Of course I can. And I know the perfect place to take you.' He took his hand from hers and instead hooked it beneath her blonde hair, pulling her face towards his, their lips almost touching. She could feel the heat from the fire, from his hand on the back of her neck.

And then he kissed her.

Nicole

Her hands shook as she spooned coffee granules into the glass jug ready for the coffee maker.

'Here, let me do that.' Kent took over. 'You've had one hell of a shock tonight.'

Nicole twisted her loose hair around her fingers and up the back of her head into a twist, securing it in place with a clip lurking on the kitchen counter. 'I'm just glad you and Jackson showed up when you did.'

'Your neighbour had heard a commotion and was busy telling the doorman about it when we arrived in the building. I insisted we go up and check it out and when we stood outside your door, we knew something terrible was going on. I could hear a male voice, I heard crying. It was awful. The doorman called the police right away.' He topped up the jug with water and slotted it into the machine. 'They told us not to rush in so we didn't, but then you came out of the apartment and we had no choice.'

'You were very brave.' She took the coffee cake out of the oven, having warmed it through, and sliced it on the white rectangular plate. Funny, after what they'd been through tonight, she still wanted to wait on people, still wanted to look after her guests. 'You know, when I saw the knife, when I saw that man had Evie, the only person I could think of was your wife.'

'Cynthia?' Kent put the bag of coffee back into the cupboard.

'I thought that this is it, this is karma. An eye for an eye and all that. You'd lost the woman you loved at the hands of Noah, I was about to lose the closest thing I have to family from the same single stab wound.'

Kent's eyes held emotion, although she couldn't quite tell what he was thinking. 'You know, I've never been one to believe in karma.' He smiled at her, poured four mugs of coffee into the red vessels lined up waiting on the kitchen countertop. 'I think that life can sometimes be shitty … so shitty it hurts, so crap that sometimes you want to die.'

She gulped at his honesty, at the indirect reference to his wife's death.

'But I also believe you can come back from the darkest of places without someone or something lurking in the wings to take it away from you. I believe we make our own destiny, our own futures. We are in control.'

'You always did seem in control.' She took out plates, ready to serve the cake. She'd never felt in control, not since the day Noah had run out on her. Since then, she'd never regained her confidence. She felt a hand on her shoulder.

'Nicole, you've got to stop blaming yourself for what happened.'

Tears sprang to her eyes. 'I can't, I just can't. I'm a mother, I should've been able to protect him, stop him from turning bad. You've done it with Jackson. He could've gone off the rails when he lost his mother at the hands of my son, but he didn't. He's turned into a fine young man. Noah should've been the same.'

When the tears fell, he spun her around to him and let her cry into his chest as he stroked her hair and quietened her.

'Don't you see, we're the same, you and me?' He looked deep into her eyes.

'How are we the same? I'm weak, you're strong. I'm an emotional wreck, you're in control.'

He hooked the curl of hair that insisted on falling down behind her ear again until it obeyed and stayed put. 'We both put our children first in our hearts and minds. You did your very best and I did mine, no matter what life threw at us. We're both parents, we both always will be. And we both used distractions to cope with our grief. I threw myself into the business, into making money. You threw yourself into looking after people, strangers on the street, Evie and everyone else you've helped.

'We *are* the same, Nicole. And I loved you for so many years.' He lifted a hand to her face, tilted her chin towards his. 'And now I have something to ask you.'

He sank to one knee. 'Nicole Capra, will you marry me?'

Chapter Twenty-Six

Kent

The city streets were muffled in snow on Christmas morning. Lights twinkled merrily; cars slowed to a crawl as they pulled up and disgorged family members with armfuls of presents, faces of joy and the sounds of laughter. And inside the bay window lit up with the golden glow, in the townhouse on the Upper West Side, the house that looked no different from the outside, it was a new beginning for a family brought together in the most difficult circumstances.

'Great job wrapping those pigs in blankets, Jack.' Kent patted his son on the shoulder as he passed by and turned up the volume on the iPod. Bing Crosby's 'White Christmas' filled the kitchen as Jack wrapped the last strip of bacon around a sausage.

'Thanks, Dad.'

'Do you think it's too early?' Kent held a bottle of champagne aloft.

'It's Christmas,' Jack smiled. 'Of course it's not. Take it easy though,' he warned.

Kent rolled his eyes. 'As you say, it's Christmas. But yes, I'll take it easy.' He lined up two glasses next to the poinsettia he'd bought on December 8th even though he'd never known the significance before then. The night he'd spent at Nicole's apartment after Jack had taken Evie home to recover from the shock of the police, the violence that could have been, Nicole had told him more about Noah, and instead of seeing him as the boy who'd killed his wife, Kent had seen him as the son Nicole had lost. He'd wiped away her tears, shared her pain.

'Every year,' Nicole had told him, 'on my birthday, December eighth, Noah bought me a poinsettia plant. It started when he was seven years old, the first time he'd saved up his allowance and chosen something for me himself. He said it was the most beautiful, cheerful plant and it reminded him of me. And he also said it was the start of the Santa season when a poinsettia was in the house,' she'd smiled.

She'd bought two every year since he'd died—one for her home and one for the Churchills. 'It felt like Noah was with me every day,' she'd said.

Now, in the townhouse, Kent poured the champagne and took the glasses through to the living room on a tray. Evie and Nicole were chatting animatedly in front of the fire, their smiles as bright as the flames, as rich in their content. Since the night they'd feared for their lives at the hands of Evie's uncle, all four of them had bonded in a way Kent never would have foreseen. He'd learned about Evie's life, what she'd been through, what had driven her to run from home. Evie had learned about Noah, his link to Cynthia, the hurt Jack had felt losing a parent and having the other immerse himself so much in work he forgot what it meant to be a father. It wasn't about the fancy things, the designer clothes he could buy, the holidays he could pay for or the booming company. It was about the little things, and nothing could be truer today.

'Oh, tell me we're not,' Kent laughed, handing out the champagne when he spied the Twister game box on Nicole's lap.

'Oh yes, we are!' Evie put her champagne glass on the side table and excitedly took the lid from the game, pulled out the mat and the spinner, and with Kent's help moved the coffee table and the rug. She lay the mat down in the space created just as Jack came back into the room.

'Pigs in blankets are in the ov … What on earth is going on here?'

'Just in time.' Evie dragged him over to the mat. 'We'll let Nicole be spinner, seeing as she only has one functioning arm, and the three of us will play.'

Kent tipped his head back and laughed, and as he put a foot on one colour, his left hand on another, he relished the sounds of female giggling that hadn't been heard in these walls for so long, the sound of his son, happy. And most of all, as Jack fell against Evie and Kent toppled into them both, he relished the simplicity of a family life he had so missed and was looking forward to resurrecting once again.

The family lunch was everything Kent had hoped for: crazy, disorganised, and a whole lot of fun. Nicole had agreed, right there in her apartment that day, she'd actually said 'yes!' to being his wife, something he never thought would happen in his wildest dreams. And in a few months, she would move in with him to start their new life together.

Kent unveiled the plum pudding he'd made from scratch this year. Plum pudding for dessert became a tradition the first year Nicole had worked for him, and it had lasted until the first Christmas without her. After that, Kent had barely been able to look at a plum pudding let alone eat it. But this year, it was back, and he was glad he'd made the extra effort.

'Dad, I'm impressed. No, I'm floored!'

'Jack,' Evie admonished.

‘It’s all right, Evie. I’m not exactly domesticated, and I did have a little help.’ He winked at Nicole and picked up the bottle of brandy. He drizzled alcohol across the top of the pudding and let it run down the sides. Then he picked up a box of matches as Nicole closed the drapes and turned off the lights for the full Christmas magic.

The pudding lit up the faces of people brought together this year in circumstances nobody could’ve predicted and a cheer went up around the room.

‘You’ll be cooking at the shelter next,’ Jack laughed as he helped Nicole pass out the plates of plum pudding. ‘How’s it going down there?’

‘It’s going well. I’m on the top of the leader board in darts now.’

‘He’s quite the competitive player,’ Nicole confirmed.

Kent had been helping out for the last few days and had to admit rolling his sleeves up and getting involved was nothing like he’d ever suspected. The regulars were friendly; they all wanted to talk to this new recruit. Some kept their heads down, ate and left. Others thanked him for taking over the lease of the building; some sang Nicole’s praises, much to her embarrassment.

‘Will we be seeing you two there tomorrow night?’ he asked Evie and Jack.

‘You will.’ Jack passed a bowl of dessert to Evie.

Father and son had different lives now. They had two women who completed their world, and instead of working night and day to make more and more money, they had realised the importance, the significance and the pleasure of helping other people, sometimes in the simplest of ways.

As they sat enjoying their dessert, one by one groaning at how much they’d eaten and how full they were, Kent knew he was in a place where he was content. He couldn't change the past, but he could look to the future, and with Nicole by his side, that was more than he could ever want.

Jack

'Take the corners slowly,' Evie insisted as they drove out of Manhattan towards New Haven. 'My dinner is still sloshing around in my belly.'

All the green space was covered in white, but roads had been cleared by snowploughs. The sun reflected off the snow on either side, brightening the inside of the car as they travelled all the way to his property.

'I wonder if Dad and Nicole are "playing Twister".' He raised a naughty, quizzical eyebrow.

'A. That's revolting, that's your father you're talking about,' Evie laughed. 'And B. I think they'd vomit if they tried to even move.'

They turned into Jack's street, slowing as kids scrambled past them. Three girls, triplets with ebony hair pushed beneath crimson hats, squealed past them, each dragging a red plastic sled behind them.

'Looks fun,' said Jack as he pulled into the driveway. Todd was already out with a shovel, clearing the path.

'Todd,' Jack jumped out of the car. 'Merry Christmas, buddy.' He shook his hand, patted him on the shoulder. He felt more like a big brother, especially today with it being Christmas. He didn't know what Todd would do once he was on the straight and narrow, but he hoped they could at least stay in touch; maybe become friends. Already he'd secured him some work up at Nate's farm next year at the start of fruit picking season, and hopefully it would have a waterfall effect and other jobs would come his way.

'Hey, Evie,' Todd called out as Evie made her way over from the other side of the vehicle. 'What are you both doing here? I thought you were having a huge family celebration.'

'We did,' said Jack, 'but you wouldn't come to us and I wasn't going to let you have Christmas on your own. So we'll keep you company for a couple of hours.'

Evie brandished the Tupperware containers filled with Todd's portion of Christmas dinner.

'Wow.' His eyes betrayed him, and Jack knew he was glad they'd come despite his adopted nonchalance. 'I don't know what to say.'

They went inside to microwave the turkey dinner for Todd and spend some time with a boy who'd lost his way in life but was somehow finding the right path again, just like Jack was.

Braydon hadn't shown his face in The Diamond Touch since that day, and Kent had given him a generous payout for so many loyal years at the company. Sometimes money really did help, and although Jack knew it wasn't the answer to everything, it certainly was necessary at times. Jack would've rather gone over to Braydon's place and beat the living crap out of him, giving him no money whatsoever, but he let his father handle it in his own way. And he wasn't interfering in his relationship with Nicole either. They had his blessing, although they didn't need it, and Jack had accepted the invitation to be best man at their wedding in early June. His father had told Nicole he'd be able to use contacts and get the Plaza, but Nicole had told him she wanted simplicity, close friends and family only, and they'd agreed to head to Sicily where they would honeymoon and where Nicole had scattered Noah's ashes. It seemed fitting if they were going to start again, to get to know one another and the intricacies of their lives.

Evie had been the biggest surprise of all. In the minutes he'd first met her, his life had begun to alter, and in the time he'd gotten to know her better, everything had changed. He wanted to share his days with her, his thoughts, his fears. And most of all he wanted to be there for her. He watched Evie now as she chatted to Todd while he poured the reheated gravy across his Christmas dinner. She looked up and smiled at Jack.

It was a smile that said they were both in it for keeps. And he couldn't be happier.

Evie

'Todd's a nice guy,' Evie said as they drove from New Haven towards Hollyhock Farm. 'You should be proud.'

Jack turned into the main street of Hazelbrook. 'I am. He's a great kid.'

'I don't just mean you should be proud of Todd. You should be proud of yourself too.' She looked at him until he turned to her and returned her smile. Whatever life you'd come from and whatever direction you were heading in, everyone deserved a second chance to make a change, to make amends, to become a better version of themselves.

'Jackson Churchill, I was wrong about you,' she admitted out loud.

He slapped the steering wheel. 'Hallelujah! I knew you'd have to admit it eventually!'

'Yeah, don't push it. I can easily change my mind back.'

'You won't.'

'You sound confident. What have you got planned?'

'Just you wait and see.'

Evie warmed inside at the thought of what he would do.

Jack slowed and pulled to a stop outside a store that looked empty. 'Would be perfect for a jewellery store, don't you think?'

'Or a wedding dress store.' She grinned.

Jack reached over and ran the back of his hand down her cheek. 'Or maybe it could be both. Diamonds and dresses kind of go together.'

'Yes, I suppose they do.' She put her hand on his and held it in place.

'We could make it a family business.'

'On one condition,' said Evie. 'It's a business that doesn't drive a family apart.'

'Deal,' he said. 'Come on, let's go. I've got plans for you, Evie Jefferson.'

She grinned as they continued on their way. When they reached Hollyhock Farm, the house was covered in a layer of snow, like frosting on a cake. Twinkle lights ran from one side of the porch to the other, pointing up in the middle when the roof pitched high. It was beautiful out here. So quiet, so magical.

They bundled into the house. Nate and Julia had gone to her sister's for a couple of days so they had the place to themselves, and Evie felt safe, secure, with her man at her side. That night after Uncle Brett had forced his way into the apartment and terrorised them, Jack had taken her home to her basement apartment. He'd stayed over, insisting on taking the couch, but in the middle of the night, still unable to sleep, she'd crept out of bed and woken him, taken him by the hand and led him back to the bedroom. It had felt the most natural thing in the world. Her life had changed the instant she met the Churchills; even when they'd banished her, it had been the start of something good without her knowing it, and that night was the start of something even better. It was the start of a future with Jack.

'What are you thinking?' Jack wrapped his arms around her waist now and nuzzled her hair. 'If you're thinking of taking me to bed, I've got plans for that later, but we have something else to do first.'

'Cheeky!' She giggled and spun round to kiss him. Their first time had been tender, intimate and powerful, but since then sex had become more fun as they began to trust one another more and more. When she'd told Lizzy they'd slept together, Lizzy had thrown her hands in the air in celebration before making up a jug of margaritas. And then she'd wanted to know all the sordid details.

'I'll sleep on the couch if you're not careful,' she teased him.

'You will not! You couldn't stay away from me the first night, you're not capable.' He still liked to tease her about it, and she suspected he'd be making the same joke for years to come. At least, she hoped so anyway.

'Well,' she began. 'I never thought I'd say it, but I'm starting to get hungry. I don't smell anything cooking, Jackson Churchill, so what have you got planned?'

He smiled. 'Put your coat back on.' He did the same himself.

Evie did as she was told and he led her from the house, down to the farthest field, down to the maze.

'Wow!' As they got closer the lights shone brighter against the snow covering the conifers. The lights twinkled against the crisp, icy white flakes, creating a stunning, magical picture of the maze before them.

'Ready?' he asked.

'For what?'

'To find the middle, of course.'

'You're serious? It's way too dark!'

'Chicken.'

'Oh!' She took her marks next to him. 'You're on, mister.' When he grinned she grabbed his arm. 'Hang on a minute, you've got a distinct advantage. You know the route.'

'I'll give you a head start.'

Evie unwound her scarf from her neck. 'We'll go one better than that. You can do it blindfolded!' Laughing, she pulled the woollen scarf across his eyes and double-knotted it at the back of his head.

'This is ridiculous,' he concluded, arms out in front of him.

'On your marks …'

'Get set …' he added.

'Go!' they yelled together.

Evie took off along the first path of the maze. The lights had been strung along every conifer; goodness knows how many metres it'd taken, how many batteries were powering the white lights guiding her way.

'Damn!" She giggled, another dead end. She spun around to find Jack the same way too. 'Wrong way,' she laughed, standing on tiptoes to plant a kiss on his lips. The blindfold was firmly in place, she still had a chance. But when she went to run off, he pulled her close to him.

'You're not going anywhere till you kiss me properly.'

They must've stood there in the little squared off area, the dead end, until Evie's cheeks were numb with cold, her lips tingling from his kiss.

Eventually she pulled away, giggling. 'And go!' And off she went again, turning this way and that, determined he wouldn't catch her. She wanted to win, she wanted to get to the middle first, find the centre. She turned left … another dead end. She tried right instead, which took her along quite a way, and she guessed it was right again at the end. The lights and the moon were guiding the way and she tried to jump up on the spot and see over the conifers, but they'd grown too much and she couldn't see a thing.

It was only one more wrong turn before she achieved success and found herself at the centre of the maze. Stepping forwards, into the square big enough to fit a picnic table and allow space on the grass to sit and enjoy the victory of completing the maze, she saw a picnic basket and beside that, a bottle of champagne in an ice bucket.

'Ha!' She yelled. 'I'm here already, loser! Where are you?' She laughed into the night air, turning round on the spot to feel the flakes of snow fluttering down from the sky.

And then Jack grabbed her from behind. Still blindfolded, he pulled her into his arms, his breath warm against her face as they both recovered from the chase. She lifted the scarf from his eyes and didn't look away from him once.

'Hungry?' He looked down at her, the moon highlighting his silhouette.

'Starving. What are we having?'

'Open the basket. I'm hoping there's everything you could possibly wish for in there.'

She took him by the hand, over to the table where she unfastened the catch on the basket and lifted up the lid.

But the hamper wasn't bulging with food, with deli items, with festive-wrapped morsels she'd try and love. There was only one item in the hamper, and she took it out without saying a word.

Jack took the box from her hands, sunk down on one knee and opened the lid. The moonlight bounced off a pink diamond and Evie's mouth fell open.

'This might be too soon,' said Jack, 'but I feel I've known you years. It just took me time to get to know the real you, realise you are the woman I'm looking for. And whether we get married right here in this maze or somewhere else, I won't care, as long as you're by my side. I'm in love with you, Evie.' He took the ring from the bed of velvet, and Evie thought her heart might stop. 'You changed me without knowing it, Evie Jefferson.' Soft flakes fell on his face and one in his eye. 'Now, it's pretty cold down here and the snow is seeping through the knee of my jeans, so if you could answer quickly that'd be great.'

Evie pulled a face. 'I'm afraid I can't.' He looked completely devastated. 'You see, you broke your promise.'

'What do you mean?'

'You were supposed to take me on a date and resist spending a fortune. I'm thinking the ring was pretty expensive.'

He smiled and pulled her against him. 'That's where you're wrong. It was Mom's ring and it means the world to me to be giving it to you.'

Her smile rivalled all the lights on the trees put together. 'Well, in that case …' She wrapped her arms around his neck. 'Yes!'

He pulled back and pushed the ring onto her finger. 'Damn, it's a bit big.'

Evie held her fingers together so the ring stayed in place. 'It's beautiful. And haven't you ever heard? Size doesn't matter.'

His laughter filled the centre of the maze until she silenced him with another kiss and he lifted her up. She wrapped her legs around his waist. 'There's just one other thing.'

'Oh?'

When he put her down she slotted the ring into the box for safekeeping. 'It's really important.'

He looked worried.

'I'm starving.' She giggled. 'Please tell me you've got some food, somewhere!'

He grinned mischievously. 'Last one to find their way back to the house can cook, wash up and do whatever the other one asks.'

She pulled her scarf from her neck and covered his eyes again. 'You're on. Go!'

And trusting in the stars and the moon, as well as themselves, Evie and Jack eventually found their way, out of the maze, across the fields and up to the farmhouse.

Tonight was the start of a very bright future for both of them.

THE END

Acknowledgements

A huge thank you goes to my husband and my two children for their unwavering support as I wrote this, my fifth novel. Writing a book demands a lot of time and effort and without their words of encouragement I am sure I would've given up many times over!

Thank you to Belinda Holmes for patiently editing my manuscript and helping me to shape the final story of In a Manhattan Minute. Belinda lived in New York for many years and so her feedback was invaluable.
Thank you to Stephanie Box, whose proofreading is always so thorough and enables me to deliver a polished novel to my readers. Stephanie was able to give me a valuable insight into American life and Americanisms and any mistakes in this book are therefore my own.

Berni Stevens, cover designer extraordinaire, has delivered another cover I love and I can't wait to work with you again, Berni.

Thank you to the other nine members of The Write Romantics, your support is invaluable. I struggled to come up with a title for this book, but In a Manhattan Minute got the vote and I'm really happy with it. I think it encapsulates the story perfectly.

Helen J Rolfe.

The Chocolatier's Secret

Will one mistake ruin everything?

Andrew Bennett has an idyllic life in Magnolia Creek, Australia. He runs a chocolate business he adores, is married to Gemma, the love of his life, and has a close relationship with his father, Louis. But when Andrew receives a message from his high school sweetheart, it sends his world into a spiral, and the relationships he holds dear will never be the same again.

Molly Ramsey is looking for answers. After her last attempt, she believes the only way to get them this time is to face her past head-on. But to do this, she has to fly to the other side of the world – and she's afraid of flying. Her search for answers lands her in an emotional tangle, not only with her past but also with a man very much in her present.

Family is everything to Gemma Bennett and she longs to have a house full of kids, but it just isn't happening. And when Andrew's past makes an explosive impact on the family, Gemma must decide whether she can accept the truth and open her heart in a way she never thought possible.

In this story of love, family ties and forgiveness, will past mistakes be the obstacle to a Happy Ever After?

What Rosie Found Next

One house, two strangers, one very big secret...

A shaky upbringing has left Rosie Stevens craving safety and security. She thinks she knows exactly what she needs to make her life complete – the stable job and perfect house-sit she's just found in Magnolia Creek. The only thing she wants now is for her long-term boyfriend, Adam, to leave his overseas job and come home for good.

Owen Harrison is notoriously nomadic, and he roars into town on his Ducati for one reason and one reason only – to search his parents' house while they're away to find out what they've been hiding from him his entire life. When he meets Rosie, who refuses to quit the house-sit in his parents' home, sparks fly.

Secrets are unearthed, promises are broken, friendships are put to the test and the real risk of bushfires under the hot Australian sun threatens to undo Rosie once and for all.

Will Rosie and Owen be able to find what they want or what they really need?

Handle Me with Care

Does true love come along more than once in a lifetime?

Maddie Kershaw doesn't think so. She lost the love of her life in the 9/11 attacks, and since then has hopped from one casual fling to the next. But when she delivers an erotic cake to a one-hundredth birthday party by mistake, she meets Evan and starts to believe in second chances … until she realises there's a risk of getting hurt all over again.

Evan Quinn is serially single, yet when he meets Maddie he feels an instant connection, so much so that he confesses on their first date that he may have testicular cancer. Was it a mistake to tell her? He wants Maddie more than he has ever wanted any other woman. But he doesn't want her pity.

With the odds stacked against them both, finding love won't be easy. But beneath the Australian sun, a Happy Ever After could be worth fighting for.

The Friendship Tree

Why do good girls fall for bad boys?

Tamara leaves London and puts ten thousand miles between her and her ex. But as she vows to start over, she meets Jake – and life gets more complicated than she could ever have imagined.

Jake is the direct competitor for the family business, and a man with a dark secret, and Tamara struggles to fight her attraction to him as she deals with secrets of her own and an ex who refuses to give up.

Tamara is soon drawn in to the small community of Brewer Creek where she becomes the coordinator for an old fashioned Friendship Tree – a chart telling people who they can call on in times of trouble. And before long, she realises the Friendship Tree does a lot more than organise fundraising events and working bees; it has the power to unite an entire town.

Should you ever try to run from your past?

Printed in Great Britain
by Amazon

29861472R00189